"I was going to make us a couple of sandwiches. I hope you didn't tire yourself out too much."

"That's sweet. But I'm more than capable and I've been vegging out on your couch for most of the morning, so it was good to have something to do."

"I can see that."

He hadn't commented on the drip. Or rather, lack of drip. After urging her to take a seat, Brigg brought over their food.

A strong hand rested on her shoulder. "How are you feeling? I meant to check on you earlier, but the phone lines have been ringing nonstop."

The compassion in his tone warmed her heart. And the heat from his hand rubbing circles on her shoulder created a slight sizzle that was messing with her libido because she was zing-zanging from the physical contact. "Oh, I'm all right," she said breezily. "I have a few weeks to go before this baby shows his face, so it's all good."

"That's good to know." He sat adjacent to her, his long legs grazing against her own. She squeezed her legs tight together and focused on shoving food into her mouth. It was either that or groan from the contact.

Their hands touched. On cue thunder cracked.

Really?

Dear Reader,

I am so pleased you chose *Twenty-Eight Dates*. I am so glad that I am able to take you to the fictional town of Love Creek, Florida, and continue the Harrington men series. I love writing sassy heroines and Courtney did not disappoint. Like all of us, she was a product of her childhood and had past grief to overcome, so I think many readers will be able to relate to her journey for independence. But this story is also about a second chance at love—a strong hero like Brigg was the perfect person to help her achieve it. I love his sense of humor and their friendship made my heart smile. I hope you are as entertained by this summer romance as I was while creating it. I would love to hear from you. Please consider joining my mailing list at michellelindorice.com.

Best,

Michelle

Twenty-Eight Dates

—

MICHELLE LINDO-RICE

HARLEQUIN

SPECIAL
EDITION

HARLEQUIN®
SPECIAL
EDITION™

Recycling programs
for this product may
not exist in your area.

ISBN-13: 978-1-335-59457-0

Twenty-Eight Dates

Copyright © 2024 by Michelle Lindo-Rice

Harlequin Enterprises ULC
22 Adelaide St. West, 41st Floor
Toronto, Ontario M5H 4E3, Canada
www.Harlequin.com

Printed in U.S.A.

Michelle Lindo-Rice is an Emma Award Winner and a Vivian Award finalist. She enjoys reading and crafting fiction across genres. Originally from Jamaica, West Indies, she has earned degrees from New York University, SUNY at Stony Brook, Teachers College, Columbia University, Argosy University and has been an educator for over twenty years.

She also writes inspirational stories as Zoey Marie Jackson. You can reach her online at michellelindorice.com or on Facebook.

Books by Michelle Lindo-Rice

Harlequin Special Edition

The Valentine's Do-Over

Seven Brides for Seven Brothers

Rivals at Love Creek
Cinderella's Last Stand
Twenty-Eight Dates

Visit the Author Profile page
at Harlequin.com for more titles.

Thank you to Sobi Burbano, who is among my first reads, and my husband, John, my handsome muse. Thank you to my editor, Gail Chasan, and Katixa, Erin and the rest of the team at Harlequin involved in bringing my book from my head into your hands. I also shout out to my agent, Latoya Smith, who looks out for my interests so I can be free to write at my heart's content.

Chapter One

She could do this.

Courtney Meadows held back a yawn and snuck down the winding grand staircase of the mausoleum she had called home for the past year and five months. A place she would have stayed in if she hadn't overhead her in-laws plotting against her.

After her husband, Jet, died while on duty as a firefighter, Muriel and Robert Meadows had insisted she continued to live with them. Their house was considered a landmark in Druid Hills, Georgia, and with nine bedrooms and twelve bathrooms on the property, there was more than enough room for them to spread out. At least that had been Jet's response when Courtney suggested they get a two-bedroom apartment or purchase a condo since they were newlyweds instead of living with his parents. He reasoned he wouldn't be worried about her while he was at work since his parents would be there to care for her.

As if she needed looking after. Courtney and her sister, Kaylin, had been taking care of themselves since they were children growing up together in foster care.

Remembering the biggest area of contention between

her and Jet, Courtney gritted her teeth. He hadn't wanted her to continue working as a mere waitress. Never mind that he had met her while she was busing tables and asked her out. They had married within eight weeks.

Since Jet lived with his parents, he banked most of his money, so Courtney could be a stay-at-home mom. When he broached the idea, Courtney suggested they wait on children—since she had never even planned to be a mom—and take a year to continue to get to know each other while she got used to the idea. But he had been insistent and so, here she was. Eight months pregnant.

Alone.

Sort of.

She yawned again and patted her round stomach, acknowledging her constant companion. A son. A son with a pair of interfering grandparents.

Courtney had been in their floor-to-ceiling library earlier that day curled up behind the chaise longue, reading a book when Robert and Muriel entered the study. As she was about to show her face, she heard Muriel utter her name in a condescending tone. Courtney then tucked her legs close to her chest so she could listen in.

Of course, her phone began to vibrate from the pocket of her bike shorts. Courtney had pressed the ignore button and held her breath for a tense second, just knowing she would be discovered. But they continued their conversation.

Muriel stood a few feet away from her. "How long do I have to smile in Courtney's face like it isn't her fault that Jet died?"

Courtney covered her mouth to keep from gasping. And responding. And making them aware of her presence. She squeezed her legs tight, her pulse escalating.

She yearned to confront them, but she made herself stay absolutely still.

Robert poured himself a drink. "Lower your voice, dear. Our lawyer said the easiest way to get her to sign the custody papers is to play nice."

"I can't wait. Courtney isn't ready to be anybody's mom. She can barely take care of herself." Muriel snorted. "I can't wait to redecorate Ansel's room."

Courtney fought the urge to lash out. This was the same woman who had gushed to her that very morning how much she loved the gray walls and elephant theme. Courtney had spent hours choosing the furnishings and preparing the space for her son, Jayson—not Ansel.

"All in due time, dear."

Courtney folded her lips inside her mouth to keep from screaming at the calm certainty in Robert's voice. Like it was a foregone conclusion that they would be raising her child. Not as long as she was alive and breathing.

Muriel narrowed her eyes. "It's a pity we can't declare her unfit."

Robert rubbed the stubble on his chin. "Jet did say her mother had a mental illness…"

Hot tears sprung and rolled down her cheeks. She had told Jet that in confidence. Her mother had suffered from bipolar disorder and had self-medicated with il' gal drugs, which was how Courtney and her olde' ter, Kaylin, had ended up in foster care at six ar years old. The girls had learned to rely on r each other. And Courtney had remained until she had fallen in love with a dasl the color of midnight.

Never again would she allow he' her feet by a man. Especially one in

Robert held out his arm. "Let me see what Todd thinks about that." Todd Lansing was the family attorney and friend.

With a nod, Muriel wrapped her arm around her husband. Courtney watched them depart the room.

The door clicked softly.

From within, panic rang loudly.

Uncurling herself, Courtney pulled out her cell phone to check her personal bank account. She had kept it open against Jet's wishes. Good thing too, because she was going to have to get out of this place. In the early morning. Because even though his parents had been generous, covering all her expenses, they hadn't given her cash. Jet hadn't gotten around to declaring her as his beneficiary, so Todd was working on getting all that straightened out through the courts.

Or so he said. Holding on to the chaise longue, Courtney wobbled to her feet.

Todd was on the Meadowses' payroll. And if she were being honest, Courtney had been too grief-stricken to pay attention. It had taken every ounce of strength she had to get out of bed, to eat so that her baby had the necessary sustenance to survive. As long as Jet's son was taken care of, Courtney hadn't been concerned about anything else.

She swallowed. She should have been.

Blinking away her tears, Courtney focused on the small screen. She had $237.41. If she took food from the pantry and used rest stops instead of a hotel, that should more than enough to take her from Druid Hills, Georgia, to where Kaylin lived in Fort Lauderdale, Florida. Her sister worked on a cruise ship and was away at sea, and Courtney knew where Kaylin kept a spare key.

Through dinner that evening, it took all her self-control not to show her hurt. Not to show how disgusted she was at their false concern. But she had done it. She had forced herself to eat a small portion of her lasagna, garden salad and garlic bread, nodding and smiling like she was clueless. She had even insisted on taking a picture with her in-laws under the guise that it was for her baby album. Courtney wanted to have photos to share with Jayson when he was an adult. He deserved to know his background, and she wouldn't hold that information from him once he was old enough to understand. But that was years away. Right now, she had to focus on the day-to-day. Her and her baby's survival.

After dinner, Courtney had packed a lunch bag and stuffed a small duffel bag with a few outfits along with her laptop. Then she had donned a pair of black jeans, T-shirt and sneakers. Tucking her curls under a cap, Courtney waited until it was close to four in the morning, setting the alarm on her phone as a backup. Robert was a night owl. She wanted to be sure he was in bed before exiting this place for good.

For a split second, standing in the grand foyer, cell phone in hand, Courtney hesitated. She was close to the end of her term, and her eyelids were heavy with sleep. Maybe she should wait until she delivered before traveling. Then she stiffened. She wouldn't put it pass the Meadowses to take her baby while she recuperated from giving birth. They had strong political clout, and to put it simply, she couldn't trust them not to do something underhanded.

No, it was best if she left for Florida now in the wee hours of the morning. When they were sleeping. By the time they awakened, she would be long gone.

Feeling a twinge of guilt, she placed a hand over her

pounding heart. Regardless of their nefarious intentions, the Meadowses had lost their only child. Courtney knew they cared about their grandchild. It would gut them to be excluded from Jayson's life. But these were the same people who had no qualms about snatching him away from his own biological mother.

She squared her shoulders and ambled toward the alarm by the front door. Her sneakers made squeaking sounds on the marble floor. With a slight tremor in her hands, she rested her cell on the entry table, keyed in the code and opened the front door, tensing at the chime. Slipping outside, she locked the door behind her and wiped her brow.

Whew.

The crickets and cicadas' night song this first week of June was a crescendo in her ears. Remembering the tiny frogs that liked to hang like a garland on the side of the house, Courtney cringed, hunched her shoulders and trotted down the three front steps before dashing into the dark to the right. The muggy summer morning made her crave the cool central air of the house behind her.

Entering the garage, she beelined for her twenty-year-old sedan nestled in the corner, an eyesore compared to the five other premium vehicles inside. Robert had insisted she drive the Range Rover, and Courtney was glad she had begged them not to junk her trusty Kia. Despite the dings and scratches, it had been her ride for five years, her second vehicle now at thirty-one and the first she had paid for with her own money. Unlocking the passenger door, she placed her duffel and lunch bag on the seat before darting to the driver's side.

Courtney adjusted her seat to accommodate her expanded tummy and started up the car. She tossed her cap off her head, her tendrils damp against her face, then took a moment to bask in the blast of the air conditioner before putting the car into gear.

Keeping the headlights off, Courtney crept down the gravel on the driveway, her pace slow, her heart thumping with the precision of a drummer boy. As soon as she turned out of their property, Courtney turned on the lights and accelerated.

Pumping her fists, she yelled, "We did it, Jayson!" A fierce kick made her stomach jump, and Courtney smiled. Patting her stomach, she said, "You feel it too, little guy, don't you? Freedom. Wait until you're out of there. Then we're really going to celebrate."

With each mile, her worries melted away like an ice pop in the sun. Her neck muscles relaxed, and the tension oozed from her body. A tension she must have been carrying around for the past seven months following Jet's death. She hadn't realized how constricted she had been. How…constrained. Courtney straightened, anticipation injecting energy into her being. She was now wide awake. She couldn't wait for the sunrise, for the first glimpse of a new day, a new beginning. A new life with her son.

Chapter Two

On days like today, Brigg Harrington reminded himself he had become a police officer to help other youths as he had been helped as a teen. But he hadn't been like these modern teens making bomb threats at the middle school near the ending of the school year. Brigg had been pulled from his post as a school resource officer at Love Creek High to assist with evacuating the nervous gaggle of students and teachers during the chaotic lunch hour. Thankfully, his captain had allocated the task of easing the minds of the worried parents to the superintendent and town mayor while dealing with the vicious Florida heat. The sun's rays had seared his exposed skin with laser-like precision, and he regretted not wearing sunscreen.

Brigg had had to change out of his wet, sweat-stained uniform for a clean one before working the rest of his shift doing traffic duty on highway patrol.

Exhaustion cloaked his body like a warm blanket. He took a sip of coffee, needing a shot of caffeine, although his fatigue was more mental than physical. Three thirteen-year-olds had been arrested. Brigg hadn't relished putting handcuffs on their wrists and reading them their Miranda rights. It was a part of the job, but his heart had constricted when seeing the fear in the young men's eyes and their tear-streaked faces. He wished he could have given them a stern warning, but the boys had actually placed two homemade bombs in the bathroom stalls as retaliation against their bullies. His stomach knotted remembering the change in the atmosphere when it had become evident this was no harmless prank. Brigg had been stupefied. He knew those boys and their families, had seen them waddling about in Pampers under the town sprinklers when they were toddlers, so he was beyond flabbergasted at their actions. The most Brigg had done during his senior year in high school was steal candy and chips from one of the two quick-stop stores in Love Creek, Florida. And that had been a major to-do.

The shop owner had called Brigg's father, Patrick Harrington, plus there had been a police officer in the next aisle. A police officer who fortunately decided to mentor instead of punish. Beckett Sparks was almost a second father to him, a work father, because Patrick Harrington didn't need a substitute. He was among the best there was.

Lightning flashed, followed by a crack of thunder and then heavy plops of rain. Within seconds, Brigg was in the middle of a downpour. He wasn't worried though. Within in a matter of minutes, the rain could end and they could have clear blue skies. That was Florida weather for you. Squinting up at the skies though, Brigg saw huge dark clouds. With all the commotion earlier in the day, he hadn't thought to check the weather. Pulling up the weather app on his phone, Brigg's eyes went wide. There was a tropical storm farther out, and most of the area was under a tornado watch. According to the app, it could be upgraded to a hurricane. June heralded the beginning of the hurricane season, so it was a definite possibility. But he chose to focus on the key words: *could be.*

He looked at the time and exhaled. Thirty minutes to go before the end of his shift at 4:00 p.m. He had felt every hour of this ten-hour workday.

Settling into the leather of his patrol vehicle, Brigg rubbed his jaw and yawned. Sleep was a siren fanning at his eyes. Twenty-eight minutes. Then he was off for three days. Seventy-two glorious hours of just him and three of his six brothers—Caleb, Drake and Ethan—fishing and cutting it up on Hawk's yacht.

Brigg hoped the weather turned and the weekend would bring nothing but sunshine. He could already smell the scent of the sea-foam, feel the lull of the vessel and see the shoals of fish while he and his brothers engaged in some good-natured ribbing.

No women allowed.

It was supposed to be all seven of them lounging about, but two of his older brothers, Lynx and Axel, had honey-do lists now that one was married and one was engaged. Both had bowed out. Then Hawk, his eldest brother and NFL quarterback, started seeing someone and dropped out. The relationship was new and fresh, which meant Hawk was spending all his spare time with Arie. But Hawk had left the keys, and his place would be stocked and staffed with a chef and housekeeping. Brigg smoothed his pants leg. It wouldn't be the same without all seven of them though. Unlike Lynx or Axel, Brigg wasn't getting married or engaged or doing long-term relationships like Hawk. As far as he was concerned, love was for suckers and he didn't eat lollipops. Besides, he thoroughly enjoyed being a serial dater. When he had time to date.

Which was almost never.

He was too tired. Yep, at the ripe old age of twenty-nine going on thirty, Brigg was tired of the dating scene. Or rather, the pretense. Because there were women out there who only cared about the number of zeroes in his bank account, his penis size and how long they could milk both. Ask him how he knew. That's why he had stopped swiping right or left and had deleted the myriad dating apps. He couldn't be bothered anymore.

If he had to describe himself, he would say he was a no-nonsense, by-the-book kind of guy. He liked his own company, though he had entered the world with a womb-mate. His fraternal twin, Caleb, lived nearby, and though they spent time together, growing up in a house with all those siblings made Brigg crave his solitude. That's why he didn't mind the hours he spent in a vehicle waiting for the unsuspecting speeding motorist.

Swiveling the mount to bring his laptop closer, Brigg pulled up his recorded statements from some of the other students at the middle school. After rereading them, Brigg submitted his paperwork, along with the digital photos he had taken while on the scene. There would be hundreds of others from other officers, but Brigg knew the importance of a single photo and a different angle. During his nine years on the force, he had seen where a tiny piece of evidence had acquitted or condemned. Plus, though tedious, it was good police work. He tapped the steering wheel.

Twelve minutes. Plus, the rain abated somewhat.

Just as he slammed the lid of the laptop, a call came in, and he was quick to answer when he saw who was on the line.

"Hello, Cap," he said, greeting his former mentor, now

captain. He rarely called him by his first name, though Beckett had urged him to do so many times.

"Just calling to check on you. Don't know if you heard, but in the next town over, a young woman parked on the side of the road was hit by a semi. She's in critical care at Love Creek Hospital. That's how we heard about it."

"No. I didn't hear. Is she…?"

"It's out of our hands, now." Beckett's voice sounded grim. "Be careful out there."

Brigg's heart squeezed when thinking of that woman's family. "Thanks for looking out for me, sir. With this weather, I may not be going anywhere. If so, I'll be working."

"All right, but you're still taking that vacation when this all dies down. And Tara and Violet are looking forward to having you at dinner next week." It had been months since Brigg had taken time off. His captain emphasized that an odd day here and there didn't count and that it was important for him to relax and recoup.

"I will."

Brigg looked at his watch and smiled. Just as he started up the truck, a burgundy sedan shot past. He clocked it at seventeen miles above the speed limit. The last ten minutes of his shift too. Of course, it wouldn't go any other way. He sighed and moved to turn on the patrol lights when he heard a loud bang, and the unmistakable squeal of the tires.

Great. His seventy-two hours off would be about sixty-eight once he was finished here. That's if he was lucky.

He reminded himself his profession wasn't just about making arrests or giving citations but included helping someone stranded on the side of the road during hurricane season. Even if that person had been going forty-two in a twenty-five-mile-per-hour zone. Brigg drove the few feet to where the vehicle had stopped, grabbed his raincoat and jumped out of his SUV right into deep mud.

A huge crack of thunder was accompanied by even more rain.

With a grunt, he wiped his boots and stomped over the car. The headlights were on, and the wipers swished back and forth, furiously fighting the torrent and failing. Brigg stood off to the side and rapped on the window, careful to avoid the splatter of water from the wipers. The window rolled down with slow precision. He squared his shoulders and looked into the eyes of one of the most beautiful women he had ever seen.

Lightning bolt.

She had high cheekbones, a nose as cute as a button, and her skin appeared smooth and soft like cocoa butter. She had hair the color of copper stuffed under a baseball cap and a pair of hazel eyes framed with long lashes. But those pouty lips distracted him. They looked inviting and…kissable.

For a second, Brigg was speechless. Her mouth was slightly ajar. Brigg took in her spiked lashes, wet from the rain or from crying? Immediately, he prayed it was because of the rain. That he could handle. Then her expression changed to quizzical while he reigned in thoughts akin to popcorn popping around in his brain.

"Do you want my license and registration?" she asked, her voice sultry and low. Now she looked at him like he was addlebrained.

Brigg bent so she could hear him over the rain. Water from the wipers whipped him across the face, and he saw her cover her mouth, her pupils wide. The abrupt onslaught shocked him back to his senses. Jumping back, he folded his arms and yelled, "Turn off the windshield wipers."

With a jerky nod, she complied. "Sorry." He could see her clenching her cheeks to keep from laughing. Normally, Brigg would crack up at his misfortune, but he didn't find his internal reaction to her amusing. If he had to put a name to it, he would call it attraction, but his job superseded this unexpected case of…whimsy.

Frowning, Brigg stuck out his hand. "License and registration." Once she handed them to him, he gestured for her to wait, though it was evident she wasn't going anywhere, and stomped back to his vehicle.

Punching in her information in his laptop, Brigg waited for the results. He held her license in his palm. Her name was Courtney. Nice solid normal name. His eyes slid back to the screen, and he breathed a sigh of relief. Good to know he hadn't been jolted by a convict or serial killer.

Then he raised an eyebrow. Her registration had lapsed over six months ago. That meant she had driven all the way from Druid Hills, Georgia, with expired tags. Brigg sighed. Technically, this was a misdemeanor, which could be sixty days in jail, plus a five-hundred-dollar fine. A quick scan showed she had no prior arrests or violations, so he decided to write her a ticket instead. He opened the door to his vehicle.

Thankfully, the rain had eased to mere sprinkles and the sun peeked through the clouds. Since he wasn't sure how long that reprieve would last, Brigg hurried back to her car. That's when he saw the steam coming up from the hood. That's right. On top of having to cite her for improper registration, Brigg would have to help sort out her defunct vehicle. He had hoped the loud bang had been the result of a flat tire, but it was evident there was much more going on. In weather like this, it could be hours before a tow truck arrived. For a brief second, he considered calling backup, but his replacement was a rookie.

He'd better handle this himself.

As a result, when Brigg's eyes met hers a second time, the only thing his brain registered was annoyance. Deep annoyance.

Chapter Three

It was bad enough he had an imposing large frame, but now he was glaring at her as if she was an irritant. Courtney hurried to roll down her window.

"Your registration lapsed months ago," he said, handing her the slip of paper. Their fingers connected and she felt a minor electrical shock. Pulling her hand away, Courtney refused to look at the ticket, knowing it had an astronomical fine she had no idea how she would pay. In her defense, she hadn't had cause to renew her tags. She had been driven anywhere she needed to go. He cocked his head. "Now, what's going on with your car?"

There he was pinning those deep chocolate brown eyes on her again. For some reason that got her heart racing.

He was particularly good-looking, with skin the hue of sepia, a squared jaw and strong cheekbones. The officer had a tight lineup and fade with tight black, shiny coils.

"I don't know..." Her lips quivered. Goodness, she knew her hormones would have her balling in seconds if she didn't take deep breaths. In two, three, four. Out two, three, four.

"Is it the alternator? Or the pump?" he asked.

"One minute it was fine and then..." She gulped. A

fat teardrop began its descent and was promptly joined by others. Her shoulders shook. There was no stopping the flow. So she gave in, covered her face with her hands and had herself a good ugly cry.

She heard the officer say, "Ma'am, please don't cry," which of course made her wail even harder. She tilted her head to face him.

"I—I can't help it," she hiccuped. "Believe me, I would stop if I could. It's just that…"

He stalked toward his vehicle, and Courtney tried to reign in her emotions to no avail. All the stress of the past day was pouring as hard as the rain had been moments earlier. The officer returned with a handful of tissues. Thanking him, she stared straight ahead and wiped her face. If she looked at him and saw any level of sympathy, that might lead to an even greater crying fest. She hated having anyone feel sorry for her. But she sure did feel sorry for herself.

"Is there someone you can call?" he asked once her tears subsided.

"N-no. I forgot my cell phone." Courtney had discovered that fact hours later. Even now, she could picture the device resting on the desk by the front door. She had put it there to enter the security code and, in her haste, hadn't slipped it in her purse. Berating herself for that stupid mistake, Courtney had gripped the wheel and pressed down on the gas, willing herself not to turn around but to keep pressing forward.

He gave her a speculative glance. "Where is it?"

Disliking the suspicious tone, she answered the question through gritted teeth. "Back in Georgia." Then, because she couldn't hold her sass, she said, "Forgetting a phone isn't a crime. It's a common mistake."

For a second, his jaw jutted, but he looked at his watch. "I'm almost off the clock, but I can call you a tow truck. You're only about five miles from town, and I think I can convince Lenny to come get you."

She released a shaky breath. "I don't have any money for repairs."

Her eyes misted as the enormity of her situation sunk in. She was stranded with less than twenty dollars and no means of communication. Her heart began to pound. Most of the funds she had carried had been used to fuel this gas-guzzler. That had been an unexpected expense. Come to think of it, that should have tipped her off that something was wrong with her vehicle. Not that it would have changed her desperate escape plan.

Her stomach rumbled. And she was hungry, having eaten the remainder of her snacks an hour ago.

The officer cleared his throat. "What about a credit card?" She gave him her attention, noting the name on his badge on that broad chest read Brigg Harrington. Her pride was as flat as the puddles in front of her. She had several credit cards. However, the Meadowses had canceled them, along with her phone.

When she realized she left her phone, she had attempted to get another cheaper model, and that's when she had learned her old number was no longer in service. Then she experienced an embarrassment at the store when she inserted the credit card to buy a new cell phone. At least she'd had enough in her own account to fill her tank for the last time. Pity that the car was now out of commission. Permanently.

"That's not an option for me right now." Even if she had to walk to Fort Lauderdale—okay, now was not the time for that kind of a blanket statement. She couldn't walk any serious distance in her condition.

He bunched his fists and lifted his eyes upward. She could feel the mixture of impatience and disbelief wafting from his persona. "Who travels like this in this day and time? And am I really supposed to believe that you have no one. No one that you can call?" She kept silent because his tone suggested he was releasing his frustration and not expecting an answer. Pointing at her, he commanded, "Wait here," and stormed off.

It's not like she could go anywhere. She placed her tongue between her teeth to keep from saying that to him. Somehow, she doubted he would welcome her sense of humor.

Still, she felt horrible she was keeping him from ending his shift on time. Yet, it wasn't like she had planned this. She rubbed her tummy. She hadn't planned any of the events of her life for the past year. Peering in the rearview, Courtney could see he was on his phone, most likely radioing for assistance.

It was now dark, and any second, the rain could start pouring again. Courtney was stuck, and she had no idea what to do. Taking off her cap, she allowed her hair to fall to her shoulders, wiping her now sweaty brow. She really wanted to step out of the vehicle but wasn't sure if the cop would want her to do that.

And she wasn't about to take any chances without any witnesses around. Not that he gave off a bad vibe or anything. Still.

The humid Florida weather made the air stifling and dense. Reaching in the back seat for her bag, she pulled out a maternity tank top, then pushed her seat back to swap her T-shirt damp from sweat and tears with the tank top. That's when she noticed him standing there with his arms folded showing off well-shaped biceps. Waiting or watching? She couldn't be sure.

A blush crept up her body. "I was hot," she explained, noting the rain had petered off again.

His tone remained professional. "The tow truck will be here soon. I'll wait with you until it comes."

"Just impound it. I can't afford to fix it."

He dipped his chin. "Lenny will work out something. Don't worry about that now. The more pressing thing is you need a place to stay. There's a town shelter, but it's late, and with the weather, I can almost guarantee that it's at capacity."

Then why suggest it? Again, she kept that thought to herself. His matter-of-fact tone grated her nerves. "Officer, maybe you can cancel the tow truck and I can stay here in my car?" Even as she spoke the words, she knew that wasn't feasible.

"That's not safe. Your car is a dark color and there are no streetlights. Parked as you are, you could get hit and seriously injured by a passing truck or car." He gestured for her to come out of the vehicle. "We can try the next town over to see if they have boarding for the night." His mannerisms suggested he couldn't wait to be rid of her.

Resigned, she stuffed her hair back under her cap, snatched her bag then looked around for the baby bag. An image of the bag she had packed since month five resting by her bedroom door came into her mind. She groaned. She had meant to take it on her way out the door, but it was obvious she had forgotten. She sighed. Pregnancy brain was real. She gathered her other meager belongings and pushed the door open, giving it the usual shove. Then holding on to the door frame, she carefully maneuvered herself out of the sedan.

The cop's eyes bulged. He pointed a finger and sputtered in an accusatory tone, "You're pregnant?"

"Yep," she quipped, enjoying seeing the unflappable man appear caught off guard. "Good to see your observational skills are on par." Oh, boy, her sarcasm and wit tended to go in overdrive when she was scared or hungry or broke. Didn't take much to loosen her tongue. She needed to dial it back though, considering this man was her source of rescue.

"How far along are you?"

"I'm eight months."

"Yet, you would have had me leave you here on the side of the road?"

Frustrated, she flailed her arms. "I don't know what else to do. I've been driving for hours, and if this piece of crap had just held out for a little longer, I would have been in Fort Lauderdale with my sister." Touching the car, she said, "I'm sorry. You're not crap. I'm just frustrated."

An eyebrow rose. "I thought you said you had no one."

"Nothing gets by you, eh?" she shot back. "Well, for your information, I didn't lie. My sister works for a cruise ship, and I've got about fourteen days or so before she returns."

He studied her for a beat before calling the town shelter. Hearing they had no space, he then called two others in two nearby towns. All stated he should try tomorrow. He pressed his lips together and ran a hand over his fade before groaning.

There was a crack of thunder. She lifted her head, and a plop of rain landed on her nose. Another drop hit her forehead.

Placing his hands on both of his hips, he declared. "You can stay with me. Just for tonight." He sounded ungracious making that generous offer, and for a second, Courtney was tempted to say no.

"Don't do me any favors, sir."

"Don't give me any sass, ma'am." Her mouth dropped. He was quick on the comeback. She would have laughed if her situation wasn't so sorry. The rain began to come down, soaking her shirt and hair. "Get in my truck," he said in a much milder tone.

With a nod, she waded through the puddle, her sneakers dipping into mud. She opened the passenger door and dropped her belongings on the floor. No way was she riding in the rear. The last time Courtney had been inside a police vehicle, it had been with her sister as they were being taken away from their mother. Fighting back that terrible memory, Courtney climbed up into the front seat, eyeing him, daring him to tell her she couldn't.

Fortunately for him—and her—he didn't say a word.

Chapter Four

This woman had him breaking all his rules.

Brigg pulled into his driveway next to his personal SUV and turned off the engine. He lived alone and he liked his solitude. The thought of sharing his space with a stranger put him on edge. But after hearing about that woman getting hit by the semi, Brigg couldn't abandon this pregnant lady, especially not in this storm.

The entire ride over, Brigg tried to think of alternate solutions, but none came to mind. He doubted he would be able to sleep with her all up in his space. She had a clean record, but that didn't mean that Mrs. Meadows was law-abiding.

Maybe he would chill on the couch. That way, if she got any ideas…

She cleared her throat and place a slender hand over her stomach. He still couldn't believe he hadn't seen how pregnant she was, because Courtney was all baby. "Thank you, sir, for taking me in. I realize you're going above and beyond your civic duty, and I appreciate it. I'll camp out on your sofa and be out of your house once the sun is up." He heard the light tremor in her tone and realized she was feeling the same apprehension he was at spending the night with a stranger.

Brigg placed a hand on her shoulder. "First, call me Brigg. Second, you're my guest. My mother raised me too well to have you uncomfortable on my futon. I have a second master bedroom with a lock and its own bath, so you'll be comfortable."

Her shoulders slumped, and he heard her release a breath of air. "All right, Brigg. Call me Courtney. Thank you so much for your hospitality." Her voice cracked and his stomach tensed. He hoped she wasn't about to cry again. Brigg had grown up with six brothers and was used to roughhousing, but the thought of this wisp of a woman next to him crying made his palms sweat.

Opening the door, Brigg asked Courtney to wait for him. She was about five foot seven and tall enough to get out of the vehicle without a hassle, but he had stones lining the edge of his driveway and didn't want her falling. Especially since the automatic lights hadn't come on.

Brigg had converted his house into a smart home, which meant he could use voice commands or an app to operate the lights and other devices and doors. But it wasn't smart enough to handle a thunderstorm and the loss of power. Still, he made a mental note to check the bulbs just in case.

He hurried out of the vehicle and headed to the passenger side. Grabbing her bag and holding her arm, Brigg guided Courtney to the front door. They made it without mishap and he breathed a sigh of relief.

This house had actually been his mother's and was fully paid for. All Brigg had to do was pay the yearly taxes. Tanya had been a single mother raising Axel before she met and married his father, Patrick, who also had had his own place on the other side of town, where he was a single father raising Drake and Ethan. Drake now lived in his father's former home. Then, when his parents got married, adopted Hawk and Lynx, and had twins, Brigg and Caleb, they moved into their forever home.

He didn't understand why Courtney was traveling a far distance on her own. He wondered about her husband's location and if there was trouble in her marriage, which prompted her road trip to visit her sister. A road trip for which she was ill-prepared. His heart moved. Her husband must be worried. Maybe Brigg could persuade her to call the man and ease his mind.

Using his phone to pull up the Home app, he paused. Maybe her husband was in the military and away on duty. Brigg then tapped on the icon to unlock the front door. He tested the lights, relieved to see them come on, and then gestured for Courtney to enter. The last thing he would have wanted to do is have to light candles with a stranger in his residence. The door handle was loose, and he made a mental note to secure it later.

As soon as she stepped through the threshold of his three-bedroom home, Courtney exhaled. "You have a lovely house," she said. The interior was painted in neutral tones, and most of his furnishings were black and gray. His mother had added touches of color with art pieces and vases sprinkled throughout, and Hawk had personally made a sculpture that Brigg had set on a special display stand.

He splayed his hands. "As you can see, the house is a split-open concept with the living area on your left, and the kitchen is straight ahead. If you keep going left, there's the guest room, where you'll be staying, which is a master suite. But there's a bathroom right off the hallway you can use now."

She gave a jerky nod.

Chuckling, Brigg directed her to the half bath located on the right hallway that led to his office and bedroom. She dashed off, and he willed himself to ignore the trail of mud on his white tiles.

Before stepping farther inside, Brigg undid his boots and left them by the door. He should have used the garage. But his brother Ethan had begged Brigg to store his newly purchased Sling for a few months while he awaited another parking spot at his apartment complex. So, Brigg had gotten into the habit of entering through the front door.

Padding the short distance to the eat-in kitchen, Brigg placed Courtney's bag on the round table and then put on the electric kettle. He had purchased a package of ginger tea with honey that he believed his guest would enjoy. His cell vibrated and he saw that it was Lenny.

Just picked up the car.

Good. How much to repair?

Much more than it's worth.

Brigg was afraid that would be the case. Okay. Drop it here. You can bill me.

Got it.

The kettle began to whistle, and the stopper popped up. Pouring two cups of tea, Brigg rubbed his temples, then frowned. Courtney sure was taking a long time in the bathroom. A past case where a woman pretending to be pregnant and stranded on the side of the road so unsuspecting helpers would get robbed hit his mind. Brigg paused. She was really small…and she could be going through his medicine cabinets while he stood here getting ready to entertain. His long legs stalked over the bathroom, and he rapped on the door.

"Are you okay in there?" he asked, harsher than he wanted to sound.

"Y-yes." He heard the toilet flush and the faucet turn on before she opened the door. "I…I was washing up a little." Peering over her head, Brigg scanned his bathroom to see if anything was missing. She scuttled past him. "I didn't take anything."

Her affronted tone made him apologize. "I didn't say you did."

"You didn't have to," she shot back, her attitude frosty. "Why don't you go count the ear swabs and toothpicks to see if I used any?"

Her ridiculous words kindled his fury. "Listen, don't get defensive. You were in there for a good while and I got…" He tried to search for a word other than *suspicious* and couldn't find any. Brigg shrugged. "Whatever. Let's drop it. Do you want some ginger tea?"

"No, I don't want any tea." She rushed to get her bag. "I'm out of here. I'd rather sleep on the street than stay somewhere where I'm not trusted."

"Don't be rash."

Her head lolled back. "Don't chastise me. I'm not a child."

"Well, what do you call going out in the middle of a thunderstorm?" Seeing her mouth pop open, Brigg drew in deep breaths. He had only known this woman about an hour, and she was needling him in ways he had never experienced before. He was a fraternal twin and considered the goofball of the two. Caleb was the serious one. Yet here he was getting mad at a complete stranger. This was unlike him. To be fair, he hadn't been himself since meeting Courtney. Every action he had taken since coming into contact with her was out of his norm and his comfort zone. He was generally even-tempered, cool under any situation. The opposite of how he was behaving now.

Tucking her bag under her arm, Courtney glared. "Did you go through my bag while I was in the bathroom?"

His brows rose to his forehead. "Are you out of your mind?" He jabbed a hand to his chest. "I uphold the law to the point where I get paid to prevent doing that very thing. How dare you accuse me of doing something like that!" See now, this was what he got for being nice and for helping some random woman off the street. Wait till he told his brothers about it. *Humph.* Knowing them, they would crack on him for hours. He had better keep this faux pas to himself.

Courtney cocked her head. "How does it feel to have the tables turned? Doesn't feel good, does it?"

"All right, bet." His signature response when he didn't know what to say or to indicate his agreement. Thunder boomed and there was a flash of lightning. The electricity flickered but stayed on. *Whew.*

The stubborn woman headed to the door. For some reason, he loathed to see her leave. Maybe it was because as an officer of the law, he would most likely be involved in her rescue if she ventured out and fell into danger. In a softer tone, he said, "You might as well wait for your car to arrive." On cue, there was a downpour. "I wouldn't advise you to stand outside in this weather. Think about your baby."

Standing by the door, her hand on the knob, she hesitated. "I can be quick-tempered when cornered. If it's okay with you, I will wait until my car comes."

"That's fine. I'm sorry for not trusting you." Brigg stuffed his hands in his pockets. Her eyes lowered to below his belt before she tore her gaze upward.

"And I'm sorry for saying you went through my bag when I know you didn't."

"How do you know for sure I didn't?" He crooked his head toward the kitchen. "Come have tea."

They made their way over to the open space and Brigg handed her a mug.

"Do you always ask so many questions?" she asked, taking a sip.

"I guess so. Why do you ask?"

She chuckled. "There you go again. You can't help yourself."

They smiled. "It comes with the job. I spend a lot of my day asking questions."

"I get that." She blew on the hot tea.

He took a gulp of his. The liquid seared his tongue, but he loved it piping hot. He could already feel his insides warming and settling. "So now, back to my question. How do you know I didn't touch your bag?"

She giggled. "Because the zipper is broken."

Laughter bubbled from the pit of his stomach and deep into his chest before he released it. Seconds later, she joined in. "Courtney Meadows, meeting you has been eventful and memorable."

She lowered her lashes. "That sums me up in a nutshell." A loud yawn escaped followed by a stomach growl.

Patting her tummy, she said, "I think this little one is ready for a nap."

"And some food," he said, admiring the blush across her skin.

Mindful of the circles around her eyes, Brigg showed her the spare bedroom, pleased he had purchased a queen-size comforter and sheet set with matching curtains. It was gray, red and white, and he could attest to the fact that Courtney would find it soft and inviting. He had a blue set in his own master suite on the other side of the ranch house. Checking the bathroom to make sure there was enough supplies, Brigg excused himself.

Before he rounded the corner, she called out to him, wringing her hands. "I can't thank you enough for taking me in, or rather, us." Her voice hitched like she was about to cry.

Wagging a finger, he warned, "Now, we're not having any of that. No crying. I'd rather you be snarky and snappy over sniffling any day. Get an hour or two of rest. I have plenty of food when you're ready to eat." If he felt a sense of anticipation at seeing her again in a few hours, Brigg would never admit it to anyone, least of all himself.

Chapter Five

The sense of security she felt upon entering Brigg's home scared her.

The only other time she had felt this with the opposite sex, she had married him. Jet had been a wonderful albeit somewhat controlling partner, but she had ended up losing him while he had been trying to save a life during a three-story fire. The person had survived, then her husband had succumbed to smoke inhalation.

Snuggled under the covers in Brigg's spare room, Courtney reminded herself of the devastating outcome of being with a man in uniform. Just as her in-laws had done several times. Whenever they could, Robert and Muriel would drop in conversation that Jet would be alive if Courtney had talked him into leaving that dangerous profession. What they refused to understand was that Jet loved his job. It had been his second love, next to her. She couldn't say she loved him and ask him to give up his passion. Not when she had no clue about hers.

Her lack of passion made Jet her everything. Her center. He had captured her heart in a matter of days, and she would have been content to just be his wife— forever. Jet had advised her on many occasions to choose a career path, but she hadn't felt pressed, thinking she had time. Time was a joke. When Jet died, she had been gutted. A mistake she wouldn't make again.

Yet, under the cover of darkness, Courtney admitted she found her rescuer physically appealing, and she enjoyed their verbal sparring. A sign she might be attracted to him, which was normal and healthy. An indication that her hormones and her eyes were still intact. But nothing would come of it. Not that Brigg would even look her way, considering she was carrying another man's child. Not that she wanted him to. She still wore her wedding ring for two reasons: it deterred most men from approaching her, and it helped her maintain her last connection to Jet.

Courtney inhaled. There was an aroma creeping into the room that made her mouth drool. The baby kicked in her womb, a demand for her to get out of bed and feed him. It had been hours since her last meal. She sniffed again. Goodness, whatever that was smelled amazing. Tossing the covers aside, Courtney trounced out of the room. Before going to sleep, she had taken a long shower and donned a sensible two-piece cotton pajama short set and slippers. She rued leaving her sexier sleepwear in Druid Hills, but she had needed to pack light. Anyways, it's not like she could be scantily dressed in this surrounding.

She traipsed past the living room, which had the large screen television turned on to a sports game and headed toward the kitchen, fussing with the neck of her pajama shirt. As she grew closer, the clamor of pots and the cling of utensils became more pronounced, right along with the delicious smells. Her belly sang, anticipating the first taste, and her mouth watered, ready to savor whatever goodness Brigg had cooked up.

It was pitiful the highlight of her day would be what she ate for dinner. But there it was. Joy in the small things.

"You woke up right on time," Brigg said with a smile. "I warmed up some chicken stew and some white rice that my mom made. I didn't cook it, but I am really good at heating things up. I use the pots to do that, or they would never get used." He cleared his throat. "By the way, your car is at the repair shop. Lenny, the tow truck owner, said there was some flooding on the other streets, so he went there instead."

"Okay, thanks for letting me know." She licked her lips. "Dinner smells amazing. Me and my baby thank you in advance." Courtney watched his eyes fill with curiosity and squared her shoulders, preparing herself for the inevitable question of her husband's whereabouts. But instead, he turned off the burners on the stove.

After serving a small scoop of rice on two plates, Brigg dipped the ladle in the stew and gave them each a good portion. Holding the plates in his hand, Brigg walked around the counter and placed them on the small table in the eat-in kitchen. Then he held out the chair and invited her to sit. "What do you want to drink?"

"I'll have a bottle of water if you have any." She gathered a couple of napkins and put one by his plate and then hers. She heard the refrigerator door close, a drawer open and then cutlery ping before Brigg returned with knives and forks.

He took the seat across from her, and they dug in.

She moaned. "This is delicious…"

Mouth full of food, Brigg smiled. Soon the scraping of their cutlery were the only sounds, and Courtney racked her brain for something to say, some mundane topic that would fill the silence while they enjoyed the meal.

He picked up a remote from the center of the table and turned on the small television above the round glass table. He tuned to the weather station. The volume was low, but there was a reporter standing in the rain, gripping the microphone and swaying under the tempestuous winds.

She dabbed at her mouth with a napkin. "Turn it up, please."

The reporter stated that there was a new tropical storm brewing that would become Hurricane Norma in a few hours. It was scheduled to hit landfall in about sixteen hours, which was ample time for her to come up with a plan and get to Fort Lauderdale to hunker down until the hurricane passed.

"I've got to get out of here," she said, scraping her chair to stand. "Maybe I can take a Greyhound to Fort Lauderdale." If she could work up the courage to brave the weather.

Brigg shook his head and motioned for her to sit. "They are evacuating down that end, and everyone will be going up north to Orlando to find shelter. Not to mention the highway is going to be gridlocked. There will also be the mad dash to the stores and massive panic. Your best bet would be to stay right here in Love Creek."

Courtney plopped back in her chair. "Stay where? I imagine the shelters will be overcrowded."

He raised an eyebrow and gave her a look like she was daft to even ask. "You think I would kick an expectant mother out on the street in this weather?" The silent, *you should know me better than that*, hung in the air. But she didn't know him at all to make presumptions.

"Maybe I can go to a nearby school or something." She untwisted the cap and took a swig of water.

"You'd rather sleep on the floor than wait it out here?" Now he sounded affronted.

"I don't want to assume." She stabbed her fork into the chicken and plunked it into her mouth. She hated being in this position. If she had a job, she would have her own money saved, and she wouldn't be in this predicament. At the mercy of a complete stranger.

Now that she was about to become a mother and independent of her wealthy in-laws, it was time for her to take the necessary steps to earn a substantial living so that her son would be well taken care of. She swallowed a feeling of bitterness. The Meadowses had encouraged her to stay at home. Maybe to cripple her. To keep her from being financially viable. She remembered how they had discouraged her from seeking employment, all part of their plan to prove her unfit. But once she was with her sister, she would get herself together. She wasn't going to depend on anyone for a handout.

That plan had no bearing on her present, however.

"Fine. Since you need to hear the words, please shelter here." His words intruded on her musings. "No point in the spare room going to waste. If it puts you at ease, I would do this for anyone in need. This house might be modest, but it is sturdy, built to code and able to withstand category-five winds. It's not marked as a flood zone."

"How do they know that for sure? Isn't the true test an actual hurricane?"

"This isn't my first storm. I've lived here all my life. Most of the time, we're out grilling or playing football, especially when the eye passes."

Her mouth dropped. "I can't imagine that."

He chuckled. "We'll be fine. I have candles, water and cans of soup, tuna, beans. Plus, I bought a backup generator, and if needed, I have family nearby." He then gave her the code to his Wi-Fi so she could connect her laptop. As she was joining his network, Brigg's cell pinged, and he took a quick glance at his phone. "There's my mother now." Another ping. "And my brothers." Then he explained. "We have a group chat, and we're all checking in to make sure we have ample supplies."

He sent a quick text and then placed his phone face down on the table.

"Are all your family here in Love Creek?" she asked, thinking of her sister. Kaylin was on a ship heading to Alaska, so she would bypass the storm. But Kaylin had no idea that Courtney had been making the journey to Fort Lauderdale. As soon as she could, she would alert her sibling that she would be heading there soon.

"Almost all. My twin—"

"You have a twin?" she asked, fascinated at the idea of there being two gorgeous look-alikes.

Wiping his mouth, he dropped his napkin on his plate and leaned back into his chair. "Yes, I'm fraternal. We are polar opposites. Caleb has the same height and build like my dad and works as a lawyer for the school board. Actually, all of us work for the Love Creek School District in some capacity. During the day, I'm a school resource officer, and after that—"

"You hand out tickets to unsuspecting, innocent women."

His lips quirked. "I hand out tickets to drivers with expired registrations."

She averted her gaze, enjoying his comeback. She

imagined many of the women in town soaking up his charm as she was. She rubbed her tummy.

"And might I add that I didn't cite you for speeding. You were going about seventeen miles above the posted limit. But I gave you a break."

Oh, yes, she had been speeding… "Thank you. I plan on paying my ticket as soon as I have the funds."

His phone rang and he stood. "I have to take this."

She nodded and gathered their plates to be useful. Taking them to the kitchen, she filled the sink, then washed and rinsed them before placing them on the dish rack. Then she wiped the already spotless counters before returning to watch the news. She already missed her new companion, hearing his low rumble while he talked to…a girlfriend perhaps? No way was he single. She felt a twinge of inexplicable…jealousy.

She twisted her wedding band.

Jealousy? For a man she had just met. Ridiculous. Drying her hands, she marched into the guest room and pushed aside her curiosity about Officer Brigg Harrington. Pulling out her laptop, she decided to send her sister an email. She heard a boom and peered out the window to see thick dark clouds across the blue-gray skies.

Returning to her laptop, she noticed there were two messages from her in-laws in her inbox. Her hands shook as she opened the first communication. It was Robert asking if she was okay and letting her know that she had left her phone at the house. Hitting Delete, she then read the other, which made her shiver. It was Muriel letting her know that they had canceled her credit cards and stating that she had no right to take Ansel away from them. She vowed to find her, threatening that she would regret it.

Heart pounding in her chest, for the first time, Courtney was glad she had broken down in this small town. The Meadowses knew about her sister. They might have someone on the lookout for her there. This—this is what she needed to be thinking about. Not the handsome man in uniform who was her unwilling host.

A heavy downpour followed that dark affirmation. She wrapped her arms around herself, trying to be calm.

For now, she was safe here. She repeated that until she believed it. Love Creek would make a good temporary hideout while she calculated her next move. Because there was no way she was going to sit back and allow her son to be taken. Jayson would never spend nights crying, yearning for his mother, wondering why she wasn't involved in his life.

Besides, she had finally gathered the courage to look at how much she owed for that ticket. She needed a job to pay off the fine. Another reason to stay here.

Firing off an update to her sister without disclosing her location, Courtney then pulled up an employment site. The hurricane wouldn't last forever. In time, the storm would pass, and after that, she would get a job.

Chapter Six

Shaking shutters, howling winds and the clap of thunder were the music of the hurricane he had heard played many times before. He knew that symphony well. Hurricane Norma had arrived and, according to the news, was leaving a path of devastation across the Southeast.

Lying in his king-size bed with his arms folded behind his head, Brigg resisted the urge to go check on his visitor. It was a little past 3:00 a.m., and he hoped Courtney was asleep, but since she wasn't a native Floridian, he figured she was awake. And possibly terrified.

It was no use. He had to look in on her.

His feet thumped across the floor as he ambled across the hall from his bedroom. He wrapped his hand around the door handle and paused as a possibility dawned. She could think he was at her door for a different motive. This was booty-call hours.

But she's pregnant.

Yet no less desirable.

Brigg rocked back on his heels. She had spunk and sass, which was like having AC on a muggy day. A cool breath of air. Talking with her, he felt excitement he hadn't experienced in a while. Moving from her door, he went into the kitchen to put the kettle on. He would have to trust that if she became concerned, she would seek him out. In the few hours in her presence, he knew Courtney had no qualms speaking her mind.

If it hadn't been his job calling, Brigg wouldn't have taken the call during their conversation at dinner. He found he enjoyed seeing her brows furrow or her eyes flash while she spoke. He was pretty sure she didn't know it, but Courtney wore her thoughts on her face. He could read every expression. And even the brief flash of curious desire when he had stuffed his hands in his pants pockets.

Which deepened his questions about her husband.

It didn't escape his observation that she hadn't asked to use his phone to call her spouse. There was no frantic urgency to reach her baby's father. Unless she'd had an affair... That could explain a lot, including her traveling solo. Maybe she was on the run.

Naw. No way was she a cheat. She didn't give off those vibes. He had been in the police business too long. Too suspicious.

There had to be another explanation. Normally, Brigg would ask. But he was a refuge for a member of the opposite sex in the storm. Those dynamics made him hold his tongue.

The kettle sang.

Taking two cups out of the cupboard, Brigg decided to make two hot cocoas. Being pregnant meant plenty of bathroom trips and late-night snacking. She would find her way into the kitchen. He wasn't a gambler, but this was something he would bet on.

He washed his hands at the sink, squeezing the spout tight to stop the tiny drip, before reaching for the pound cake on display.

Sure enough, just as he sliced a piece, the guest door squeaked. He heard a shuffle of feet before she appeared.

"I couldn't sleep."

"Figured as much. I made you some hot chocolate, and if you give me a few seconds, I'll give you a generous piece of cake." He went to get another plate. He had tried out a recipe for pound cake that his mother, Tanya, had given him, and to his surprise, it had turned out better than edible.

Her eyes brightened. "That sounds marvelous. The thunder boomed and woke me, and I haven't closed my eyes since." She scurried to sit at the table. Her hands drummed some rhythm on the tabletop. She started to hum "We will, we will rock you" while pounding out the beat.

Brigg joined in, singing the lyrics.

She laughed. "I can't believe you know the words to that song. I only know that one line."

"Yeah, well, my mother was a fan of Queen, and my father is a football fan. A love he has passed on to all his sons. One of us ended up playing pro football. You ever heard of Hawk Harrington?" Adding whipped cream to their hot chocolate, Brigg then placed her nighttime snack in front of her before retrieving his own. The way she rubbed her hands together and moaned with delight, you would think he had given her a stack of cash.

After biting a huge piece of cake and stuffing it in her mouth—she hadn't bothered to use a fork—Courtney nodded. He reached over to wipe the excess from the side of her face. She swallowed. "Of course, I know Hawk—the beast of the NFL. My husband, Jet, was a huge fan. He had a Hawk jersey that he wore every time his team played. I'm pretty sure I have it in my possession." She patted her stomach. "Saving it for my son."

She spoke about her husband in the past. Like he was no longer here. Brigg dipped his fork into the moist cake and tasted a piece. *Mmm*...just as good as the last time.

"Is your husband deceased?" he asked, his tone gentle.

"Yes," she exhaled. "Jet died in the line of duty about seven months ago."

"Oh? I'm sorry to hear that. My condolences for your loss." Her choice of words registered. "He was a fellow policeman?"

She shook her head. "A firefighter." Brigg thought she would share more details, but she tasted her hot chocolate and turned the conversation by asking if he was married.

"No. Every now and again, I reenter the dating scene, but—" he shrugged "—I'm single. By choice."

"Is it because of your profession?" Something about her tone suggested that question was more than just a natural flow of their conversation.

Stretching his legs, he decided to elaborate. "Being a police officer means that people entrust you with their lives every day." He pointed her way. "Case in point. Though you are in a bad situation, I doubt you would've accepted my invitation to bunk out here if I didn't have a badge. There's honor but also a level of confidentiality that I have to maintain." Her eyes flashed registration and understanding. "Well, my last girlfriend didn't understand that. She is a reporter at the news station."

"Ahh…"

"Yes. She is very ambitious and wanted a prime-time slot, which meant she wanted me to give her the inside scoop if I covered the mayor or if I was a part of a crime scene. We're a small town, and we don't have too many high-profile cases, but we've had an SAT scandal at one of the high schools that went viral."

"Wow...that must have been something." She tapped her chin. "Wait, I think I heard about that. If I remember right, the principal was a woman, and people were demanding she be fired or something."

"Yes. My father was the superintendent at that time, and my brother was her temporary replacement."

Courtney's brows rose. "Small town."

"Yep. So, Pilar wanted me to tell her where Shanna— that's the principal's name—where she was hiding." He waved a hand. "I refused. Then, when Shanna married my brother Lynx after she had been cleared of any wrongdoing, Pilar wanted to be my date. When I refused, because I knew it wasn't about coming with me, that it was trying to get info for the paper, Pilar threatened to leave, and I didn't stop her. I was relieved actually."

"That's awful. Not your feeling relieved but her using manipulation."

"Yeah. I think the only reason she dated me is because of my family." He chuckled. "I told you about Hawk, who's an NFL player, but Axel Harrington is also my brother."

Her mouth dropped. "You're related to *the* Axel Harrington—the movie star? Get out. My sister is a huge fan. Kaylin is not going to believe this." She gave him a look of admiration. "Man, kudos to your parents. It sounds like they did a bang-up job." She cocked her head. "Are all of your brothers as successful as you are?"

Brigg's chest puffed. The fact that she saw him as successful when he had just told her about Hawk and Axel impressed him greatly. "Yes, I guess you could say so. My twin brother, Caleb, is an attorney. I've got another,

Ethan, who was an Olympic athlete…" He trailed off. "Our parents didn't give us a choice. My dad constantly told us that we had to be productive citizens."

She gave a sad smile. "Sounds like you all had some good parents."

"Yes, they are the best. We're a blended family." Her tone suggested she had had the opposite and his heart squeezed. Brigg knew he was blessed, and he didn't take his upbringing for granted.

She smirked. "I figured, once you mentioned Hawk, but I didn't want to pry."

Brigg then explained his family heritage. "Hawk and Lynx are adopted." He paused to get her reaction. Growing up, whenever he had introduced his brothers, Brigg always had to brace himself for the questions.

However, all she said was, "Interesting… Where do you fit in?"

"I'm the baby," he said, pointing to his chest. "Well, myself and Caleb. We're number six and seven. So, my Mom had Axel, Dad had Drake and Ethan, and they both had Caleb and me."

"And that's the way you became the Harrington bunch?" she supplied.

"No, we're the Harrington men."

She dipped her head. "Must have been interesting growing up in a house with no girls."

He chuckled. "We had a lot of fun. My mom might feel differently. I finally have sisters though, since Lynx is married, and Axel is engaged."

She jutted an index finger in the air. "Oh, yeah, I remember reading about Axel in the papers. It was like a real-life Cinderella story. His fiancé is stunning."

Picturing Axel's assistant and soon-to-be wife, Brigg

smiled. "And sassy. She doesn't hesitate to put Axel in his place. Maddie is the best thing that ever happened to him."

Courtney gave Brigg a light jab. "Sounds like you wouldn't mind that happening to you."

"No. No." He held both hands up. "It would take an act of nature from the man upstairs for me to enter a serious relationship again. I'm good with an occasional date or two." Then he swerved the question her way. "What about you? Do you think you'll ever get married again?"

Courtney twisted her wedding ring. He doubted she noticed how many times she played with that piece of metal. "Why mess with perfection? I don't think lightning will strike twice." He heard her breathy tone, and for some reason, his stomach clenched. She sounded like she was still in love with her husband. She patted her tummy. "I think I'm good with taking care of my son. Besides, I've got other pressing priorities, like getting money so I can fix my car and get out of here once it's safe."

He didn't want to stress her by telling her that her car had choked out its last breath. But then he thought of his mother and Shanna and Maddie. They would be furious if they felt coddled. So, he let her know what Lenny said and prayed she wouldn't start crying again.

"I had a feeling…" Her eyes misted, but she didn't fall apart. "That's why I plan on getting a job."

His brows rose. "A job?" He just stopped short of adding, *How far along are you?*

The overwhelming urge to help her, to meet all her needs, pressed his heart, and he almost opened his mouth and offer to take care of it for her. However, that wasn't his place, and the fact that the thought had entered his mind was confusing—an internal discussion for another time. He really wanted to say that he didn't think she should be working in her condition. But once again, he held back. Brigg wasn't about to get bopped in the head. Instead, he said, "Let's just take things one step at a time. It will all work out. In the meantime, you're more than welcome to stay here."

She placed a hand on her chest. "That's generous of you, but I don't want to impose."

"A necessity is not an imposition. My house is your house."

"You might regret that."

"I wouldn't say it if I didn't mean it." His cell pinged. "That's my job again. I had this weekend off, but they were asking for volunteers to help with stragglers stuck outside." The wind howled its fury.

"In this hurricane? Won't you be putting your own life in jeopardy? That doesn't make sense." Thunder boomed. Her eyes were wide and filled with fright. For him.

He shifted. "Yes, it comes with the territory. Not everyone follows the rules and stays inside. You'd be surprised how many people brave the weather regardless of the warnings."

Brigg grabbed his phone and stood, resisting the strange urge to explain himself to her. To put her mind at ease. Bidding her goodnight, an image of those troubled hazel eyes followed him into his bedroom. Maybe her worry was because she was pregnant. Then he slipped out of his pants and shirt. He couldn't very well leave her here. She could go into labor anytime. It was no use. He couldn't leave. He called in and apprised his boss of the situation. He knew he had done the right thing. Done his duty.

This was precisely why he wasn't in a relationship. He

didn't want to have to answer to anyone. To explain why he took the risks he did. It wasn't for a paycheck. It was because he knew he didn't want to do anything else with his life. His career, his choice.

If at times he felt...lonely in this house, well, it was worth it. No matter how cold the space in the bed was next to him, he was good with his life the way it was, and for now, he had no reason to change.

Chapter Seven

Courtney had misspoken. She knew that. She had no right to voice her opinion on his job habits. It wasn't her place.

That's why, much later that same morning, she vowed to bite the inside of her cheek before she commented on Brigg's everyday life. Instead, she would show her gratitude for him opening his home by helping out as best as she could. After that pep talk, she showered using the lavender body wash in the bathroom and dressed in a pair of leggings and an oversized T-shirt.

The house rattled and shook from the heavy winds. It had been hours, and the hurricane didn't appear to be losing strength. She was pretty sure the damage in Hurricane Norma's wake would be extensive.

When she entered the kitchen, she saw the lawman seated around the table eating a bowl of oatmeal with a glass of orange juice. He too had showered—the smell of citrus strong in the air—and had donned his uniform. Her eyes roamed his well-defined physique in the neatly pressed ensemble before landing on his badge.

"Good morning, again," she said, ignoring the sudden tightening in her shoulders. That had been Jet's very last meal. He hadn't made it home. Fear enveloped her and though she knew it was irrational, Courtney found herself fighting back tears. Drat these hormones. She sniffled and turned away from the sight, urging herself not to make comparisons.

"How was your sleep?" Brigg asked, unaware of the fear growing within her at the speed of ants running to sugar. All she could do was nod in response.

To keep herself busy, she headed for the pound cake and cut herself a huge slice. When she joined Brigg at the table, his brows rose. He stuffed a spoonful of oatmeal in his mouth.

"I'll be working from home on desk duty."

"You're not going out?" she said breathily, trying her best to sound unaffected.

"No. I'll be handling and covering low emergency 911 calls."

"Oh, okay." Her heart loosened.

"There are lots of downed trees, people are losing power and water in the other town over, so some are braving the weather and coming here. All our schools are doubling up in capacity."

"Wow. It's so bad out there."

He pointed upward. "Yeah. Put it this way. This house is supposed to be soundproof."

"Whoa."

"Yes, Norma has been upgraded to a category four. Even though she hit landfall, she hasn't weakened. Our captain said we're to all sit tight for now. Only a select few and some of the National Guard are out in this weather."

"Any idea when it should subside?"

"Hopefully later tonight. But that's just the beginning. The cleanup will take months, not to mention the insurance reports and claims. We will be working non-stop for a solid six months at least. FEMA plans to set up offices at our mall to provide assistance and food." His phone chirped, and Brigg took a final gulp of his orange juice. "I'd better get to it. I'll be in my office. If you need anything, reach out."

"I'll make sure not to disturb you."

"Don't worry about it." His chair scraped as he stood, gathering his bowl and glass. "I didn't give you a tour, but my office is down the hall, the first door on your right. My bedroom's farther down on the right, and I do have a lanai," he said, pointing to the sliding doors, "but of course, I would advise against going out there in this weather." He placed both items in the sink and proceeded to wash them.

"Mind if I snoop around in your fridge?" she asked.

"Not at all. I've got peaches, plums, grapes...already washed and they should be nice and cold." His phone rang, and she could see he wanted to answer.

So, she shooed him off. "See you at lunch." After finishing her cake, she cleared the sink, took out a package of chicken tenderloins to defrost and ate a large peach before settling on the microfiber couch in his living room to watch a movie and then the news surrounding the hurricane. There was a newscaster standing near the town entrance wearing a raincoat being tossed about like a feather in the wind. Behind her, the rain pelted, and if Courtney's eyes were seeing right, a lanai—an actual lanai—had rolled across the screen.

"You need to get home," Courtney mumbled before turning off the tube. She wandered over to the sliding doors intending to open the blinds but realized Brigg had put the shutters down. She went to peer out the front door. The sky had blackened with purple and gray hues. She could see a flash of lightning and the trees dipping and swaying under the forceful gusts. Rubbing her arms and closing the door, she was thankful Brigg had asked her to stay.

She heard the low rumble of his voice helping people on the phone, and he had ventured out to help himself to an orange. But the calls had been nonstop. He was bound to be hungry. Which reminded her. The chicken. The least she could do was feed her host, and this was soup-making weather.

A quick search of the pantry revealed that Brigg had celery, carrots, potatoes, egg noodles, flour, bouillon cubes and chicken broth. She had all the ingredients she needed. Within fifteen minutes, Courtney had the vegetables chopped, the chicken diced and the soup pot gurgling. Snapping her fingers, she went to see if Brigg had corn on the cob.

There were three in the vegetable drawer of the refrigerator. Shucking the corn, she cut them in three and tossed them into the pot along with the vegetables and noodles. Next, she made quick work of rolling out the dough to make small dumplings. Then she covered the pot and placed the timer on for ten minutes since Brigg had an induction stove. *Yum.*

Her stomach growled and the corners of her mouth moistened. She couldn't wait to eat.

Courtney had just finishing preparing a quick salad when her ears perked up. She heard a high-pitched plop and frowned. Maybe she had left the tap on. She went over to the sink to investigate. Sure enough, there was a tiny drip. She returned to the pantry, which doubled as a laundry room. She might have seen some tools on a shelf above the washer and dryer. Sure enough, there was a case of tools and a drill. Upon further investigation, she realized Brigg had purchased all the items he would need to repair the faucet.

She rubbed her lower back. Maybe she should leave well enough alone. Then she spied the receipt inside the plastic bag. Her mouth dropped. The receipt was about a year old. There was no way that sink had that drip for that long…the water bill would be outrageous. She rocked back on her heels. She could fix his sink in less than hour.

Grabbing the bag and tools, she decided to go for it. Saving his water bill would be a great way to show her gratitude. Besides, now that she knew about it, the drip would annoy her. Back inside the kitchen, she crouched to the floor to turn off the water under the sink. Being eight months pregnant made it a balancing act. Good thing she practiced yoga.

The timer went off.

Great. She didn't relish the struggle to get back on her feet so soon. She grabbed the sink and used it as a support to hoist herself to stand before turning off the stove. Huffing, she wiped her damp hair off her face.

Then, with a determined grunt, she returned to her task. Thankfully, she was repairing a faucet and not working under the sink. Courtney placed her tongue between her teeth and used a screwdriver to loosen the screen to remove the handle. Then she snatched the smaller of two wrenches to take off the cap. She had to take out the cam, washer and ball, as well as the seats and springs.

Exhaling, she massaged her neck muscles. Then she arched her back and did a couple mini squats. Her stomach growled, but she ignored it. She would gorge on the soup as a reward for getting this done.

After stretching her arms, she took off the seats and springs. Digging in the bag, she saw Brigg had replacement seats, springs and O-rings. Perfect. She replaced them all. Her chest heaved from the effort, but she was done. Tossing the empty packages in the trash, she repacked his toolbox and returned it to the pantry.

Now to turn on the water supply. She groaned, unsure if her legs would hold up this time. Maybe she could bend over instead of squatting. Maintaining a precarious balance, she managed to turn the nozzle and not end up sprawled on the floor. A quick test and she was satisfied the leak had been repaired.

Whew. She rubbed her stomach. Now for soup.

Turning around, she yelped at the man standing a few feet behind her. "Brigg, how long have you been standing there?"

"Not long…" He avoided eye contact. "I followed my nose. What's that I smell?"

"Soup. Chicken noodle."

Not long was relative. She busied herself by getting the salad and balsamic vinaigrette out of the refrigerator, all the while wondering if he had seen her with her butt perched in the air. An unappealing sight. Correction. An embarrassing, unappealing sight. She was pretty sure a blush was spreading across her cheeks. Not to mention her chest was heaving, bringing attention to her enlarged breasts.

"Thank you, but you didn't have to. I was going to make us a couple of sandwiches. I hope you didn't tire yourself out too much." Brigg got utensils, two bowls and salad plates out of the cupboard and proceeded to serve their meals.

"That's sweet. But I'm more than capable, and I've been vegging out on your couch for most of the morning, so it was good to have something to do."

"I can see that."

He hadn't commented on the drip, or rather, lack of drip. After urging her to take a seat, Brigg brought over their food.

A strong hand rested on her shoulder. "How are you feeling? I meant to check on you earlier, but the phone lines have been ringing nonstop."

The compassion in his tone warmed her heart. And the heat from his hand rubbing circles on her shoulder created a slight sizzle that was messing with her libido, because she was zing-zanging from the physical contact. "Oh, I'm all right," she breezed out. "I have a few weeks to go before this baby shows his face, so it's all good."

"That's nice to know." He sat adjacent to her, his long legs grazing against her own. She squeezed her legs tight together and focused on shoving food into her mouth. It was either that or groan from the contact.

She had heard from other pregnant women at Lamaze class that their sexual urges had been in overdrive since pregnancy, but of course, she had been too busy grieving the death of her spouse the past few months to think about sex. Yet a few hours in close proximity with a man, a virile man, and she was in heat. Not that she could do anything about it. Tell that to her pulsing— *Nope. Stop thinking about it.* She shifted her legs slightly and reached for a napkin the same time he did.

Their hands grazed. On cue, thunder cracked.
Really?

Tapered fingers curled around hers and squeezed. "It's just a little thunder, or as my father says, God's talking," he drawled out, his voice sounding low and sexy, which made her focus on his lips. Plump lips. And his talking about thunder made her wonder what kind of thunder he had packing. *Goodness.*

Slowly, she removed her hand from under his and wiped her mouth. She didn't want him to think she was affected by something as simple as a touch and a squeeze of encouragement. Despite her racing heart, erratic pulse and wayward mind, she attempted to engage in normal conversation.

She jabbed her fork into her salad. "If the newscaster is right, the worst of it will be over in a few hours."

"Yes, but then comes the recovery. There could be downed lines, flooding, search and rescues... There's no telling when schools will reopen. A lot of people in the next town over have lost water and electricity, so they might be seeking refuge here. Though we might lose power too. Then we'll have to worry about people passing out from heat stroke." He knocked on the wooden table. "Thankfully, we've been lucky so far, but we just have to be prepared for what happens and remain positive."

Wow. Courtney could have ended up stranded on the side of the road. Alone. For the first time, she was thankful her car had broken down before the hurricane hit. She reached over to grab his arm. "If I hadn't gotten stuck..." She stopped before she got too emotional. "I'm glad I'm here with you."

Brigg patted her hand. "There's a reason for everything. It will all work out." After a moment, he stood. "I've got to get back to work, but lunch was delicious. You put your foot in that soup. I can't wait to have some more later." He pointed at his empty bowl. "Don't tell my mom I said this, but you're giving her some stiff competition."

His words of praise enfolded her like a warm blanket. "I love cooking," she said, standing to gather their empty dishes and already mapping out the next meal. All because the man said he loved her food. She had taken a few culinary courses and had dabbled in some baking but hadn't completed the certification.

"Then we'll make a great team, because I love to eat."

Chapter Eight

Now why had he used the word *team*? That's the question that stayed in the back of his mind the entire time he worked over the next few hours. He could hear the pots clanging and the sounds of chopping while Courtney prepped their dinner. Brigg had gone back out there to tell her she didn't need to cook anything else since he was quite content with leftovers, but she waved him off, mentioning the words *pepper steak* and *mashed potatoes*. Of course, he hadn't argued.

His mother had texted to see how he was faring and to report that they were hunkered down with Ethan and Caleb. Brigg was glad his brothers had gone to stay with their parents. Patrick and Tanya Harrington were pretty active and independent, but he still worried.

The aroma of some good home cooking teased his nostrils. That woman knew how to throw down in the kitchen. Something Brigg appreciated. He was what he would call a good intention shopper. The customer who went into the grocery store and picked up all kinds of meat and produce because he just knew he was going to eat it all. And he had visions of himself whipping up gourmet dinners. Yet he found himself pulling into his mother's driveway to get a container to go several times during the week.

(1) It was quicker. Easier with his work schedule.

(2) He couldn't cook that well.

He had hundreds of YouTube videos saved but had yet to master any of the numerous recipes. It wasn't for lack of trying. It was because he was a tad bit too creative, adding random ingredients just to see what would happen. Big mistake. But at least he had made a decent pound cake. And that was due to his mother making him vow to stick to the recipe.

His cell rang. It was his brother Axel calling from LA on his next movie set. "You good? I'm making my rounds."

"Yes, I'm at home." Brigg didn't mention his unexpected house guest. "I spoke to Lynx earlier, and he and Shanna are fine as well. Lynx wanted to go to the high school, but Shanna convinced him to stay put."

"Smart woman. I'm glad you're not out there in that hurricane weather."

"No, I'm more directing calls and setting up evacuees with shelters and housing." The people of Love Creek were generous, opening their homes to others in need.

"If you need to use our place, you know the code," Maddie chimed in. Axel must have his phone on speaker. Axel had a mini mansion about fifteen minutes from him.

"I don't think it will come to that." Just then, he heard a loud bang and a crash that shook the house. "Bro, let me call you back. It sounded like something hit the house." Jumping up, he propelled himself outside the room, his heart thumping in his chest.

"Okay, keep us posted."

Disconnecting the call, he shouted out to Courtney, "Are you okay?"

"Yes, I'm good." Her voice was distant enough for him to believe she was in her room. He rushed in and glanced around, but all appeared to be well. "What happened?"

"I think a tree fell and hit the side of your home."

Brigg opened the door leading to the garage with Courtney not too far behind. He looked up to see that the roof had caved in near the garage door, but Ethan's Sling seemed fine. He wondered if there were more trees down or about to come down.

"I'm going outside for a minute to check things out," he told Courtney, closing the door behind him.

"But it's bad out there."

"I won't be long."

He could hear the wind whistling, but Brigg threw the door open and ran out to investigate. His legs bent as he fought the force of the downpour, clutching the side of the house for support. He cupped his face with his hands and dipped his head around the corner. Sure enough, a large tree from the neighbor's yard had smashed his garage, mere feet away from the bedroom where Courtney slept. Brigg's car was spared, but his AC unit had sustained damage, though it was still running. Feeling like he was being watched, he whirled around to see that Courtney had followed him outside. "You shouldn't be out here. It's too dangerous."

Rain splatted her hair against her face. "I was worried." Standing there with her eyes wide, Brigg felt an urge to comfort her and yell at her for putting herself and the baby at risk.

He did neither and ushered her back into the house

and shoved the door closed. The door handle felt even shakier, and he made another mental note to change it out for the other one he had purchased a couple months ago.

They stood facing each other, dripping on his mat like bedraggled rats. The rain pelted against the door, and the only other sound was that of their heavy breathing. "It's not as bad as I thought, but you can bunk in my room." There were more large trees on that side, and he couldn't chance one falling on her. The implications of his words sunk in.

Her pupils dilated. "With you?" Was that desire swimming in their midst or his own sudden attraction reflecting back at him? Brigg told himself it might be wishful or, perhaps, stupid thinking. Images of her wrapped in the sheets of his bed filled his mind, messing with his equilibrium. It had been a minute since he had shared his bed, but he wasn't about to proposition a pregnant woman.

"I'll sleep on the futon in my office."

"I couldn't put you out of your room." Her breath sounded raspy.

He stepped back. "I'll be okay."

She patted her damp curls. "I can camp out on the couch."

Yes, that was a safer bet. "We'll both do that." That way he could keep an eye on her and keep her calm. Brigg didn't want to scare her, but he knew from experience there was a direct correlation between bad weather and labor. Maybe it was the low barometric pressure or the physiological stress, but the hospital's labor and delivery ward had doubled up their rooms to accommodate the number of women giving birth. Brigg didn't want

Courtney added to that number or, worse, to have to deliver a baby himself.

"Are you ready to eat?"

Oh, if she only knew… *Whew.* "Yes. I could eat." And he wasn't talking just about food. He would love a taste of her lips. That unbidden thought alarmed him. It didn't help that she was looking at him like…like…he was a piece of fruit. She actually licked her lips. Dangerous. This was Netflix-and-chill weather. No. This was him transposing, reading more into her innocent comments to fan his wants. He had to put distance between them before he acted on his baser impulses and possibly got slapped. He would avoid Netflix and break out the board games. Plus, he had a thousand-piece puzzle somewhere in the back of his closet. They could engage in practical pastimes.

"I'd better get changed."

Tugging on her shirt, she said, "Me too. I'm soaked."

"Meet you back here in ten?"

In his room, Brigg kept his gaze off his king-size bed and reminded himself why he wasn't in a relationship. Reminding himself it was his choice.

Gathering two sets of blankets and the games, he moved the coffee table and rearranged the living area so they could spread out. Courtney came out of the kitchen dressed in her jammies holding a heaping plate in each hand. Brigg got two folding trays from behind the couch to hold their dinners.

Then the lights went out.

"I've got candles and flashlights," Brigg said. Within minutes, he had a few candles lit, and they ate their food under the candlelight. Courtney snuggled under the covers, and the scent of vanilla and lilacs filled the space, creating a bubble of intimacy around them. To the casual observer, they appeared to be lovers enjoying a romantic meal.

Time to shred that mirage.

He made them both cups of hot cocoa adding a generous amount of whipped cream and then asked if she wanted to play Phase 10.

"Can we talk instead?" she drawled out, cupping her mug.

"What do you want to talk about?" He settled next to her.

She shrugged. "I don't know. Tell me about your childhood, or we can tell each other scary stories." Without the electricity, the Florida heat would be vicious. A bead of perspiration was already lining her forehead. The house was going to get warm and the hot beverage wasn't helping. A quick glance outside showed the rain had tapered off a bit. Maybe the storm was finally passing on.

He stretched his legs. "Not much to tell about my past, except that I have the best family in the world. Grew up in a house of educators who are sports fans. You name it, my dad watched it. And so did we. And my mom had us watching musicals, so we were well rounded." Courtney laughed at that. "I know that's how we ended up with Hawk in the NFL, Axel in the movies and Ethan an Olympic swimmer."

"Wait, when you said Ethan was your brother, I didn't register that he was *the* Ethan Harrington. I should have known. He was supposed to be the next Michael Phelps until his injury." She slapped her leg. "From now on, anyone famous with the last name Harrington, I'll just assume they are related to you."

He chuckled. "Not all. That's it. I promise."

She gave him a look of admiration. "I know I said it before, but I'm impressed. I mean, I love to hear that all of you, as Black men, are successful. And I know Hawk and Lynx aren't Black, but they are invited to the cookout."

Brigg cracked up. "You're hilarious, but yes, I am proud of us, and our parents have a lot to do with how we turned out. Believe me. I'm one of the babies, so I didn't even realize we were a blended family until I was about to start middle school. I didn't get the impact of my parents adopting two white brothers until my first year of high school. One thing's for sure—I never doubted that I was loved, and having lots of siblings means you've got automatic best friends, automatic acceptance and you're never alone." He waved a hand. "Now, there's good and bad to that though. Sharing a bunk bed all the way through elementary school wasn't fun."

He then regaled her with Hawk getting bitten by a bee on his butt, Axel's embarrassing pimple and Ethan peeing in the pool at the amusement park when they were kids. He and Courtney laughed so hard it was like they were old friends.

Brigg couldn't wait for his family to meet her... *Wait.* She wouldn't be there long enough to meet his fam.

"Your family sounds amazing. I wish I could say the same for mine though," she said, her tone light. "I had a nomadic childhood. My mother was a drug addict and did whatever she had to to feed her habit." Courtney sipped her hot cocoa and then divulged, "That's how she ended up pregnant with me and with my sister, Kaylin."

Understanding dawned. Brigg squeezed her hand. He knew of a couple mothers in that very situation, and it broke his heart. Courtney continued her tale, very matter-of-factly.

"She tried to take care of us, I think, as best as she could. I have vague memories of my mother combing my hair and giving me ice cream. But she couldn't kick the habit. In fact, when I got older, I learned that me and my sister were taken away because I stuck myself with one of her needles. My mom rushed me to the emergency room, and they called Child Protective Services." This time, when she took a sip, she got a whipped cream mustache.

"Wow. You could have died." Brigg used his thumb to wipe the residue off her upper lip. She tensed for a second before relaxing under his touch.

"I almost did. Which is why I wanted to wait to have children." So her pregnancy had been unplanned, Brigg noted.

She brushed at imaginary lint on her pajama top. "The last time I saw my mother, it was from the back of a police car when I was six years old. Both me and my sister were placed in our first foster home. Luckily for us, our social worker managed to keep us together. We pretty much stayed together until I married Jet."

"Sounds like you and your sister are really close," he observed. "So, how did she end up on a cruise ship?"

"Ahh, you remember that?" Then she rolled her eyes. "Of course you do, you're a cop. You probably ask questions in your sleep and wake up with answers."

They shared a laugh. He loved her sense of humor. His family really would get a kick out of Courtney. It was really too bad she would be gone soon.

"Unlike me, who didn't go to college, Kaylin got her degree in hospitality management—"

"I've never heard of that major."

"Oh, yes, most of the resort and ritzy hotel managers have their bachelor's degrees. Ensuring that a hotel, resort or cruise ship runs smoothly takes someone with leadership and business management skills. They have to make sure there is enough food and beverage to run the ship, oversee guest services, housekeeping and all that stuff that makes a cruise memorable and fun."

"You seem to know a lot about it."

"I was supposed to enroll with her in the courses… But I wasn't sure if that's what I wanted to do." She lifted her shoulders. "My sister has an aptitude for languages and is fluent in Spanish, French and Italian, which is a bonus. She's now an assistant manager over guest services. Kaylin calls me a *Jill of all Trades*, which of course means…" She trailed off, avoiding eye contact.

He knew the rest of that saying. Brigg used his index finger to lift her chin so she would face him. "You're still young. You'll figure it out eventually."

She patted her exposed stomach since her shirt had ridden up, and her face grew serious. "I have no choice now with Jet gone."

"How did you two meet?" he asked softly before sipping his hot cocoa. It was ice cold, so he put it back on the tray.

"On a cruise ship. I was one of the waitresses in the VIP suite." She scoffed. "Then when we got married, he begged me not to get a job, though I've been working since I was thirteen—off the books at first—all the way up until he met me. Or, as he liked to say, he rescued me." Her voice held an edge of bitterness. Sounded like there were some thorns in their happily-ever-after, but there was no perfect relationship, so he couldn't read too much into that. Besides, the way she said Jet's name all breathy and squeaky told Brigg how much she had loved her husband.

She threw off the blanket and stood. "It's way too hot in here." Holding out a hand, she asked, "I'm sure it's much cooler outside on the lanai."

The storm had petered out to light rain, and it was beginning to feel like a sweaty sneaker in here. He looked at the time, shocked to see it was well after midnight. He eyed their dirty plates and mugs and groaned on the inside. They would hold until morning, he told himself. Scooping the blankets in one hand, he accepted hers with the other.

The minute their hands made contact, the lights came on.

Chapter Nine

She had never begged a man to sleep with her before. But now she had, and she would do it again, without regrets. Courtney had awakened two mornings in a row with Brigg right next to her. The storm had passed, but there had been flooding, so they hadn't ventured out. Today, though, she knew their respite had come to an end.

This morning, she had just completed her breathing exercises and her gentle stretching and felt as content as the birds singing outside her window. The sun beamed through the shades, giving her a great view of the man snoring near the edge of the bed with his back turned away from her and facing the wall.

Once the electricity had come on, Brigg had offered her the use of his room again. Visions of the roof falling had pushed her to plead with him to share the bed. It was big enough for the both of them, and she had used spare pillows to build a fort between them. Pillows that now lay scattered on the floor and at the foot of the bed.

She inhaled, appreciating Brigg's familiar citrus, woodsy scent and his broad shoulders. Her hand itched to press against those strong muscles bulging through his back. At some point in the night, he must have tossed the white T-shirt he had changed into before coming to bed. She lifted his covers to see if he was still wearing his plaid pj's. He sure was. He had a firm, squeezable rear end. *Nice.* With a light grunt, he shifted onto his back, giving her an unrestricted view of his impressive endowment.

Oh, my.

The sun wasn't the only thing on full blast this morning. She dropped the blanket like she would a bad grudge. The whoosh was all it took for him to jump awake.

He pinned those chocolate eyes on hers. "You all right?"

After that sight, she was so not all right. "Yes." She giggled. "I've never seen anyone go from snoring to alert so fast."

"Comes with the job." He swung his legs off the bed and stood away from her. Then he checked his phone. "I've got to report to the station in a couple hours."

"Can I hitch a ride to the nearest diner?" she asked.

He picked up his shirt off the floor and slipped it over his head. "You hungry?" His pectoral muscles clenched from the effort. What was that? An eight-pack?

"Yes, but I have to get a job. I told you that before, and you said one step at a time. The hurricane was step one. This is step two for me."

That made him pause. "A job?"

"Yeah, you know that thing where you do some sort of labor in return for compensation?"

"I know what a job is. My question is, why do you feel you need one?" He folded his arms.

"Um, how else am I going to get my car fixed? I have to seek gainful employment."

"Let me text Lenny and see if his shop is open."

While he did that, Courtney reached for her backpack and ambled into his bathroom and turned on the showerhead. She used verbal commands to adjust the mode to the power-massage settings, undressed and stepped inside, relishing the feel of the water on her back.

One thing she knew from spending time with Brigg was that he loved taking showers. His bathroom was on another level. Brigg had told her that his brothers had renovated and expanded the master bath as a birthday gift. It featured his and her sinks, double toilets, an imported oversized bathtub and a monstrous shower. It had smart gadgets and two sets of showerheads. Courtney spent a solid fifteen minutes under the running water. Brigg had different kinds of body washes, shampoos and the most luxurious-feeling towels that she had ever used. And the water stayed hot. The entire time.

She turned off the spout, her skin wrinkled like a prune, and made sure to spray the shower cleaner Brigg kept on a shelf in the corner of the shower. After wrapping an oversized towel around her, she towel-dried her hair and brushed it with a detangling comb, intending to let it air dry. She had finished the last of her curl cream, so she put it up in a messy bun and prayed there was an ethnic beauty supply store in town. Then she dipped into her backpack and took out a pair of maternity jean shorts and matching shirt before shoving her feet into flip-flops.

"Good news," Brigg said once she had returned into the bedroom. "Lenny was able to order the parts to fix your car."

She tried to appear nonchalant at the fact that he was shirtless and had a towel wrapped haphazardly around his waist since they were literally roomies. He didn't seem to notice that she hadn't answered, but her hormones were giddy at the full frontal outlined underneath that towel.

"Great. That's a weight off my shoulders. Hopefully, I'll be able to rustle up the cash to pay him and to get out of here." She couldn't stay here past a month or so with her hormones raging.

He clenched his jaw and shuffled that fine behind into the shower.

Eleven minutes after leaving his house, Courtney and Brigg entered a local mom-and-pop restaurant while she tried to process some of the devastation from Hurricane Norma. On their way, she had spotted downed lines, two-feet-high flooding on some streets, fallen trees and various degrees of property damage. Yet Brigg had assured her that it wasn't as bad as it appeared, especially once the debris had been cleared and trucks were already out.

There was minimal damage to the shopping area, so businesses were open. Both gas stations had cars lined up circling the block. Brigg had told her that it was mostly drivers from surrounding towns who had driven over to fill up on gas. He had a full tank and a couple of red containers in his truck.

"What can I get y'all?" a woman in her midthirties asked. She had bleach-blond hair that hung lifeless on her shoulders and darkened raccoon eyes, which were in direct contrast to her chipper greeting. Her name badge read, Princess. There were only five other patrons in the establishment, which was good, because it meant they would get served quickly.

Brigg ordered an omelet and Courtney the pancake special.

"Is there a drugstore around here where can I get

some toiletries?" Courtney asked Brigg once their meals had arrived.

"Yes, there's one a block over. I can take you if you'd like."

She waved a hand. "You don't have to. I can walk. Besides, I need the exercise after being cooped up in the house the past couple of days." She didn't add that she had the full intention of stopping into every venue to enquire about employment.

More customers came in, the bell clanging as the door swung back and forth. Princess called out for them to choose their seats as she was wiping the tables. From where Courtney and Brigg sat, she could hear the banging and clatter of the kitchen staff. Another good sign.

"If you're sure… It might be a couple hours or so before I get back," Brigg said, bringing her mind back to their conversation.

Courtney nodded and looked around. The restaurant had tripled in guests, and even though two other servers had finally arrived, they were struggling to keep up. Problem for them. For her, possibilities. "I'm positive. You can meet me back here. I'll be more than ready for lunch in a couple hours."

After settling the tab, Brigg left, but not before pressing a bill into her hand. Courtney breathed out a thank-you, but her chest tightened. She was a grown woman. Having to rely on a virtual stranger for her basic necessities was mortifying. Plus, it made her feel beholden to him, like she had been to her in-laws. No way was she living that on repeat.

With a crook of her finger, she called Princess over. The restaurant was now at capacity, so she hoped Princess would be able to talk for a moment.

"May I speak to the manager?"

"She'll be here in above five minutes," she said, smile firm. And, yes, she was still staring. "Did you have a concern about the food?"

Courtney could see a hint of worry in the other woman's eyes. "Everything was delicious, and the service impeccable." Throughout breakfast, she had observed the employees and liked what she saw. They were restocking as needed and were efficient, timely and courteous. The customers were happy, coming in and talking like only regulars would. The overall aura appeared to be that everyone helped each other and got along well. She liked the vibe and knew she would fit in here.

The woman preened. "We are the best in town. Everyone says we have the best food and the best pies. In fact, if anyone ever needs catering, they call us. We're committed to five-star service every time."

"This sounds like a great place to work," Courtney said.

"The best, and the tips are great."

Courtney hid a smirk. She had a feeling the woman would say that. "Well, I am hoping your boss will allow me to work in this fine establishment." Princess's eyes dropped to Courtney's protruding stomach. Then she locked eyes with Courtney. "I really need a job," she whispered, allowing herself to be vulnerable.

"I figure you must if you're asking when…" The other woman pointed at Courtney's bump. Her voice held compassion.

"My car broke down two days ago, right before the hurricane, and without money to fix it, I'm stuck here. It's in the repair shop, but I've got to be able to pay for it."

"Oh, poor dear. Well, don't you worry yourself. I'll talk to Nancy. See what we can do."

Courtney's eyes filled, mostly due to her hormones and not because she wanted to play the pity card. "Thank you. I've got plenty of experience. I can jump in and work the floor or the kitchen."

Princess placed a hand on her hip. "What's your name and when can you start?"

"Courtney, and today if you need it." Her heart thumped. "I hope Nancy hires me because I don't know what I'm going to do if she doesn't. I'd understand though." She placed a hand over her stomach.

The door chimed and a petite woman entered. At a glance, it appeared Nancy might be in her first trimester of pregnancy. Princess gave a wave and hollered for her to come over to their table. Nancy came over, and before Courtney could start talking, Princess took control.

"This is Courtney, and she's new in town and needs a job to get her car out of the shop. She says she's got the skills, and we sure could use someone with Paula out for surgery. Especially since we have the catering gig coming up."

"You'll be on your feet a lot," Nancy said, sizing her up.

It had been a minute since she had been a server but she was desperate. She didn't want to depend on Brigg to bail her out. She didn't want him seeing her as a charity case. Plus, she was grown and a mother-to-be. "I can do it. I'm fit," she said. "It's great exercise for when I go into labor."

"Humph, I'm just past four months pregnant, and my doctor has been telling me to walk, but all I seem to want to do is eat bonbons. It doesn't help that my hubby waits on me hand and foot." Nancy patted her tummy. "At the rate I'm going, they're going to have to roll me into delivery."

They shared a laugh. Courtney's heart squeezed. Jet had been really attentive as well before he passed.

"Try yoga," Courtney urged.

Princess excused herself to tend to her customers. Courtney drummed her fingers on the table while Nancy deliberated.

"All right, you're hired, but you need to make sure you stay hydrated and rest when you need. And if it's too much, say something."

Courtney's heart lightened. Thank goodness for small towns, because this had to be the most unusual interview she had ever been given. Nancy hadn't asked much, but she had keen, intelligent eyes and probably filled in the blanks. Courtney appreciated that neither woman had pried or asked about her baby's daddy.

"Thank you so much. I can jump in anywhere."

Nancy reached across the table to rest her hand on Courtney's. "Don't overdo it." Then she named an hourly rate and ran through her expectations before having Courtney complete the usual hiring forms.

"Thanks for giving me a chance."

"We pregnant women have to stick together. Once we get your background check completed, you should be good to start. I can ask my cousin at the sheriff's office to get you in today if you'd like," Nancy said.

"Yes, thank you." Courtney's eyes welled and she dabbed at them. "I appreciate your help."

"Pshaw. Now, never mind with all of that. Do you need a place to stay? We have a space above the shop if you want to take a look at it. We use it for storage, but we're in the process of converting it into an apartment."

Courtney's shoulders snapped up. "Sure."

Nancy walked her up a small set of narrow stairs, both women holding on to the wall for support. When Courtney got to the top of the landing, she looked around and swallowed. She eyed the stack of cartons lined up against the one window in the room. The space was large and open, bigger than she thought it would be, but it would need some thorough cleaning and AC. The renovated bathroom was a pleasant surprise. Large, airy and clean.

Nancy said, "There's no central air up here, but we're meeting with the HVAC installer later today to get a quote to run the cables and get the wiring done."

The heat was obnoxious, which meant until they installed the ventilation, Courtney would have to open the windows. Good thing there were screens. Hope filled her chest. Even with everything the way it was, she could move in here. Then Nancy went to turn on the water. Nothing.

"Plumbing's out."

Courtney's shoulders deflated. It looked like she was going to have to ask Brigg to let her stay on.

"Sorry." Nancy shrugged.

"It's all right. Thanks for thinking of me."

They picked their way down the stairs. "So, we're probably looking at a week before it's ready. Help yourself to some of that pie. It's heaven in your mouth, and your baby will thank you for it. What are you having?"

"A boy."

Nancy's eyes flashed. "Me too. Maybe they'll be best friends."

Courtney planned to be long gone by the time Nancy

delivered, but she nodded. She had learned to never say never to anything. Three days ago, if someone had told her she would flee her in-laws in Druid Hills, Georgia, break down, sleep—literally sleep—with a stranger after knowing him for one day and end up working at a diner in a small town, she would have laughed in their face and told them they were crazy. But Courtney had done all those things, and if she had to for her independence, her peace and her child, she would do it again.

Chapter Ten

"I was going to drive over to your place if you didn't show your face today," Brigg's mom said, embracing him. His mother smelled of candied apples. She had grown out her former pixie cut to shoulder length, and she had a rigid workout plan that made her look like she was in her forties and not in her sixties. Brigg had quite a few inches on her, but he enjoyed the security he always found in his mother's arms.

Especially since she had scared all of them when she passed out the year before due to vertigo. That had been one of the most terrifying days of his life, making him realize how short life was, so Brigg made sure to visit twice a week.

"You know I was going to come to see my favorite lady," he teased once she had released him. After dropping Courtney off, Brigg had driven in the opposite direction to his parents' home. His father, a retired superintendent, was with Lynx and Shanna at the district office dealing with school closings. Since the schools were closed, Brigg would head to the station once he left here.

Tanya slapped his arm and went to serve him a slice of key lime pie. "Save your flirting for the ladies. Speaking of which, when are you going to start dating again? Both Axel and Lynx are settled and happy, and I wish the same for you. You can't keep coming to our events solo. What about one of the teachers at your school?"

"Mom, can we not do this today, please?" He sighed. "I told you I'm not about to get handcuffed to any woman."

"Marriage doesn't come with shackles. That's the myth. It frees you to love, be loved and to be your authentic self with your life mate. There's no pretending, and you get to share your hopes and fears with someone who cares for you deeply. Love is powerful." She placed a huge slice on the plate. "Don't you get lonely in that house of yours?" She slid the pie his way before pouring him some lemonade.

He ignored the memory of Courtney snuggled in his bed that very morning. She smelled of jasmine and shea butter, and it assailed his senses at night. "We can't all have what you and Dad have. It's not that I'm not open, but you won't believe how many girls are only looking for a good time." He shrugged. "I simply choose to oblige them, to honor their wishes."

She gave a small laugh. "Quit messing with me."

Brigg picked up the knife and cut his slice of pie in half. Courtney would eat this up. He gobbled down the rest.

"What's that all about?" his mother asked, pointing at his plate.

He hadn't realized until then what he had done.

"Just saving some for later." Or for someone. He wasn't about to tell his mother that and get her hopes up. Generally, his parents didn't get involved in any of their love lives, but ever since two of his brothers had settled down, his mother had been nudging the rest of them to do the same. Well, that's why Brigg didn't play dominoes. He wasn't about to fall.

"When are they going to get that tree off your garage?" Tanya asked, changing the subject. Brigg relaxed his shoulders, glad she was done trying to get him hooked up. She was now wiping down the counters. His mother never stood still.

"No idea. I've called a few tree hauling services but am still waiting on a call back." Thinking of the tree on the garage made Brigg remember he needed to check with Lenny again about Courtney's car.

"I'm sure they're swamped. I'll have to replant my roses, but other than that, everything is still standing." Her brown skin stayed bronzed, a testament of the amount of time she spent in the sun.

Brigg didn't mention that Hawk was already going to take care of that task. His brother planned to drive down from Miami with a truck full of rosebushes. They had worked it all out in the brothers' group chat. Axel and Maddie were flying back via private charter to help. Although, if he knew Axel, his brother was going to hire someone and pay them well to do it.

He kissed her cheek. "I'll go clear the debris from the yard."

"Thanks, son."

"No problem. I don't want you going out there to do it yourself."

After stacking and tying most of the light branches in his parents' yard in a pile for recycling, Brigg made his way to one of two stations in the town. This was the main station, but they had put up a hub on the edge of town because of the increased crime rate in the area.

The population in Love Creek had grown since their new mayor had taken over.

Brigg strolled into the station fist-bumping or nodding at his fellow officers. In the morning roll call, everyone had been accounted for, and none had reported significant property damage. He passed two other desks before getting to his own. On his right, there was a stack of folders of cold cases that he liked to review and hoped to solve. Brigg had cracked one so far. On his left were sticky notes and a small pile of paperwork he needed to complete. Plus, there was Courtney's ticket. The benefits of being in a small town was that he could talk with his boss and the judge to see about getting it dismissed. And with the court next door, he could get it done in under an hour.

Or…if he did nothing, that would mean she would have to stick around longer to pay the fine. The minute that temptation hit his mind, Brigg shunned it. That would be disingenuous. He couldn't allow his selfish desire to have Courtney stay in Love Creek motivate his actions. The sanitation department had declared that roads would be cleared within twenty-four hours. The only thing keeping her from leaving was her car.

Which reminded him. Brigg pulled Lenny's information and gave him a call. Lenny didn't answer, so Brigg left a message. Then he reviewed his paperwork on the teenagers' arrests once more. His captain's office was across from his, so when Beckett popped his head out, Brigg gave him a wave. The captain beckoned him over.

Beckett's cheeks were red and his chest heaved. "I need to talk to you." His voice sounded grim. Brigg wondered what he could have done to upset the other man. He wasn't behind on his paperwork. Brigg followed him inside his office, greeting Queenie, the captain's secretary, as he passed her desk. Beckett grunted at her, and he shook his head. Beckett had one flaw, and that was he treated his admin with disdainful authority. Queenie was in her forties and dressed in an understated manner—to keep in the background as much as possible, Brigg suspected. But Brigg and the other officers knew she was the backbone of their department. If you needed anything, you asked Queenie. There was little she didn't know.

As soon as he entered, Brigg saw that Mayor Adrian Angelos was also present. He had the brawn of a linebacker and the brain of a scientist, having graduated as a mechanical engineer before heading up the town after his father's passing, since the town didn't have a second in command. It had been an unwilling appointment but a fulfillment of a dying father's wish. Brigg liked to believe that town's boom had more to do with Adrian's aggressive plan to build up the community, but the fact that he was also single and dubbed the *Greek Adonis* might explain the sudden boom. Plus, he was well respected by all, including Brigg.

At thirty-eight, Adrian was about the same age as Hawk. His records as a football player and hockey player had been highlighted in the town's paper when he took over for his father.

Normally Adrian had a ready smile, but not today. He sat in one of two large armchairs, and his face appeared solemn. Brigg wiped his sudden clammy hands on his pants, a sure sign of his nervousness. Whatever was going on wasn't good.

"Have a seat," Beckett said, returning to sit behind his imposing desk. He was a man of average size, but that didn't make him any less intimidating. Brigg remembered the first day of his hiring nine years ago and how sweat had poured from his body even as his chest puffed with pride at working for his mentor. He hadn't felt that way again until right now.

Brigg settled into the other armchair.

Adrian leaned forward. "I'll just get to it. There is a video that was sent to us by Pilar Hernandez documenting a case of police officer violence in our town and—"

He held up a hand. "Pilar and I ended on decent terms, but if this is some sort of a revenge video, I am denying any allegations. I have never been abusive to anyone, and if you see my face, then I am going to say it's fake. Photoshopped."

"She didn't mention you," Adrian said. "This was about twenty years ago, and she's citing it as racial profiling against a Dominic Jones."

Brigg reared back into his chair. That time frame eliminated any possibility it was him. Therefore, he had no clue why he had been called into Beckett's office.

"She claims the officer in question is me," Beckett chimed in. He held his head between his hands.

Brigg jumped to his feet. "No way. I don't believe it." He faced the mayor. "There is no way Cap would do anything like that. He supports Black youths, and I can vouch for that. Pilar's...ambitious. Tenacious when she wants a story." Short of calling her outside of her name, that was the best he could do.

"Pilar wanted a statement, an interview, but we declined," the mayor said.

"She threatened to go live on the air tomorrow with footage. If things go sideways, I might have to place Beckett on administrative leave until we figure this all out."

Beckett wiped his forehead with the back of his sleeve. "I can't figure out where this video came from."

"Why is she doing this?" Brigg asked. "Why come after someone over something that happened all that time ago?"

The mayor stood and paced the room. "Somehow, she learned that I was considering Beckett as chief of police. I'm determined to find her source, but in the meantime…"

"Well deserved," Brigg said. He registered the mayor trailed off and was looking at him. So was Beckett.

"Which is where you come in," Beckett said, never meeting Brigg's eyes. "Adrian asked me who I think could take my place if I have to be placed on leave while all this is investigated, and I didn't hesitate." He pointed toward Brigg. "You're my man."

"But I'm not even a lieutenant," Brigg protested. "And there are several detectives who would jump at this opportunity and do a better job than I would."

"My choice," Beckett said. "You have the drive, the compassion and the instinct to lead this department."

The other man had broached Brigg several times about taking on a higher role. Brigg had yet to accept. He wasn't after a title. He just wanted to serve his community.

Adrian glanced at his watch. "I have a meeting with Pilar in about a half hour, and if we can't come to an agreement, she's breaking the story tomorrow." His voice was as steel. "I will do all I can to change her mind, but she's adamant, sees this as her chance for a promotion."

Sounded just like Pilar. Brigg's chest tightened. He didn't relish the task of being the one in charge, even if it was to be a temporary situation. Still, he wasn't about to say no to his mentor. "If I have to step up, I'll do my best to fill your shoes. I give my word."

Beckett gave a nod. "Thanks. I'm sure you'll do fine."

Before he left, Brigg decided to ask about getting Courtney's ticket dismissed, quickly explaining about her pregnancy and her getting stranded during the hurricane. Both the captain and the mayor were more than happy to oblige. Brigg departed their office in high spirits, envisioning Courtney's relief over not having to pay that fine.

It wasn't until Brigg was leaving the police station that he realized Beckett hadn't insisted on his innocence. His stomach plummeted. In fact, his boss seemed resigned; his demeanor was that of a guilty man. His heart protested. Before he could marinate on that improbability, Caleb called. He caught up with his womb mate, and before long, they were joking and laughing. But the dread lining his stomach never abated. There was more to this story. He felt it. And this was one time he hoped his instincts were wrong.

Chapter Eleven

Courtney felt like she was on an episode of *Pimp My Ride*. That couldn't be her car on the lift. Courtney tilted her head back and exclaimed, "I can't believe this! How on earth did you get so much done in such a short time?"

The tall mechanic with a shock of ginger hair blushed and gave a little shrug. "I live upstairs, and when they said we had to shelter in place, I got bored. I figured I might as well get started on this. My sons helped me with the body work. It was a good teaching exercise."

"I don't even know what to say."

Lenny lowered the ramp so she could get a better look at what he had completed. First off, all the dings had been smoothed out, and it had been repainted. There were new tires and hub caps, and the interior had been redone. Oh, the interior was simply divine. The bucket seats and rear had been given an overhaul with leather seats. She placed a hand on her chest. "Goodness, this is amazing."

"We have a new transmission and engine coming over the next few days. There will be no more breaking down on the side of the road for you when I'm done."

Tears brimmed. This was monumental. She sniffled, "I don't know how I'm going to pay you for this."

He waved a hand. "Brigg's got you, ma'am. He's handling the bill."

Courtney seesawed between being grateful for Brigg's generosity and feeling resentment at his knight-in-shining-armor complex. The subject of her thoughts sauntered inside, looking like the hero of a romance novel come to life. In this case, the hero had a small white bag in his hand. She swallowed at the sight of his broad chest and powerful thighs in that uniform. Her insides tingled as he drew close. She cupped her stomach protectively.

Lenny went back to work on the car, whistling an Earth, Wind & Fire tune.

"I figured I would find you here. I went by the diner, but Princess said you had already left." He led her off to the side so they could talk in private.

She locked eyes with him. "I promise I will pay back every dime."

Brigg nodded. "I know you will. We'll work out a suitable payment plan. But for the record, you don't have to."

Her shoulders relaxed. She was glad he hadn't demanded she let him settle the tab and respected that she was capable of paying her way. Her heart warmed. Brigg went over to inspect the car, looking in the trunk and under the hood. He and Lenny mumbled to each other and bobbed their heads before shaking hands. Courtney would have wanted to join in their conversation, but she had a much bigger concern. Her bladder. She had a sudden urge to pee, so she crossed her ankles and tried to think of the desert, a plateau, anything to keep her mind off water.

Brigg looked her way and surmised the situation. "All right, Lenny, just keep me posted on everything." Brigg placed a hand on her back and led her down the street to the secondhand clothes store. "I know the owner," he said, speed-walking. "When I used to patrol this beat, Mary was real good about letting me use her restroom. It always smells like apricots."

Sure enough, a couple minutes later, Courtney was inhaling the fruity smell as she relieved herself. Once she had washed and dried her hands, she wandered the aisles to find a couple more outfits, a wide-brimmed hat and a pair of new Crocs on sale. She and Brigg were the only two customers in the store. There was a section for clothing, household goods, furniture and antiques.

Eyeing a sheer stretchy nightgown that satisfied her inner sexy, Courtney gave in to temptation and grabbed it, rolling it up to keep it away from Brigg's prying eyes. The man was too observant for his own good. While she shopped, Brigg chatted it up with the owner, Mary, a woman who looked and acted like Mrs. Claus. She still had the bill Brigg had given her and would use that to purchase her goods.

Of course, when she went to ring up her purchases, Mary couldn't find the tag for the nightgown. Courtney's heart raced, watching her begin to unroll the garment.

"Uh, it's okay, you can just put it back." She reached for it, but Mary was too fast.

"No worries, dear. I'll find it." Holding it up, Mary adjusted her glasses and then turned the gown inside out. Courtney felt her face grow hot. This would be a good time for Hurricane Norma to return and blow her out of here. Of course, Brigg stood there taking it all in. She thought she heard a low chuckle, but she wasn't about to look his way to be sure.

"Ah, here it is," Mary said before trying to scan it with the gun. After three attempts, Courtney pleaded with her to put it back. Mary patted her hand. "It's okay. It will only take a few seconds." She then input the numbers in one by one while Courtney exhaled.

Mercifully, Brigg did decide to step away, checking out an antique chessboard. She wanted to scold him and say that's what he should have done long before, but then he would know for sure she had been bothered.

Mary took her time folding each article of clothing while keeping up a steady stream of conversation. Courtney drew deep breaths and answered where appropriate, reminding herself that this was the blessing and curse of small-town life. Everything here moved at a slower pace, which was a plus, but the downside was *everything moved at a slower pace.*

After promising to stop back the next day, Brigg guided Courtney out of the store, holding the door open. A young woman with a stroller dipped through the entrance. There was a screaming infant inside. The harried father wasn't too far behind, toting the baby bag and a toy. Courtney turned to watch them. Realization slapped her in the gut, and she froze for a beat. She would never have a moment like that with Jet. He wouldn't be there to experience all the joys and woes of being a first-time parent. He would never lay eyes on his son.

"You okay?" Brigg asked.

"Yeah..." She straightened. "Yes."

She dug in her bag for the hat and plopped it on her head. The sun heated her skin, reminding her that she needed to get her toiletries. This time she was in and out of the store in less than five minutes, and Brigg waited outside.

As soon as they were on their way back to his home,

Brigg said, "You looked sad when you saw that family entering Mary's store."

"Yes. Hearing that baby yelling like that made me wonder if I'll be able to cope with the temper tantrums." She peered out the window and confessed, "I don't know what I'm doing. I've never been around babies, and now I'm going to be a mom. What's worse, Jet isn't here. I'm all alone."

"I'm sorry to hear that." Brigg's voice held compassion, which chipped at her composure.

She felt his hand on her shoulder and tensed before resting her head against the passenger window. Closing her eyes, tears leaked down her face, and her shoulders began to shake from the overwhelming onslaught of emotions racking through her body while the truck rambled beneath her. Courtney wrapped her arms across her midriff and cried, hating that death had rotten timing. Hating that a part of her hated Jet.

Hated him for dying and leaving her to figure everything out.

The truck stopped moving. Then her door was open, and Brigg undid her seat belt before lifting her in his arms. She clung to him and cried like she never had before. Of course, she had been heartbroken at Jet's death, but Courtney had had to keep it together, remain strong. And that's why it was so confusing how fast she unraveled.

Once they were inside, Brigg held her, taking her over to the couch. She cradled against his chest, welcoming his strength. Finally, she straightened and wiped her face. Her brain registered she was on Brigg's lap and that the hardness she felt beneath her wasn't from his weapon.

"I'm sorry I was a bumbling mess just now," she said, scooting out of his lap to sit beside him on the couch.

Brigg cupped her face with his hands. "Don't apologize for crying. You have to release your pain. It's no good keeping it bottled up. I don't think that's healthy for your baby." Then he grabbed a napkin off the coffee table to clean her face. "I'm sorry you lost your spouse. But you're not alone, you have m— You have your sister, right?"

She nodded, playing with her shirt. It sounded like he was about to say he was there for her at first before he self-corrected. Courtney didn't blame him. He wasn't about to take on the responsibility for another man's child. Not that she wanted him to.

"I'll be right back." Brigg was out of the house and back again in a dash, returning with two bags. One was her clothes and toiletries, and he had the same white bag from earlier. He placed his on her lap.

Her eyes swung to his. She held it up. "What's this?"

"You'll see."

Reaching inside, Courtney pulled out a new cell phone. It was the latest model released less than a month ago. Her mouth dropped. "Whoa. This is expensive. My IOU is growing faster than I can process." Placing the phone back inside, she set the bag on his lap. "Brigg, this is too much. I can't accept this."

"Nonsense." He put it on her thigh. "This is a need, not a luxury. Consider it a birthday gift. It's all set up and ready to go. I added you to my plan until you can get your own."

It was obvious he had thought of everything. She was touched by his thoughtfulness. "My birthday was last month…"

He smirked. "I know. I saw your license, and you're

about a year older than me. I'll be thirty this September. Happy birthday. Besides, it's more for my benefit," he said, straightening his legs. "Things might get hectic at work, and I need to be able to reach you. Plus, I imagine you want to reach your sister."

"Thank you," she said, dipping her chin to her chest. She patted her hair, positive it was a hot mess. She had put it up that morning without brushing it out. "But you could have just bought a cheap throwaway phone. You're spending like you're related to the Rockefellers."

"No. I'm a Harrington." Every syllable he spoke held pride. "We do nothing second best."

Courtney plugged in the phone to charge, accepting Brigg's gift and reflecting on how he spoke about his family with such certainty. She had never had that. She rubbed her tummy, resolved to ensure her son felt stable and secure in her love. She couldn't wait to start her job. It was a small beginning, but it would lead to new and greater possibilities. Possibilities she never dreamed or saw as attainable before her son.

On impulse, she rushed over to Brigg, hugged him and planted a kiss on his cheek. "Thank you so much for the gift and for taking me into your home and into your life." Her lips tingled from the contact.

He placed a hand on the same cheek and kept it there. Like he was in shock. Stupefied. His other hand reached behind her neck. There was no misinterpreting the warmth in his eyes. Courtney leaned toward him and then the baby kicked. Brigg must have felt it because his eyes went wide.

"Did he just…?"

Plopping beside him, Courtney guided his hand to her

abdomen. Jayson kicked again. "I think he likes you," she giggled.

"You think so?" Brigg asked, his voice filled with wonder.

"Yes, for sure." *But not as much as I like you.*

Now both his hands were on her belly. "Do it again, little man." Of course, Jayson complied. This was the time of day that he was overly active.

"He does like me," Brigg said, laughing.

"Yes, he does." *And so do I.* Courtney just didn't know if it was because of her libido, her gratitude or…something more.

Chapter Twelve

For the first time in he couldn't say when, Brigg wanted to bring a plus-one to a family event. The problem was his family would think it was a date. And it wouldn't be a date-date. It would be a gesture to include the female companion staying in his house.

The embossed invitation to Axel and Madison's wedding—because Axel was too bougie for an evite—had been in his mailbox when Brigg and Courtney returned from the diner. Courtney had wanted to eat there again and he noticed her chatting it up with Princess. The wedding was less than a couple weeks away because Axel had wanted to keep their venue location secret, thus the last-minute mailing. Not that he and his brothers hadn't known all the plans from months ago.

He stood in his home office, flipping the invite on the palm of his hand while he mulled on the alphas and deltas—as Caleb would say—of bringing Courtney to his brother's wedding.

He scoffed. A few days ago, he didn't know this woman. And now…now she was all he thought about. Okay, that was an exaggeration. He had to look out for her because (1) she was in her last trimester, and (2) she was stuck in a small town.

Still, there was a buzz when he was around her. A light hum of electricity he couldn't deny.

Like when he had returned to get her from the diner. She had a thousand-watt smile and she glowed. Glowed. His breath had stopped for a second. Literally stopped. He'd had to remind himself she was pregnant and grieving, then take a breath. 'Cause the straight-up truth was she was fine as all get-out. Might as well admit it.

And there was nothing he could do about it. 'Cause his mom had raised him right. Figures, the only woman to peek his interest would be taken—by a baby in the womb! There was no such thing as keeping it simple with him. He'd laugh if his heart wasn't completely tripping.

Brigg froze. *No. No. No.* His heart had nothing to do with this. If anything, this was lust. It had been about five New York minutes since he had been with a woman. *Yes. That has to be it.* And when was the last time he had worked out?

Tapping the envelope in hand, he went to seek out the woman of too many of his thoughts for his liking.

She was in his kitchen licking an ice cream cone. He stopped. Really? And they were sharing the bed again tonight. Though the storm had passed, he didn't trust her sleeping in that room until he had assurance that that side of the house was secure.

She took another lick. That's it. He was going to the gym tonight. Since he had a late-night shift, Brigg had slept on the couch the night before, and it had left him with a backache. He wanted to be back in his comfortable bed. *With Courtney?*

Brigg cleared his throat. Ever since they almost locked

lips, and he was pretty sure they would have if the baby hadn't kicked, Courtney popped into his mind at the oddest of times. "Look what I have," he teased, waving the envelope.

She paused mid-lick. "What?"

"It's an invitation to Axel's wedding."

Her eyes flashed. "Get out. I didn't hear anything about that on social media." Her teeth grazed the top of the cone before she took a bite. And she was back to her licking. Goodness. She was eating that cone with gusto.

"That's because it's top secret, and I'd like you to go with me," Brigg replied.

Now there was ice cream all over her mouth. He placed a hand over his face and groaned on the inside. *Shoot me now. Mental note: there will be no more conversations with Courtney when she's eating ice cream.* It was dangerous for his equilibrium.

She lifted a hand and worked on finishing her treat. While he sweated and thought about gnats and the leaky faucet. *Wait.* He tilted his head and gave a listen. Nothing. No ping. Ambling over to the sink, he bent over to investigate the spout.

"Did you fix this?" he asked.

"It wasn't a ghost," she said, wiping her mouth with a napkin. She made a show of coming over to wash her hands and turning off the tap.

"Thank you," he said.

"The not-so-observant cop." She chuckled. "You're welcome."

"I've been meaning to get to that."

"Well, now you don't have to. Figured I'd earn my keep."

"Incredible. You really are a *Jill of all Trades*."

Courtney rolled her eyes. "Ugh. Don't start. I should have never told you about that." She wiped her hands with a paper towel. "Now, about your invite. While I would love to come with you to what I am sure will be the wedding of the century, I can't commit to going."

"Can't?"

"No, 'cause I got a job and I may have to work." She sounded really pleased with herself. Skirting around him, she walked toward the living area.

He followed her, feeling like a puppy nipping at her heels. "What do you mean you have to work? When did you find time to get a job? I was gone for what? Two hours?" His voice was as high as his incredulity.

Her brows rose and she gave him a look that said, *Oh, no, you didn't. Who do you think you are talking to that way?*

Backtracking, Brigg lowered his voice. "Forgive me. I was caught off guard, and I'm concerned about you working so far into your pregnancy." But what his tone said was, *I'm sorry. I have no right to talk to you that way.*

To which her face said, *I know that's right. You didn't put a ring on my finger, and if you did, you still couldn't come out your face at me like that.*

He dipped his head, ending their nonverbal standoff.

"No worries. It's all good," she said, sweetly. "Repairing my car and buying me a phone are more than enough."

"I don't have a problem helping you. I'm not hurting financially." He splayed his hands. "You repaired my faucet."

"And you're letting me stay here in your bed—for free." She squared her shoulders. "I don't want to take advantage or be a burden."

"I would do this for anyone." Okay, that was not the

truth. He didn't take just anyone into bed. In fact, he hadn't taken anyone to his bed in a while. Whatever. Courtney was being stubborn.

"Well, I'm not anyone." She jabbed a finger to her chest. "I have to work. I want to work. I'm going to work."

"Fine. Suit yourself." He stalked off and went into his office to call Caleb. When his brother answered, Brigg exhaled. He tried to make the call about checking on Caleb's welfare, but his bro knew him well.

"Why do you sound so aggravated? What's going on?"

"Give me a minute."

"Take your time, dude. Call me back." His brother clicked off.

Knowing he was too agitated to whisper, Brigg changed into a tank and shorts, dropped his phone in his back pocket and left his uniform in a puddle on the floor. He rammed his feet into a pair of socks and old sneakers, then shoved his earbuds in. Though the floods had dissipated, the roads were still wet and muddy.

The niggling fear of Courtney going into labor during his absence almost made him stay. Almost. He told himself that even if she did, it would be hours before the baby came, so he would be all right, Brigg passed the living area where Courtney was watching a sitcom and stormed toward the front door.

He almost tore the already shaky handle off the door trying to slam it so Courtney would know he was furious. Furious that she had gotten a job. Furious that because of her *job* she wasn't going with him to his brother's wedding.

The heat slapped him in the face and he almost took his butt back into the house. But he had to get rid of this restless energy. And he didn't want Courtney seeing him return so soon.

Speed-walking, he called Caleb and spewed. The bright blue skies and sunshine were in direct contrast to his mood, but it meant he could stay outside. After making Caleb promise not to tell Ethan or Drake, Brigg told him from beginning to end about the very pregnant, obstinate, pigheaded, stubborn source of his frustration. He had to have walked a good two miles by the time he was finishing expounding on the tale.

"Then she has the nerve to say she's working to pay me back," he huffed. "I didn't ask her to do all that. I didn't ask her for anything." Except to go to the wedding with him.

"So, let me get this straight," Caleb said. "You're sharing your bed with a stranger off the street?"

"Yes. I can't have her in the guest room when the ceiling might collapse. The roof over the guest room might be compromised for all I know."

"Why didn't you just move her bed into your office?"

Brigg paused in front of a well-manicured lawn where two squirrels dashed back and forth, and he wiped his face. His body was drenched with sweat. "I didn't think of that." Drat his brother and his reasonable mind. The squirrels scampered across the street and out of sight.

"Didn't want to think of that, most likely."

"Malarkey," Brigg said, moving again at an even faster pace. "In my defense, there was a hurricane raging and I was acting fast."

"Mmm-hmm."

For a good thirty seconds, Brigg heard nothing but Caleb's laughter in his ear. "What's the 'mmm-hmm' about?" His left eye was jumping.

"You sound like Axel and Lynx before they fell."

"Fell where?"

"Don't play dumb," Caleb snorted. "Fell in love."

"Love?" He burst out laughing, ignoring his now thumping heart. "Boy, I thought you were the smart one. It's a mere ninety-six hours and you're dropping the L-word on me. What part of 'pregnant widow' did you not understand?"

His brother cracked up. "I'm beginning to recognize the signs, bro. I guarantee you're going to be calling me crying. Crying 'cause you're in love."

"I can't stand you. I should have never called you."

"Wait till I tell Ethan and Drake. You guys are dropping like flies."

"You said you wouldn't tell them. I can't believe you're having a laugh at my expense. Stay on track. I am expressing my concern about a helpless woman's welfare." He started to make his way back to his home. He had been gone for over an hour, and he needed to check on her.

"The woman you told me about doesn't sound helpless," Caleb shot back. "She's doing what anybody would do in her situation."

Brigg released a long sigh. "I guess. I just don't like it."

"Yes, because you want to play knight in shining armor and rescue your damsel in distress, and she won't let you. Admit it, this woman has gotten under your skin, and now you want her under you."

He was all right with that position or she could be on top. He didn't mind. Wait. No. Caleb was planting images in his head. "Shut up."

"When am I going to meet her?"

"I would say at the wedding, but she's not coming."

"Quit pouting and get over your tantrum, and we'll talk tomorrow. I've got some paperwork to do." Caleb was the Love Creek School District attorney and was always working on some case. When he wasn't working, he was reading. Thinking of the defunct fishing trip, Brigg promised to arrange another.

"See you at the wedding," Caleb said. "And take two aspirins before going to bed."

"Why?"

"To prevent your heart from falling."

Brigg said, "Don't quit your day job, because that pun was beyond corny."

"I'm going to be laughing about this for days, and I'm calling Axel and Lynx as soon as I hang up to tell them the good news."

"You swore not to tell."

"You said not to tell Drake and Ethan."

"Why are you so literal?" He was now outside his own front door.

Caleb was quick with the comeback. "Why are you in denial?"

Click.

Brigg rested his hand on a shiny new handle, one he had meant to put on. Courtney. So while he had been stewing, she had been calm and up to pure good. Anger washed over him in waves and he thrust open the front door.

Chapter Thirteen

Courtney could tell Brigg's location with each bang.

Bang. The front door.

Bang. The bedroom.

Bang. The bathroom.

Courtney sat on the couch and fumed. Brigg had stormed inside like an Avenger dripping in hot sweat, and she'd tensed her shoulders, ready to take him on. But instead of yelling at her, he was pouting.

A grown man throwing a tantrum, stomping around the place like King Kong. Just like Jet had on many occasions. Freezing her out until she caved.

Well, it hadn't worked for the man she'd married, so it sure as honey wasn't going to work for a man she'd known for less than a week. She had lived this script and knew the play by heart. The bedroom door crashed against the wall, causing her to jump. She clutched her stomach. *If that man bangs that door one more time...* She turned up the television to listen to the news.

Brigg's feet thumped on the floor as he headed into the kitchen. She bit the inside of her cheek to keep from cracking up at his antics. She was not going to change her mind, so he might as well give it up. She heard rustling and clanging before the sounds and smells of popcorn filled the house, causing her mouth to water. Her baby kicked. Suddenly, there was nothing she wanted more in the world than popcorn.

Brigg walked into the living area holding a bowl of buttery goodness, plopped next to her and exhaled.

"I'm sorry," he said, placing the bowl between them, staring at the television. She lowered the volume, tempted to ask him to repeat that. "This behavior isn't even like me. I'm usually cool and even-tempered. I have no right trying to dictate your moves or take out my disappointment on you." He reached over to take her hand and give it a squeeze.

And, this wasn't the usual script. He was apologizing? And disappointed? "About what?" she asked him.

He lifted his shoulders. "I don't even know." His voice and mannerisms were room temperature. *Hmm…* She was learning more about Brigg. His anger cooled quickly. Unlike Jet, who could stew for days. Or even longer.

"Is it the kind of job I'm seeking that disappoints you?" she asked, picking at an imaginary lint.

"No. No. Why would you think that?"

Why indeed? She shrugged. "Just wondering…" If he felt the same way Jet had.

Courtney turned in his direction and squeezed back. "I accept your apology. I'm beyond grateful for you opening your home to me, but if it means I have to do as you say, then…" She trailed off and dug into the bowl for a scoop of popcorn with her free hand, since their hands were still joined.

He faced her. "No, it doesn't. And my mother would knock me upside my head if she saw my actions just now.

Although she might take pity on me if she knew the reason I was misbehaving."

Something about his tone made Courtney believe he wasn't talking about her pregnancy. The warmth in his eyes stirred a longing in her chest, and she wondered if she was misreading the signs. He released his grip, scooted close, placing the popcorn on his lap and dipped his head. Her heart thumped. Then he rested his head against hers. They exhaled at the same time and faced the television screen, sharing popcorn. She turned up the volume.

They had survived their first argument without nasty words.

A bitter memory stoked in her mind. The memory of Jet insisting they have children though she had told him her preference to wait until they had adjusted to married life. They had argued for days until she caved.

Patting her stomach, she didn't regret her pregnancy. Not one bit. It was the flash at satisfaction on Jet's face when she had shared the news that ate at her. For him, it had been all about getting his way, keeping her at home, her feelings insignificant.

She hadn't spoken to him for a week, her emotions seesawing between delight at her bundle and anger at his plan to keep her dependent on him. An anger Jet couldn't understand and refused to apologize for when the outcome had them both excited. His motto had been *All's well that ends well.*

And soon, her excitement had outweighed her animosity, and they were at peace. Neither of them could have known Jet would be gone just a few weeks later, never having seen his child. And she had been left with his most precious gift.

"Brigg?"

"Hmm?"

"I wonder if you would let me stay here a few weeks while I—"

"Yes," he interrupted. "You've grown on me."

She smiled. Her heart lightened. "Thank you."

"You can stay as long as you like and take all the time you need. I'll always make room for you." Then he went right back to his popcorn, unaware that his words were like hot butter on her heart. She opened her mouth to talk about paying rent, but he beat her to it. "And don't think about paying me to stay here. That's not up for debate, friend."

Friend... That's right. That's what this was. That's all this was. They had escalated from roomies to friends and had...plateaued. Maybe he had stopped the almost kiss by distracting her with the baby. That was his way of being nice, of letting her down easy. She quashed the secret hope that he would see her as...more. Her heart must have forgotten that her belly was rounded with another man's child. But Brigg hadn't. And she couldn't either.

Just then, a curvy Latina came on the news. Courtney felt Brigg stiffen beside her, his eyes riveted on the screen. *Pilar Hernandez.* Red lips. Stunning. Brigg's ex.

He pointed. "Can you turn it up?"

Sure she could. Fighting back jealousy, she complied, not paying attention to what Pilar was saying. Instead, Courtney snuck glances at Brigg, hating how entranced he seemed. Like he had regrets. Like she was the one who got away.

"She really did it," he said, speaking through his teeth. No, that wasn't affinity. He sounded disgusted. Courtney paid more attention to the reporter's words.

"...didn't comment on the allegations against his candidate for chief of police, Captain Beckett Sparks, but he did say—"

The camera flashed to a muscular man of Greek heritage who looked like he should be in a bodybuilding club rather than lead a town. "Captain Beckett Sparks is a man of honor. He has devoted his life to this community and to help our youths, and I stand behind my decision."

Brigg huffed. "I know that's right." Courtney squeezed his arm.

"Stand by his decision?" Pilar asked. The lens zoomed in on her face. And that zit on the bridge of her nose. "Captain Beckett Sparks isn't who he says he is. Please note, the clip you're about to see is very graphic and could be a trigger for anyone who has suffered any abuse."

A crackly video appeared, and Courtney scooted to the edge of the couch. Brigg leaned forward, his head on his hands. You could see someone punching a young man repeatedly, then he handcuffed him before punching him some more. Another officer ran over to him, grabbing his shoulder, but the officer shrugged him off and continued to punch the youth. Then the screen went black and Pilar reappeared.

"The actions of that officer left the young man paralyzed for life. Beckett Sparks is not the man for the—"

Brigg grabbed the remote and turned off the television. "I can't believe she would smear Beckett's reputation like this when the man in the video cannot be identified through that footage." He shook his head. "Beckett was my mentor, the entire reason I became a cop. I don't believe that's him. He would tell me. He would. I know he would."

Courtney rubbed his back. "Do you think she would do that without proof though?"

"Yes, I do. Pilar is an opportunist. She's all about making it big and doesn't care who gets hurts in the process." His bitter tone made Courtney wonder if Brigg was over her, as he claimed.

"He has a family. I can't imagine how his wife and children must feel."

"I can't imagine the network would clear this piece if she didn't have proof."

"Whose side are you on?"

She lifted her shoulders. "I can't pick sides when I don't know the situation. I don't have the same history you do. Plus, you sidestepped my question."

"Fair enough." He clasped his hands. "And I think Pilar can be very convincing when she wants something."

"You're making this about her."

"This isn't about her." He spoke through gritted teeth. "Why are you obsessing on her?"

Courtney didn't respond to that. Instead she asked, "If he's innocent, why isn't your captain right there next to her denying it?"

Her question must have pierced him, because he jumped to his feet. "I'm going to give the captain a call." Courtney watched him go, admiring his loyalty. But her heart feared for him, wondering if his loyalty might be misplaced.

With Brigg locked in his office, Courtney decided to pull up her email and check to see if her sister had responded or if she had been cleared to work. Nancy said she would email. She padded into Brigg's bedroom and retrieved the laptop off the nightstand on her side.

Her side? Her side?

Wow. Courtney's stomach twisted. She had no claim to any part of Brigg's bed. She perched on the edge of the bed and brought up her messages. There wasn't any from Kaylin, but there was another from Jet's mom.

Where are you? I promise you'll regret running off and leaving us like this. We deserve to know our grandchild. He's all we have left of our son.

"Yeah, well, you would have taken my son from me," Courtney muttered after reading Muriel's message, though guilt pressed her heart. She did want Jayson to know Jet's parents, but inviting them back into her life was asking them to take over, and Courtney was loving this crazy path to reestablishing her independence. She wrapped her arms around herself. She couldn't chance losing herself, not when she was loving this woman she was finding again.

Chapter Fourteen

From inside his office, Brigg heard the sound of beep-ing, like a truck backing up in his yard. He left another voice mail for Beckett and dashed outside to investigate.

The driver began to lower the huge crane to lift off the tree. It took a few tries, but within fifteen minutes, the tree landed in the back of the truck with a huge thunk.

"How much do I owe you?" Brigg said, pumping his fists. "You don't know how glad I am that you finally got to me."

"The bills all taken care off," the driver said.

"I don't understand…"

Courtney chose that moment to come outside.

"You and your wife have a good rest of your day. And congratulations," the man said before jumping into his truck. After a toot of his horn, he was on his way. Brigg shot a glance at Courtney to gauge her reaction. She lifted her hand to give to wave at the departing truck. She didn't seem upset at the driver's assumption. Brigg, however, found himself wishing that the driver's words were the actual truth.

He wouldn't mind being somebody's dad. *Whoa.* Scratching his head, he said, "I have no idea who did this." He turned to survey the damage. "I don't think the repair will take more than a day or two to get done. We were fortunate. The insurance company rep is supposed to come by some time tomorrow."

"That's great news," she said with a smile.

Just then, a large pickup truck turned the corner. You could hear the bass from the music playing in the vehicle. Brigg folded his arms. "Ah, I should've known."

"Known what?"

"You're about to see."

As expected, the vehicle pulled into his driveway and parked behind his SUV. A variety of different colored rosebushes filled the truck bed. The tinted windows didn't reveal the occupant. Brigg kept his eyes on Courtney because he wanted to see her reaction when his brother stepped out. The door opened slowly and Hawk came into view. He had on a pair of shades and a hat, his travel disguise.

Courtney gasped, placing a hand over her mouth. "You're Hawk Harrington."

"That's right." He grabbed a bag from the back and swung it over his shoulder. Hawk was coordinated, wearing custom-made sneakers designed to match his shorts and team jersey. He had grown out his jet-black hair so it hung on his shoulders. Hawk had a scar across his face, which only served to romanticize him with the ladies, adding to his mystique. Brigg had lost track of how many memes had been created in Hawk's honor—the newest fad being women posing next to him and calling themselves his wives. There had been a collective sigh across the nation when the media outlets heard he was dating a supermodel.

Courtney gaped for a few seconds before slowly releasing a breath. She scurried over to Brigg's side and grabbed his hand, squealing with excitement. "You didn't tell me he was coming." She patted her hair before shrugging.

Brigg's heart eased. He was worried how his houseguest would react to meeting the Beast of the NFL in person. So far, she appeared starstruck but calm. And she wasn't ogling Hawk. She was holding Brigg's hand tight enough to cut off circulation, but she was next to *him*, and he was enjoying the scent of jasmine.

Hawk's eyes zoned in on their joined hands before snapping back to Brigg. "Whoa. Did you forget to mention something? Am I about to be an uncle?" Hawk was one of the few people who made Brigg feel small and spoiled. When he was a baby, Hawk had been his caretaker, and Lynx had helped with Caleb. As they grew, that never changed. Sometimes Brigg wondered if Hawk thought he was his father even though he was only eight years older than Brigg.

"No. No. Courtney is…a friend."

"He rescued me from the hurricane," she said.

His brother snatched him in his arms to give him a tight hug before giving him a noogie. "Will you quit it?" Brigg huffed, trying to extricate himself out of Hawk's grip. In his peripheral, he saw Courtney punching Hawk on the back, laughing and begging Hawk to let him go. She had come to his defense. Not that it would help any. But still.

One heavy push got his brother off him. His chest heaved. "You play too much."

Hawk cracked up. "I missed you, baby bro." Crooking his head in Courtney's direction, he mouthed, *We'll talk later*, before heading inside. He dropped his bag by the front door. Courtney excused herself, scooted past them and headed to his bedroom. Of course, Hawk caught that. He gave Brigg a look.

"Mom knows you're here?" Brigg asked, striving for normalcy and to ward off the questions about Courtney as long as he could.

"Not yet. I needed to get that tree off your property. I've got some men coming to fix the roof tomorrow. Insurance is too much hassle." Hawk raised an eyebrow. "Need anything else done?"

"Nope. Courtney fixed the door handle."

"You sure?" he asked.

"I know I can procrastinate on the household chores, but I'm good."

"Mom knows she's here?" Hawk asked, heading over to the refrigerator to get a bottled water. He should have known his brother wouldn't leave the subject of Courtney be.

"No. Only Caleb. Although I think he might have blabbed to Ethan and Drake," Brigg said. "Actually, I think it's weird they haven't popped by, unless—" he studied Hawk "—you're here to investigate. You knew," he accused, giving his brother a playful shove.

"Yep." Hawk didn't deny it. His cerulean blue eyes held mirth. "Caleb called me. Told me you were hitting the roof because your new housemate got a job."

"I just don't think it's wise in her condition. She starts in a couple days."

"You seem mighty protective about a woman you just met." He leaned against the counter and took a swig of water.

"Well, she isn't just any woman." Brigg sighed. He had leaped right into that confession trap.

"I knew it." Hawk pointed. "You're next."

"Quit messing around. Don't forget I saw you and Arie all hugged up in the gazebo."

His brother's face reddened. "If you had come ten minutes earlier..." He trailed off. "Well, if you must know, I'm planning to ask her to marry me."

"No way." Brigg snickered. "I can't believe you're going out like that. We were supposed to be single together."

"It's all about finding the one you can't let go," Hawk said, running a hand through his hair.

Curious, Brigg asked, "Is that how you feel about Arie?" Hawk was real even-keeled about this relationship. He wasn't acting like he had lost his senses like Axel and Lynx had. Sure, Brigg wasn't an expert when it came to what love should look like, but he at least expected Hawk to show passion, excitement, or at least yammer on about Arie. Instead, he was just so...cool.

"I'm ready to settle down. Start a family." He tossed the bottle in the recycle bin.

He noticed Hawk didn't answer the question, and Brigg was going to express his doubts, but then his cell phone rang. It was his boss. Holding up a finger, Brigg went into his office to talk to his captain.

"Sorry I'm just returning your calls, but it's been absolute chaos since Pilar did that interview," Beckett said once he had answered the phone. "I've been on the phone with Adrian the past couple hours." The captain sounded exhausted and worn out.

Brigg's stomach clenched. "It will pass, Cap. Today's hype won't matter tomorrow."

Beckett sighed. "My wife. My daughter. My career. I could lose it all."

"You're not going to lose anything," Brigg shot back,

hating the resignation in his captain's voice. "We're going to fight this and win."

"There's no winning the truth, son."

It took a moment for Beckett's words and their implications to register. "Wh-what?" Brigg gripped his phone. "What are you saying to me right now? There's no way you could have done this," he yelled.

"I'm afraid it's true." Beckett sounded bleak.

"But…" He shook his head. "The man in that video does not line up with the person who rescued me, gave me a chance. I don't believe it." His jaw clenched. "I think you're being coerced and pushed out of office because of your age."

"Oh, if only that were the case." Beckett gave a sad chuckle. "You were my redemption. A way to assuage my guilt, to atone for my terrible mistake." The other man broke into a sob. "I tried to apologize to that young man and his family, but they didn't want to see my face. Refused my money. Told me they hoped I suffer for the rest of my life. And I was suffering—I suffered," he wailed. "Until you."

Brigg placed a hand on his heaving chest. "So, I was a substitute? Like one Black man is expendable for another?" he choked out, feeling used. Betrayed.

"No, you're twisting my words," Beckett stammered.

Brigg legs buckled and he dropped into the chair. He bent over, weighed down by Beckett's confession. "I can't believe this." Images of the young Black man being beaten by a merciless cop—a cop he had looked up for years—flashed before him. "Why?" he tore out. "Why did you do it?" Even as he asked, he knew why.

Beckett's voice dropped to a whisper. "Because I thought he was another dead-end kid in the neighborhood, and I *really* thought he had robbed the owner of the store. A man my father's age who had died of a heart attack because of some punk who didn't want to get a job."

For a beat, Brigg processed those words. Disappointment and disillusionment coursed through his veins. How could he have been such a poor judge of character? The man in the video had pummeled the handcuffed defenseless youth like he hadn't intended to stop. Like the person on the ground wasn't a fellow human. Tears pricked his eyes, and his heart felt ripped apart, like it had been shredded with a panther's claws.

"You're a monster," Brigg growled, curling his fists. "And a hypocrite. You lectured me so many times on brutality when all you needed to do was look in the mirror." His heart beat in tune with his anger—boiling, racing.

Beckett cleared his throat. "Son, let me explain—"

"First, don't call me son, because for you, that's a term of derision, not endearment, and second, explain what?" Brigg asked, riding on the tidal wave of his fury. "There is no need for words when there is a picture. And I see you clearly for who you are. You're the man who smiles in our faces and then goes home and tells your daughter to stay away from us. Give me the blatant racist over the one hidden by a cape any day—or, in this case, by a badge."

"If I did discourage interracial dating, it was only because I was afraid of what society would say—"

"Oh, spare me," Brigg snarled, cutting him off and ending the call. The line buzzed. If that was Beckett calling back... He looked at the screen and saw it was the mayor. Brigg thumped the desk with his fist. He needed a moment to process everything. But he was an officer and this was the head of the town. He had to answer the call.

"Love Creek needs you to step up," Adrian said, sounding hoarse.

"I—I'm not the right man for the job."

"Incorrect. You're the only man for this job. Meet me in front of the station in an hour." With that, the line went dead. Brigg sat with his head in his hands, his heart pulsating with pain, and pondered his next steps.

The door creaked and Courtney slipped inside. She came over to where he stood and pulled his head against her rounded stomach before embracing him. He wrapped his arms around her before resting his hands on her lower back. He closed his eyes and inhaled. And breathed. She didn't say a word. She just let him breathe.

It was what he needed. All he needed. His muscles relaxed. His tension eased. His anger cooled. Because he was in Courtney's arms. And only to himself would he admit that he could stay here. For hours. For days. Years. Maybe even forever.

Chapter Fifteen

Was her attraction to Brigg a dishonor to Jet's memory? Because it had only been about 210 days since she had lost her husband. She had no business pining after another man. Yet she was. It was a slow burn, but it was a burn nonetheless. The fire grew every day she was in Brigg's presence. And it wasn't just her hormones.

Brigg had texted her to put on the news to the mayor's announcement, and while she waited, she decided it would be a good time go into a wide-legged child pose while she continued her deliberation. Brigg and Hawk had left for the station in Hawk's truck. Hawk hadn't trusted Brigg to get behind the wheel when he was so devastated by Beckett's confession.

Snatching a stack of pillows, she piled them on the floor in the living room area before lowering herself across them. She relaxed her arms and cupped the pillows, then went through six cycles of breath. Admittedly, Jet had been selfish at times, and even a little spoiled, but they had loved each other. She had been happy with him.

But even though Jet loved her, he didn't accept all of her. Her humble past. There were times she wondered if he had been ashamed she had been a waitress and not a nurse or a teacher. Because he hadn't wanted her to work at the supermarket or the diner. How would it look? he had said. If she worked, people would think it was because he couldn't provide for her. His family had wealth, power, influence, and all Courtney had to do was adapt to their lifestyle. He hadn't understood her need for independence and couldn't get that she hadn't been with him for what he had but who he was.

To please him, she had caved. Because she had loved him. Had basked in his approval. Then like the wisp of the wind, Jet was gone...

Pushing off the pillows, Courtney then held on to the coffee table for support so she could stand. She grabbed a couple of tangelos from the kitchen before plopping on the couch. She stretched her legs across the ottoman and balanced the tangelos on her tummy.

Now there was Brigg. A strong, passionate man who wasn't afraid to show his anger or loyalty. He didn't mask his emotions. He was quick to apologize.

Her baby kicked. And Jayson liked him.

The mayor came to the podium, clearing his throat. She could hear the clicking and see the cameras flashing. Brigg stood a couple of feet behind the mayor, looking calm, imposing. An older, regal version of Brigg stood beside him. That must be his father. Mayor Angelos adjusted the microphone, the screech loud in the otherwise quiet background.

Courtney peeled one of the tangelos and took her first taste. Ahh, it was sweet and juicy.

"Captain Beckett Sparks tendered his resignation earlier today after thirty-five years of service to the department. After careful deliberation, I have decided to broaden my search for the chief of police position. In the meantime, Officer Brigg Harrington has graciously accepted the task of becoming Love Creek's interim captain, and I look forward to working with him."

Brigg stepped forward and the cameras zoomed in. "Thank you, Mayor Angelos, for entrusting me with the department. I will do my best to uphold the law of this town and serve this role with integrity, building community, cultivating fairness and maintaining my principles." He dipped his head and stepped back.

Courtney's heart expanded. He wore the cloak of leadership well. Her chest puffed like he was her man.

Reporters began hurling questions about Beckett and his scandalous departure, but Mayor Angelos uttered a quick "No more comments at this time," and the conference ended.

Five minutes later, Courtney received her first text message on her new phone. She didn't have to wonder who it was as Brigg was one of her only two contacts. Her sister, Kaylin, was the other.

Are you hungry? Brigg asked.

Of course, she was hungry. All the time. She quickly responded with, I could eat.

Want some soul food?

Her mouth watered. Yes. Fried chicken, mac and cheese, greens, mashed potatoes.

Got it.

She debated whether to send the next text but decided not to think too much. Just act. After a few tries, she settled on You were amazing, Captain Harrington. And handsome. She chewed her bottom lip. Was *handsome* too much? Whatever. She had already sent it, so there was no use obsessing. Several painstaking, slow seconds went by.

It's Interim Captain. And thank you, beautiful.

Beautiful. He'd called her beautiful. Her heart lifted and she felt her cheeks warm. Okay, so they were officially flirting. Sort of. Her hands shook a little.

She ate the second tangelo and then tossed the skins into the garbage and washed her hands. Courtney then went to retrieve her laptop and pulled up her email. Her sister hadn't responded as yet. That was odd. There was Wi-Fi aboard the ship.

Scrunching her nose, she tapped on her sent messages and tapped on the message she had emailed Kaylin. Seeing nothing amiss, she checked her spam folder and then slapped her forehead. There were several emails from Kaylin.

Ugh. How had this happened? Relief seeped through her body.

Courtney clicked the Not Spam button and moved the messages to her inbox. Good. She would catch up on those later. A new message hit her inbox and her heart rate accelerated. After a quick tap, Muriel's message filled her screen.

How is the baby doing? You can't keep him away from us. We are his blood too. You must have run out of funds by now. Contact us. We have the means to take care of you.

Just as fast, another popped up.

If I just knew why you left, that would help me. I miss you both so much it's tearing me apart.

Courtney sniffled, struggling to hold on to her resentment. She reminded herself that this was the very woman she had overhead plotting to take her baby from her. But she hadn't ill-treated Courtney. Muriel was also grieving losing Jet, and he wouldn't want her to cut off his parents from knowing his child. She didn't know what to do. Maybe she could let Muriel know she was safe. That could be a start. She placed her fingers on the keyboard. But the next email made her change her mind.

When we find you, and we will, you'll be sorry.

Ugh. The woman was as mercurial as the wind.

The front door opened, Brigg entered, and Courtney slammed the laptop closed, forgetting the conversation just as fast. As soon as Brigg saw her, he smiled. She smiled back. They stared at each other before she realized he was alone.

"Where's your brother?" she asked, sounding breathy. *Quit sounding flirty.*

"He's going to stay with my parents."

"Oh." So, they would be alone. *Nice.* Her baby kicked. Okay, not quite alone.

Brigg snapped his fingers. "Which reminds me." His long legs ate up the short distance to the kitchen and he rested their food on the counter. Then he grabbed Hawk's travel bag and dashed out the door. Seconds later, Brigg was back inside, and they were back to staring.

Staring and smiling.

"I think I like you," she said.

"I think I like you too," he said.

Her heart galloped. Her palms felt sweaty. And her legs were jelly. But she wasn't taking her eyes off this man.

Brigg broke the trance by coming over to her. In a rapid motion, his powerful arms scooped her close to his chest, and she inhaled his familiar scent. She wrapped her arms around him. She felt him kiss the top of her head and her insides quivered. Maybe this was too fast. He kissed her forehead and she exhaled. Maybe this was a rebound. *No. No. It isn't.* This had nothing to do with Jet and everything to do with Brigg. He kissed her cheek and her heart fluttered like butterfly wings. *Maybe this is—* Maybe she needed to stop thinking and just go with it. He lifted her chin with his index finger. He bent his head. She tilted hers. He closed his eyes. She closed hers. And then their lips met.

He pressed deeper on her lips before sucking them. Then his tongue teased, a silent request for entrance. She groaned and opened her mouth. Once he entered her mouth, he tightened his grip and took over. He was demanding, taking, giving and igniting a thirst only he could quench. She grabbed his butt and went along for the ride.

"Brigg," she exhaled.

"Mmm-hmm," was all he said, nonstop energy.

Brigg kissed her neck, deviating between being feathery light and forceful sucking. It was like he was ravenous; he was starved for her. She could hardly breathe, exulting in being wanted with such intent, such passion. When she thought he was done and about to pull away, Brigg ran his fingers in her hair and pulled before crushing his lips back on hers.

Sensations grew, and Courtney throbbed with such intensity that she was afraid she would combust. Her hands discovered his body, his chest, his package, which added to the frenzy. He was relentless, and she was about to be overpowered by a crescendo if she didn't take a moment. She pressed against his shoulders with the palms of her hands. Instantly, he broke contact. Their chests heaved.

"That was…" She released short, raspy breaths.

His lips quirked. "Yeah, I know." Then in a blink, he banked his passion and changed the subject. Rubbing his hands together, he said, "Let's go eat."

She craved a second round of lip-locking but didn't want to appear needy. Then her stomach growled, and she was as eager as he was to sample the meal he had brought home. The food tasted sweeter after their first kiss. But when she told him so, Brigg quieted, folding into himself, and Courtney was left wondering if he had regrets. She bit into her fried chicken and moaned.

Well, too bad for him if he did. 'Cause she sure didn't.

"Relax, it was just a kiss," she said, patting his hand.

"It wasn't just a kiss, and you know it," he said, somber and unamused.

He was straight-up pouting and acting like he was afraid to look at her. Courtney shrugged and scooped some mashed potatoes in her mouth. She made sure to touch him, brush up against him, every chance she could. He was her Pandora's box, but unlike Pandora, Courtney was delighted with what she found inside. And she was oh so ready to learn more. Much more.

Chapter Sixteen

He had never kissed a woman as he had Courtney. Brigg had lost himself, felt like he was drowning under the magnitude of want and desire. Even now as they sat eating their dinner, his body yearned. Begging him to continue the onslaught. To take another taste. To savor being in her arms. That terrified him. This didn't feel like it was just physical. It felt like more. And Brigg didn't do more.

Courtney, however, had no such qualms. It was like she had a secret pleasure in seeing him tortured from these pent-up emotions and was going out of her way to add to his ache. Shoveling his food into his mouth, Brigg knew he only had one alternative: escape.

He kept his distance the rest of the night.

And for the next few days. His transition into captain came with increased responsibilities and trainings, and Brigg welcomed the work, the long hours. When he was away from Courtney, he could think, he could function. When he was around her, all he thought about was that kiss. And the fact that she was pregnant and couldn't give him the release he needed.

So, he kept things light. Friendly. Solicitous. And

though he saw confusion in her eyes, she seemed okay with him cooling things off. Which in turn made him... sad. It must be strictly physical for her then. He was a solution to her raging hormones. Or worse, a replacement for Jet. Like he had been for the captain, who was still calling him and leaving messages. Brigg didn't know why he didn't just block the number.

His roof had been repaired and Courtney had moved back into the guest room. Brigg tossed in his bed at night, and he knew it was because he wanted her there next to him. Courtney, however, slept well. Snoring. Snoring, while he wandered the house, filled with restless energy.

How did he know this? Because he had watched her. When she was sound asleep, he stood against the door-jamb and took in her beauty. Why? Because he was a grown man swallowed up under a heavy crush.

Courtney started her job at the diner that morning and gave him a happy wave when she pulled off in her rebuilt car. Brigg had taken the next few days off for Axel and Maddie's wedding. He had stood in the drive-way and watched her struggle to get behind the wheel, curling his fists to keep from rushing to help her. At one point, she bent over to adjust the seat and he had almost exploded right there in his driveway seeing that beautiful butt tucked in the air.

Living with her was maddening him, but he couldn't look away. Her pregnancy glow was an aphrodisiac. Every chance he got, he was checking her out. A sweet, sadistic torture of his doing. He should never have kissed her. Then he wouldn't know what he was missing.

His eyes looked sunken and dark from a lack of sleep. Axel was coming to get him, and he knew his brother would comment on it. So, after he was dressed, Brigg placed a warm rag over his eyes.

The doorbell rang and he ran to answer. But when he saw who stood there, Brigg was tempted to slam the door. His former captain stood before him, appearing disheveled and unshaven, and he smelled like he had taken a liquor bath. The stench of alcohol was that strong.

"What are you doing here?" he asked, then lifted a hand. "You know what, don't answer that. I don't have the time or desire to deal with you today or any other day."

"I just need you to hear me out."

Brigg looked past him and saw that the captain had blocked him in. "Wait. Did you drive here in your drunken state?" Dread lined his insides at the thought of having to arrest the former lawman.

"No. My daughter is with me."

"Please leave."

"I need a chance to explain," he croaked out.

"There is no explanation for how you left a man wheelchair-bound for the rest of his life. If you want to talk to anyone, talk to Dominic Jones."

Beckett's face went pale. Despite his harsh words, Brigg's heart moved seeing the proud man so humbled. But he steeled his heart. Beckett deserved to pay for his past actions. He had researched the young man and had learned Dominic had been on his way to college on a track scholarship before he had been incorrectly identified as the culprit for the robbery gone wrong. The only thing Dominic had been guilty of was purchasing an orange soda and a bottle of milk for his mother.

Even now, his stomach turned just thinking about it.

"I just need to…need to…" Beckett's voice broke. He wobbled and grabbed on to the door to keep from falling. Brigg reached over to stabilize him, not because he cared, he told himself, but because he didn't relish wiping blood off the pavement. Cupping the other man under the arm, Brigg led him back to his car.

Beckett's daughter, Violet, greeted him, and Brigg returned a gruff, polite salutation. A far cry from the effusive hugs they used to exchange. The other woman had been like a sister to him. Together, they got Beckett settled into the vehicle. The entire time Beckett begged Brigg for a second chance.

"He misses you," she said, touching his arm. "We all miss you." At least once a week, Brigg would be over at the Sparkses' house either eating dinner or mowing the lawn.

Brigg shirked her off, ignoring those haunting, sad eyes. "I can't stand up for a man who committed such a vicious act of violence against one of my own."

Her lips quivered. "We're like family."

He stepped back. "But, in actuality, we're not. Family, that is." Her face crumbled and he felt hollow, but he couldn't get past the betrayal.

Axel pulled into the driveway and got out. His yellow shirt was a stark contrast against his dark skin, and the sunshine elevated his cognac-colored eyes. Brigg would never admit it because Axel was already swell-headed, but he could understand why the women got all googly eyed in Axel's presence. His brother was working hard on moving past being typecast for his physical attributes by taking on meatier roles. His upcoming film was already generating Golden Globes buzz.

Strutting over to the car, Axel fist-bumped Brigg, then greeted Violet with genuine warmth and even went over to hug the captain, mumbling an encouraging, "It will be okay."

Shaking his head, Brigg stormed inside and pulled up the video. Maybe Axel hadn't seen the footage. That was the only explanation Brigg could think of for why his brother was consorting with their enemy.

Pressing Pause as soon as Axel stepped over the threshold, Brigg pressed Play.

Once it ended, he pointed out, "How can you be gracious to the man who did that?"

"Because that's in the past. He's changed. He's apologized."

"That's not good enough."

Axel dipped his chin. "Everyone deserves a second chance."

"I disagree. Tell that to DJ." That had been Dominic's pet name.

They had a brief standoff before Axel's shoulders slumped. "All right, I'll leave this alone, because today is about my bachelor party. Hawk rented a hotel suite, and he's planned out the whole day. We'll have brunch, and then we'll go fishing, play golf and we all have massages scheduled."

"Massages?" Brigg wrinkled his nose. "I'm good."

"Don't knock it till you've tried it." Axel looked around. "Where's Courtney? I've been dying to get a glimpse of her. Hawk refused to snap a pic and send it to the rest of us."

"Really? She's at the diner. Working." He grunted out the last word, still upset at the thought of her being on her feet all day. He made a mental note to get some Epsom salt and lavender, because she was going to need it when she got off her shift.

"You ready to go?"

Brigg nodded.

"Where's your overnight bag?"

"I'm not spending the night with you all. I don't want to leave Courtney alone."

Axel studied him. "According to Caleb and Hawk, you're nuts over this woman."

"I'm not nuts. She's pregnant, that's all. I would hate for her to go into labor and I'm not here."

His brother took out his cell and made a call, putting it on speaker. Hawk answered. He could hear the others in the background. "Listen, bro, change of plans. Let's eat at the diner. I don't think Brigg will survive the entire day without seeing his girlfriend."

Girlfriend? "She's not my girlfriend. It's too soon for all that." *But not too soon for that electrifying kiss, huh?*

"That sounds like a plan. Let me round up the guys, and we'll meet you over there," Hawk said, disconnecting the call.

"Listen, it's Courtney's first day, and I don't think we should overwhelm her," Brigg said. He pulled out his phone to warn Courtney about the impending invasion: Mayday. We are coming there to eat.

"We won't," Axel said, shooing him out the door. "Don't worry, we'll be on our best behavior."

He groaned, dragging himself down the driveway. "We're not in high school anymore. And you, Hawk and Ethan together will attract too much attention. I thought you wanted to keep things low-key."

"The more you plead, the more I know I want to meet her."

Brigg shut up after that. He knew there was no point, and all he could hope was that Courtney was ready for the teasing and questions.

His cell buzzed. She had responded. No worries. See you soon. XOXO.

Brigg pressed his lips together. Of course she wasn't worried. He was a dot on her life map. And in a few days, she'd leave and have her baby without giving him a second thought. So he needed to get that kiss out of his mind and see it for what it was: a onetime thing.

Chapter Seventeen

Courtney's feet and lower back ached. She went into the back room and leaned against the doorframe, drawing several breaths.

She found the Harrington men engaging and exhausting. *Ugh.* But Courtney was determined not to let Brigg see how right he was. Princess had told her several times to take a break, but she wouldn't until Brigg left.

If only he would.

The brothers had invaded the diner, and word had spread through the town quickly. The regular townies knew them from when they were kids, so seeing them was no big deal. But according to Princess, since their success and the growth in Love Creek's population, the Harrington men usually stayed on their parents' compound when they were all together. Not today though.

She didn't have to wonder why.

She knew why.

Each of Brigg's brothers had called her over to joke or ask her a random question. And Brigg? He had remained closemouthed, steadily eating, studying her from under his lashes. She knew he was looking because her traitorous body sizzled.

The air between them was charged.

A hand patted her back. "You need to go home," Princess clucked, her voice filled with sympathy.

Courtney stood. "No. No. I've got to get Hawk's apple pie and Ethan's custard."

"Those men have some serious appetites. I don't know where they put it, but I do know they are generous tippers." Princess giggled. "Nancy is going to be happy because we made more this morning than we have in weeks."

Courtney's feet could testify to that fact, but she was too tired to rejoice. She wanted to go home and snuggle under the duvet and sleep until tomorrow. As soon as the door closed behind the Harrington men, she was out of there.

"Hey, do you think you'll be able to handle that wedding the day after tomorrow?" Princess asked. "I can try to get a temp agency."

"Oh, I'm good. I'll be fine." On the inside, Courtney groaned. It was stubbornness that kept her from caving. She stifled a yawn and grabbed their desserts before trooping over to the table with a smile on her face.

Her bravado lasted through their goodbye hugs. Her heart squeezed at how much the brothers loved each other. If you didn't have the visual proof, you would think they were all blood related. That's how well they got along. That made her think of Kaylin. Her sister had emailed that her ship had docked.

Courtney couldn't wait to talk to her on video call later that day. She worked another hour before heading home. Once she did, she sunk into the couch and didn't awake until Brigg shook her.

"I made you a bath," he said, his tone gentle.

"Oh, thank you," she said, sniffling. Courtney tried to stand but her body hurt.

Brigg cupped his arms. "May I?"

She gave a small nod and the next second she found herself wrapped into his powerful arms. During the short trek to the bathroom, she fretted about getting undressed with him there. When Brigg placed her to stand, she bit her lower lip.

"Your undies are basically a bathing suit," he offered, accurately knowing her hesitation.

Not really, but she got his point. Plus, she wanted the bath more than maintaining her pride. Hands shaky, she stripped down to her undies.

He lowered her into steaming warmth of his spa tub, and she welcomed the feel of the pulsing jets on her body. Once Brigg left, she took off the rest of her clothes. Next, Brigg brought her dinner from a nearby diner. Eyeing the prime rib and brussels sprouts, she scarfed it down in less than ten minutes. He was so tender and thoughtful. Courtney's heart squeezed.

"You don't have to do this, you know," he said, tone gentle. "You don't have to work."

"I know. But I like it. I'm good," she said, pressing her lips together to keep from placing them on his.

She stayed in the tub until her skin pruned. By the time she had dried and dressed, she was ready to call her sister. Sitting on the bed with her back against the headboard, her legs spread straight in front of her, Courtney checked to make sure her laptop was fully charged.

Courtney pulled up her video-calling app and searched for her sister's contact information. Once it popped up, she tapped the call icon. Seconds later, her sister's face filled the screen.

"Kaylinnnn," she squealed, her eyes misting at connecting with her big sister.

"Hey, baby sis. It feels like forever since we've talked." Kaylin waved. Her sister had chopped her hair into a bob. They both had similar skin tones and hair. Because of that, they had been asked often if they were twins.

"Wow, you cut your hair." Courtney touched her own copper curls.

"Yes, I needed a change, a distraction. I got sick and was stuck in my cabin when we docked, so I decided to cut my ends. Only, I messed up one side, and before I knew it, I was going higher and higher." She giggled. "I had to make a hair appointment onboard to get it fixed. And voilà."

"It looks cute on you." Her lips quivered. "I missed you."

"I missed you too," Kaylin said, holding out her hands to send a virtual hug. "You don't know how relieved I am to see your face. When I got your email that you had left your in-laws, I fretted all night, wondering how you would manage being on the road while pregnant."

"Well, as you see, I didn't manage well," Courtney said.

"I know. Thank goodness, when you broke down, it was with law enforcement nearby instead of someone with less than honorable intentions."

Courtney's body chilled. "I hadn't thought of that possibility…" She rubbed her tummy. "Yes, Brigg has been a godsend. He's kind and thoughtful." She then went on to tell her of the many things Brigg had done—from gifting her the cell phone to fixing her car to letting her stay as long as she needed.

Kaylin's brows rose. "Brigg, is it?"

She scolded her wayward tongue. Good thing she

didn't mention sharing his bed or *the* kiss. The one that made her lips tingle... *No, no.* She had to savor that juicy morsel, let it marinate. Besides, she didn't want her sister getting an accurate description of her current predicament: jonesing for the hot cop while pregnant.

"He told me to call him that," she said instead. "Especially since I hunkered down here with him when the hurricane was passing through. This house was shaking, and the tree hit the top of the house. But compared to others, we fared pretty well."

"Don't try to deflect." She giggled. "You need to rewind to the part where you said his name all breathy and dreamy."

Breathy? Dreamy? Well, that hadn't worked. "I—I didn't." Wait. Had she?

"I know you," Kaylin teased, pointing to the screen. "You like him. When you wrote me about him, I pictured this older man with a paunch and a receding hairline. But hearing you sound all gushy like that, I need to get a good look at him. Send me a pic."

"How?" she sputtered. "I can't go snapping him like that."

"Is he there?"

"Yes, but what are we in, elementary school? I'm not doing that."

"All you have to do is walk out there and pretend you're admiring something in his vicinity and press the button. Easy peasy. Unless...you're scared," she taunted, poking out her tongue.

Now they were six and seven all over again. "I'm not scared. I'm grown." She refused to be manipulated.

"Nice try," Kaylin scoffed. "I need to see the man who has my sister all goo-goo gaga."

"I'm not…" She rolled her eyes. She wouldn't be if it weren't for their lip-locking.

"Yes, you are. You were like this with Jet." She mimed gagging.

Courtney froze for a beat. "Will you stop talking that loud? Brigg might hear you."

Kaylin only spoke louder. "You mean he might hear how you have the hots for him."

"Lower your voice or I'm hanging up," she whispered through her teeth.

"Fine." She lowered her tone. "But I'm excited about Brawny Brigg. Let me see that eye candy."

"How do you know he's brawny?" Courtney asked before she groaned.

Kaylin cackled. "You just confirmed it."

Courtney pretended to bite her tongue. "Me and my big mouth." She scooted to the edge of the bed, and her sister whooped. "Ugh. I'll be right back."

"I'll be here…" Kaylin drawled out.

Grabbing her phone, Courtney hurried out of the room and went to find Brigg. He was in the living room area, munching on grapes and watching a game.

"Everything all right?" he asked.

Turning on the lights, she nodded. "I, uh, might have lost an earring in the couch."

"But you haven't been wearing any." He stood and bent over to feel in the edges. She took a picture of that fine butt. Maybe her sister was onto something. She was going to need these memories when she was gone. She took a couple more before he turned around.

Snap. Snap.

He paused his search. "What are you doing?"

"Um…" She tossed her hair and lifted her chin. "My

sister wants to know what you look like, so I'm taking a few pics."

"Of my butt?"

She cleared her throat. "That was for me."

To her surprise, Brigg cracked up. "You and your sister sound like how I am when I'm with my brothers." He posed and smiled. "Go ahead and take one or two."

Holding her phone, she took a couple. "She is going to freak out when she sees how handsome you are."

"Wait. You think I'm handsome?" he asked, flexing his muscles.

She laughed. She liked him like this. But she strove to sound matter of fact. "Of course I do. If I wasn't attracted, you think I'd let you kiss me?" The question hung between them. Then she gasped, placing a hand over her mouth. "My sister's waiting on me," she said, hurrying back to get her laptop.

Brigg followed her into her room.

"What are you doing?"

"I came to meet your sister," he said.

Of course, Kaylin called out for him to show his face. They greeted each other and then engaged in small talk that made Courtney smile. Kaylin approved, which was a good sign. She had been much more reserved when it came to Jet. Not that she hadn't liked him. She just seemed to be gelling with Brigg much more.

"I can't wait to meet you, Kaylin," Brigg said, giving a wave.

"Same here. I've got a couple of things to take care off first, but then I'll be jumping on the Greyhound and heading up that way to drive back with Courtney," Kaylin said.

His shoulders slumped, which made Courtney wonder if he would miss her. Because she was going to miss him. Then he straightened. "See you then." He headed to the door, but before he left her to finish her conversation, Brigg looked at her. "You owe me a picture next." His words sounded like a promise and a challenge. Or he could be teasing.

She met him stare for stare. "Bring it," she tossed out, her chest heaving.

He gave a sexy smile. "All right, bet."

Chapter Eighteen

Coming here was like placing your hand in an anthill and hoping you didn't get bitten. Not a good idea. Even though Brigg told himself to keep his distance, he found himself in his truck outside the Jones residence with his AC on full blast.

The house had light blue awnings, buttercup yellow trimmings and a ramp. It looked cheerful and bright when the people inside had suffered loss and pain. He tapped the steering wheel, debating whether or not to knock on the door, wondering what he would even say.

What did he hope to accomplish by coming here? Brigg didn't know, but he felt compelled to.

He had researched all the Dominic Joneses in Love Creek and had been surprised to see there had been three in the town. The first was a retired military lieutenant and lived in another state. The second was a minor league basketball coach who now lived one town over. And the third had never moved.

For a reason.

Brigg sighed. When he was in the academy, he had lost track of the countless times he had received grunts and glares and called a traitor to his face by other Black people. But he hadn't swayed; he had stayed the course. Because he had wanted the blue suit to reflect honor, to reflect his upbringing, and to counteract the stereotype of a scary Black man. He didn't want to be feared but seen as a source of help and hope. But the brutal actions of one often clouded the perception for many.

Since Beckett's removal, several officers had their homes spray-painted and cop vehicles egged. Brigg intended to devote a couple hours later to strategize and create a community outreach plan. But first...

Squaring his shoulders, Brigg exited the vehicle, the stifling heat piercing his exposed arms and face, and made his way up the ramp. He rapped on the front door before he noticed there was a doorbell. He pressed it twice before wiping his brow.

The door creaked as it opened, and a head peered up at him from behind the door. "Yes? Can I help you?"

"Hello, Dominic," he said, clearing his throat. "Do you think I could have five minutes of your time?"

The crack in the door widened, followed by a whizzing sound before the other man wheeled into view. "I go by DJ. Officer, I'll tell you the same thing I told the reporters who came by. I have nothing to say about that night. I'm good, and I just want to be left alone." Nevertheless, he gave Brigg entrance, belying his words.

DJ's home was airy and bright, the scent of lemons and fresh linen teasing the air. He traipsed behind DJ into the living area. His wheelchair made a light slipping sound on the caramel tiles as they passed by the kitchen on the left. Simply put, the house was immaculate. Pictures of DJ in his early years lined the wall, and the display cabinet sparkled under the sunlight and held myriad trophies, which Brigg presumed were from DJ's days in track. They made their way into the family room, and DJ invited him to take a seat.

His eyes fell on the oversized bookcases stuffed with books. Books stacked in the corner. Books opened on the student desk.

"I love to read. Got it from my mother." DJ picked up a worn hardcover that looked like it had been around since the 1800s. "This is a classic—*Jane Eyre* by Charlotte Brontë. This was one of the first books she made me read. If I wanted to run, I had to read." He splayed his hands and gave a little laugh. "Let's just say I really wanted to run."

"Wow. That's impressive. I mostly read police procedurals and case studies," Brigg said, sitting on a firm dark brown coach. "Thanks for taking the time to see me."

"You didn't seem like the type who wouldn't come back, so..." DJ shrugged. "What can I do for you, Interim Captain?"

"So, you recognize me?"

"Yes," he scoffed. "Everyone knows the Harringtons, plus I watch the news."

The other man had a calm aura about him, an unexpected peace that made Brigg curious. "Why won't you take interviews? Tell your side of the story?"

"Because I'm entitled to mind my own business."

"I hear you. But as a fellow Black man, I'm appalled by what you went through at the hands of someone who was meant to protect the town's citizens."

DJ pinned him with a gaze. "What's it to you?"

"I'm seeking to improve relations and safety within the town, and this is one of the most egregious acts I have seen," Brigg said. "And I care." His heart hurt thinking about how DJ's future changed because of mistaken identity. Those few minutes changed his life forever.

"Look, when I woke up in the hospital and learned I would never walk, never run again, it was… I can't even put that into words. My mother stopped working to take care of me. But I was angry. Angry at God, at the cops, at my mom for sending me out to the store that day. But I was angry at myself the most."

Brigg leaned forward. "How so?"

Releasing a huge breath, DJ jabbed his finger on the table. "I heard about what was going to go down at Mr. Chin's store. I heard those boys planning to rob the store, and instead of saying something, I told myself it wasn't hurting my pockets, so it didn't concern me." He pointed to his chest. "I did nothing. If I had spoken up…" His voice broke. "Who knows? I wouldn't be paralyzed, and that man would be alive."

"You were a kid," Brigg said gently, amazed at the other man's guilt. He didn't know if he had been in DJ's situation that he would take any responsibility.

"The thing is, Mr. Chin was kind to everybody. He used to give all the kids in the neighborhood free ice pops or candy or juice. He was good people. He even let my mother keep a tab when she couldn't afford milk or cheese. Mr. Chin would be like, 'Pay me next time.'" DJ scoffed. "And you know, he never took any money." His shoulders shook. "So, I'm not being the better person right now. I'm trying to make amends for not doing the right thing."

Understanding dawned. "Is that why you didn't press charges against Cap—Beckett Sparks?"

Wiping his face, DJ nodded. "Yes, he wrote several letters begging me for forgiveness. He was at the hospital almost every day saying how sorry he was. How he wished he could make things right. He even offered to give me half of his paycheck for life. At the time, I didn't want to hear anything he had to say to me. I was too enraged. I wanted him to feel the physical and emotional agony I was feeling, wading in my own guilt. But after a while, all I could think was…" He sobbed. "At least I'm alive to be upset. Mr. Chin didn't have that choice." He grabbed a tissue off the coffee table and wiped his face. "Now, I still don't want to see that cop who put me in this chair, but I don't hate him."

"Why not?" Brigg asked.

DJ studied him for a beat before he folded his arms. "Oh, so that's why you're here. You want to hate him too…but you don't."

Brigg had been read as well as the pages of that *Jane Eyre* novel. "I don't know how to feel. I'm torn," he confessed, then volleyed a question back to DJ. "Why don't you hate him?"

"What's the point?" DJ shrugged. "Don't get me wrong. If you had asked me years ago when this all went down, my response would have been completely different. But it's been almost twenty years. If hating that man would make me walk again, I would see the purpose. Otherwise…"

"Dang, how did you get so wise?" To say DJ impressed him would be an understatement.

"Experience is a tough teacher, and I've got about ten or twelve years ahead of you."

That was it. He liked this man. Brigg could picture them becoming great friends if the circumstances had been different. "If we had gone to high school around the same time, we could've hung out. In fact, I'm sure we would have."

DJ smiled. "I have to agree. I toggled between my

parents for years, bouncing from state to state, so I don't think I was there to meet your brothers either." He then offered Brigg something to drink, pouring them both two tall glasses of lemonade. Then he asked, "What's your deal? I thought you 'men in blue'—" he used air quotes "—defended each other. Blues before bros."

"Beckett was my mentor. I don't know if I would have become a cop if it weren't for him. This man encouraged me all the way through the academy." He flailed his hands. "And now I learn it's because he was trying to assuage his guilt. I was your stand-in. By helping me, he must have felt he was helping you." Pointing between them, Brigg confided, "The situation was oddly similar, but unlike you, I stole something. But he didn't beat me to a pulp. He gave me a second chance." His breath caught. "I guess I have a weird form of survivor's guilt. Like, why did he help me and not you?"

His question went unanswered as they finished their lemonades.

"Hmm…interesting." DJ placed his glass on the coffee table.

"What?" Brigg asked.

"On one of Beckett's unwelcome visits, I remember saying that if he wanted to help me, he needed to help another Black boy. Then I cussed at him and told him to leave me alone."

Goose bumps popped up on Brigg's flesh. "Wow." He exhaled. "That's deep." He was that boy. Ten years later.

"Yeah. Let that soak in." DJ placed a hand on the gearshift for his motorized wheelchair. An unspoken signal that the visit was coming to an end.

Standing, Brigg held out a hand. "This has been an

enlightening conversation." They started toward the front door. Brigg's heart felt lighter with each step.

"Likewise," DJ nodded. "This has been the second greatest thing to happen to me since this wheelchair."

"What's the first?" Brigg asked, pausing by the door-jamb.

"Once I accepted my new life, I decided to build another talent." DJ waggled his fingers. "I earned my degrees and then developed an app I eventually sold for a cool three million dollars. I don't have to work another day in my life. I get to read and help other youths. I give to a few foundations. Later today, I'll be driving to the juvie to volunteer." He shook his head. "Too many of us in there. Got to get them out and on the right path."

Giving him a fist bump, Brigg said, "I'd love to hear about that. I think there's a way for us to work together."

"For sure." DJ gave him an earnest look. "I do get out, but I'm a bit of a recluse. It would be great to make some friends my own age. Those teens fill up my time. Plus, I'm always up for a game of basketball."

"Most def. Just know I'm not about to take it easy on you."

"Bring it."

"All right, bet. I'll call my brothers and we'll arrange something." Brigg dipped back out into the heat, this time ignoring the sun's rays. They weren't as bright as his heart leaving DJ's house. Just as he was about to get into the truck, DJ called out.

"Hey! Forgive him. Forgive him for the both of us."

After a slight hesitation, Brigg gave him a thumbs-up and hopped into his truck. He started up the car and turned up the AC. Meeting DJ had cracked the concrete resentment he felt for Beckett, and he was so glad he'd visited. Before he drove off, Brigg thought he saw a camera flash and looked around. But when he didn't see anyone, he dismissed it as a flash of sunlight, especially since there was a text from Courtney.

Your brothers are here again.

At the diner?

Yes. They got you something to go.

OMW.

Brigg put the truck in gear and made his way to the diner, a huge grin on his face. He refused to acknowledge that the sudden flutter in his stomach was because he was going to see Courtney for a few minutes. He was hungry, that was all. Ever since their playful banter the night before, there was an air of anticipation, almost like a dance-off between them, and it was his turn.

This morning, she came out of the room photo ready, wearing lipstick, her curls well tamed. The goofball in him loved to see her expectant face turn down in disappointment when he hadn't taken the pic he had promised to take.

Before heading out the door, she huffed, "Don't think you're getting a pic of me when I'm sweaty and all tired from work."

He hid a grin. Oh, that was exactly his plan. She was going to be sweaty and tired, but not from the work he was thinking about. And she was going to love every minute of it.

Chapter Nineteen

Courtney forced herself to put one foot in front of the other as she fetched water and poured tea. The other servers handled dinner and desserts. She could have been a guest at one of the most heartfelt wedding ceremonies she had ever witnessed if she wasn't so pigheaded. Axel and Madison Harrington had chosen to have their private ceremony inside the auditorium of Love Creek High. The last place the media would think to look for them. A genius idea for the venue, chosen because of its sentimental value.

From what she was told, Axel and Maddie's relationship had blossomed here when Axel volunteered to work with the high school drama team. But Princess hadn't said a word until Courtney had arrived and donned her apron. If she had known, she wouldn't have taken the gig. But at least she still got to enjoy the festivities.

The navy and ivory balloons, centerpieces and trimmings sparkled under the festive lights. She recognized the DJ from social media, and she had to say he was doing his thing.

There were a few times she had been bopping her head and tapping her toes when she needed to be serving. The high school drama team had been invited, and the teens had been on the dance floor for most of the night. She decided to place a few jugs of ice water at their tables, knowing they were going to need to cool down.

While she served, she avoided Brigg's furious glares and steered clear of the main tables. Gone was their flirty rapport over the past few days. Brigg's mother, Tanya, looking fit in a mauve formfitting gown came over and introduced herself. She took the tray out of Courtney's hands and despite her protests, served the table. Patrick came over to assist his wife after Tanya performed introductions. Her kind actions almost made Courtney dissolve into tears.

Maybe it was because his parents were now serving at their son's wedding that Brigg marched over to her and tugged her aside.

"Why would you sign up to serve here at this wedding?" he ground out, his eyes flashing and his tone incensed.

"I didn't know it was Axel's ceremony. It's a high school. What celebrity has a wedding at a high school?" she shot back, drawing attention from other guests and not caring, longing to get off her feet. Her legs burned.

"One who wants a private exchange of vows with their loved ones," he roared.

She placed her hands on her hips and used the last of her reserve energy to snap at him. "Quit shooting daggers at me with your eyes and go enjoy your brother's wedding." Brigg's parents stood off on the side observing their argument.

"How am I supposed to enjoy the festivities when I have to watch you limping and in pain?"

"I'm not limping!" she shouted. Not really. Her anger kindled more. "You know what, I'm tired of being told what to do." She jabbed a hand to her chest. "I decide what I do or don't do. And you need to respect that." She felt a pull on her arm and noticed Princess had come to her side.

"Hush now, you're making a scene," Princess whispered. "We're trying to get paid."

Courtney's comeback was quick. "Well, I would be working, but this gentleman keeps getting in my way."

"Suit yourself. I'll leave you alone." Brigg stormed off after that, and Courtney continued attending to the guests, making sure to wave at Brigg's brothers.

She felt bad for losing her temper, but her sore feet made her crankier than usual. Plus, she was hungry. A few nibbles here and there hadn't helped. Brigg kept a watchful eye, but he sulked for most of the night. Courtney kept up the pretense for another three hours before, blissfully, Princess released her.

It took sheer willpower for her to fold herself into her car and drive home. She wished she hadn't turned down Princess's offer for a ride to the event. She used a voice activation command to unlock the front door and hobbled inside.

Picking up a pillow off the couch, Courtney made her way to the hallway and placed it against the wall. Then she sat and scooted as close to the wall as she could and eased herself to her side before rolling her bottom on the pillow. She exhaled before shimmying as best as she could until her bottom touched the wall. Lifting her legs, she rested them, thankful for gravity. Hopefully, this would help to reduce the swelling in her ankles and feet. She stayed there for eight cycles of breath before working her way back into a standing position.

Stripping out of her black pants and shirt, she placed her cell phone on the nightstand. She heard a clunk behind her and turned around. Her cell phone had fallen under her nightstand and was probably underneath the bed. With a careless wave, she traipsed into the shower to wash up and then stretched out in the bed on her side. There wasn't a part on her body that didn't hurt. She felt like had walked on nails. Burying her head into her arm, she rubbed her tummy and cried. "I'll have to quit. I can't do this."

She rubbed her lower back.

The pain was something fierce right now.

Maybe she'd overdone things. She exhaled. A sharp pain in her abdomen made her cry out. Clutching her stomach, she writhed in agony. If something happened to her baby because of her stupidity, she would never forgive herself.

Hot searing pain sliced through her like a blade. Fear licked her spine and she curved on the bed. Her heart palpitated in her chest. Something was wrong and she was very much alone. She would give anything for Brigg to bust inside the house right now. Panting, Courtney reached for her phone, patting the nightstand, before she remembered she had dropped it.

"Don't panic. Don't panic," she told herself. She swung her legs off the bed and stood. Her lower back was on fire. She took a step, but the agony was simply too much, and she felt as if she were going to pass out. Struggling to remain calm, Courtney called the name of the man she had come to rely on even though she knew there was no way he could hear. "Brigg! Brigg! Brigg!" she yelled and called for him until everything went black.

Chapter Twenty

"What was that about?" Tanya asked, sidling up next to Brigg. He had known there would be no avoiding this conversation. All around him, happy couples were getting down to one of the best DJs he had ever heard in his life, and he sat here moping. The irony was his chair was in front of the big blowup of the smiling couple.

Brigg grunted. "She's a friend."

Her brows rose. "A friend?"

"Yes, and don't go reading more into it," he mumbled, "because she sure isn't."

"Watch your tone," his mother warned, picking up one of the golden bottles of bubbles to release some into the air.

Brigg turned to look at her and sighed. "I'm sorry, Mom. I'm being the Grinch of the wedding. I don't know how to lift the funk." Not even the sight of his childhood crush—Maddie's mother, Faran—had boosted his spirits. The supermodel had come over to ask him to join the line dance, but Brigg had declined.

Worry ate at him. He hadn't seen Courtney pop out hoisting an overladen tray in roughly thirty minutes.

"Who is she?" Tanya asked, finished amusing herself with the bubbles.

"She's a straggler I rescued out of the hurricane," he said, attempting to make it sound humorous, but it fell flat. Mainly because he sounded miserable.

His mother patted his hand. "Why don't you go check on her?" his mother said. "Take her home. Axel will understand if you have to leave. Where is she staying?"

"She's at my house."

Tanya reared back in the chair. "As in, she's living with you? I didn't know things were that serious with the both of you."

"No, it's not. She's staying with me until she gets on her feet. Courtney plans to head to Fort Lauderdale to live with her sister." Now that the car was ready and she had a job, he figured she would be on her way once she got paid. He didn't intend to take any money from her though. Not that she knew that.

"If it helps, she can stay with us." Tanya rubbed his back like she had done when he was a child. "We have all those bedrooms, and I would love the company." She cocked her head. "Where's the baby's father?"

He shook his head. "No, that's okay. I don't want to put you out, and the father, her husband, is deceased."

"Oh, I'm sorry to hear that. There are so many challenges being a single mother." She then gave him a pointed look, her face hiding a smile. "It sounds like you don't want her anywhere else but with you."

The truth of his mother's words sunk in. "It's not what you think. This is nothing more than attraction borne out of the fact that we're two healthy adults in close proximity. Infatuation was bound to occur."

"Infatuation. Attraction. They are building blocks for something more."

Something more? Brigg scoffed. "It isn't even like that."

Like a moth, with his mother as the flame, his father came over and flanked his other side. Tanya gave Patrick a quick rundown of their conversation.

Patrick punched his arm before dragging him in for a hug. "It's okay, son. Mightier men have fallen under the spell of a good woman."

His eyes darted between his parents. "You two are making more of this than it needs to be. I'm not under anybody's spell. She's not a witch or a siren. She's merely a woman." A sassy, independent, sexy woman, but a woman nonetheless.

"A pregnant woman who was on her feet and might be in need of some TLC." His mother gestured toward the exit. "Get. Go help your *friend*."

Patrick leaned in front of Brigg to kiss Tanya full on the lips. Her sun-kissed skin took on a rosy hue. Cupping his father's face, she said, "You ready for tonight?"

Though a secret part of him was happy to see his parents very much in love, it didn't mean he wanted to see their PDA in action. Brigg scrunched his face and stood. "Will you two get a room?"

"We did," Patrick said, waggling his brows.

"Um, I'll see you both later." Brigg strode across the dance floor cutting through the line dance to go in search of Courtney. When Princess told him that Courtney had left and that she had tried to call Courtney but didn't get her, Brigg sprinted out of the building and jumped into his car. Putting his sirens on, he sped home.

In record time, he pulled in his driveway.

Praying he was overreacting and telling himself he would laugh about it later, Brigg rushed into the house and raced toward Courtney's room, calling out for her. There was no answer, and when he bounded into her room, he saw that she was passed out, and a quick check of her pulse showed she was barely breathing.

Heart pounding like horses on a track, Brigg called 911, hoisted her in his arms, and headed out the door.

"Captain, both Mom and baby are fine," the doctor said after what felt like hours of waiting. Hearing others refer to him as Captain jarred him, but in this case, Brigg welcomed the deferential treatment.

As soon as he had entered the emergency room, they had rushed Courtney back, and he had completed the paperwork. Brigg had insurance from his job, but of course, he couldn't use that, so he told them he would cover the expenses out of pocket. He wasn't too proud to ask his older brother for help and had called Hawk, who promised he would help cover the costs of his future sister-in-law.

Brigg accepted the ribbing, especially since it meant Courtney would receive the best possible care. Turns out there was a private VIP suite he never knew existed until now. Once the staff had heard Hawk Harrington should be billed, they had been extra solicitous. Courtney was now asleep in a room with a private nurse. Brigg stood near the door watching her.

The doctor had come over to update him on her progress. "She was dehydrated and her air levels were low. We have placed her on an IV drip and oxygen. We'll monitor her overnight, but she should be good to go in the morning. I'm putting her on temporary bed rest." The physician gave Brigg a pat on the back and headed to the door. "Make sure she stays off her feet."

Brigg followed the doctor outside the room to ask, "What about the baby?"

"We have hooked up an electronic fetal monitoring device so we can track the baby's heartbeat. Don't worry. Mom and baby are in good hands."

Brigg shook the doctor's hand. "Thank you, Doctor. I'll do my best to make her comply." As soon as the doctor left, Brigg slumped, feeling overwhelming relief. When he had seen Courtney's lifeless body, he hadn't known what to think. But he knew he had felt like a jackhammer had hacked away at his heart.

He tiptoed back inside the room, her loud snoring echoing off the walls. There was a full-size bed in the corner and a chaise longue. Because he was still dressed in his tuxedo and Courtney was asleep, Brigg decided to head home to shower and change, then return and spend the night. His stomach rumbled, reminding him that he had barely eaten, having spent most of the evening occupied with thoughts of Courtney.

Pulling up a food delivery app, Brigg ordered takeout. It should arrive by the time he was showered. When he pulled up, he saw Hawk's truck and canceled his food delivery. Maybe they could grab something to eat together.

Once he opened the door, Brigg froze. All his brothers were present except for Axel, who of course, was on his honeymoon. He closed the door behind him, feeling the heat of ten eyes trained on him. As usual, when they got together, the channel was on whatever sports were in season. Like Brigg, they were still in their tuxes, but the jackets were off, the ties loosened and the shirts untucked.

Hawk, Lynx and Drake were sprawled on his couch, and Ethan and Caleb had dragged chairs from his kitchen. The men filled his small living area.

"What are you turkeys doing here?" he asked.

"Gobble, gobble," Ethan said, flapping his long lean arms, which earned him a shove from Hawk. Ethan was now a swim coach at the middle school, but he still swam twice a day, before and after work.

"How is Courtney doing?" Hawk asked.

"Both Courtney and her son are fine, and she's sleeping at the moment." Brigg shuddered. "I tell you, that was the scariest thing I've ever gone through."

"That's why we came to hang with you for a little bit and check up on Courtney. Also, we ordered pizza," Caleb said, adjusting his glasses on the bridge of his nose.

Brigg gave his twin a smile, knowing this had probably been his idea. They shared so many opposites: Caleb was a couple inches shorter than Brigg, and unlike Brigg, who was sepia-toned, Caleb was a pecan tone, and Brigg kept his hair in a fade while Caleb was clean-shaven. But they shared a bond that cemented as they got older.

"I can't stay long though," Lynx added. "Shanna needs me to stop at the pharmacy."

"Shanna, Shanna, Shanna," Brigg teased. Ever since Lynx married Shanna, there wasn't a single conversation where he didn't mention her name.

Lynx threw a pillow at him. "Your time is coming, Captain." Brigg ducked, causing it to hit the art on the wall, it tilted but fortunately didn't fall, because it had cost a fortune to frame. He shook his head. All it took was five minutes of them being around each other for them to behave like they were kids again.

Hawk snickered. "I think it's already here."

Lynx jabbed him in the chest. "You shouldn't talk. Word in the press is you're getting ready to pop the question."

Losing his smile, Hawk's eyes turned into slits. "I wish they would mind their business."

Drake came over to give him a tight hug. He was the same height as Brigg but had also inherited a lot of his mother's Native American features. Drake and Ethan's mom had passed when they were really young. "Bro, you got it bad for this girl. You were such a party pooper that we were all really worried about you."

"Since I met Courtney, I've been behaving in ways that are not normal for me," Brigg admitted. "But it doesn't mean I have it bad, to use your words, Drake. I'm attracted to her, but anything beyond that is pushing it."

"I wish I could say I understood, but this dude ain't getting into entanglements," Drake said, pointing to his chest.

The doorbell rang. Their pizza had arrived. Since Brigg was closest to the door, he grabbed the order and placed it on the kitchen counter. Soon the brothers were digging in with eyes on the game. Brigg glanced at the clock. Courtney might awaken soon, and he didn't want her to wake up without him there. He ate a couple slices and excused himself.

"Where are you going?" Caleb asked, giving him a knowing look.

"I have to get back to the hospital," he said.

"If it walks like a duck and quacks like a duck…" Drake teased.

"It can also be a goose," Brigg finished, dashing into his bedroom. Brigg was ready in under fifteen minutes. Since he had rushed out of the house with Courtney, he knew she didn't have her cell phone or her purse. So he went into her room to have a look. Grabbing her bag, he scanned the surfaces before deciding to look under the bed.

Sure enough, her phone had fallen. He reached for it and dusted it off. Courtney must have been snacking in here, because he could see crumbs on the floor. Brigg had been about to slip her phone into her purse, but since she didn't lock her phone, he noticed Courtney had missed calls from her sister, Kaylin.

A reminder that Courtney would be leaving soon... Taking a deep breath, Brigg gathered her toothbrush and other toiletries and placed them in her backpack.

Twenty minutes later, he walked into Courtney's private room and stopped short. The bed was empty, and her private nurse wasn't there either. Dropping her possessions on the chaise lounge, Brigg rushed to the bathroom and knocked. No answer. Heart thumping, he raced outside the room to the nurse's station.

"Where's Courtney Meadows?" he asked, breathless, his chest heaving. "Is she okay?"

"Calm down, Captain. She's all right," the nurse said.

"If she's all right, then where is she?" He gripped the ends of the counter to keep himself stable, all the while wondering why they were so calm.

Patting his hand, the nurse smiled. "She's in labor."

Chapter Twenty-One

Don't forget to breathe. Don't forget to breathe.

Courtney watched the TOCO monitor charting her contractions and gripped the nurse's hand. Her contractions were already five minutes apart, and according to the doctor, she was almost fully dilated. That was unusual. Courtney believed it was because of the extensive walking she had done over the past days.

Seeing the lines go up on the small screen, Courtney tried to remember the breathing exercises the nurse had walked her through, but there was no preparing for this level of pain. She had awakened in the hospital discombobulated, but before she could ask how she had gotten there, she registered the warmth seeping between her legs, soaking the sheets. Her water had broken.

She pressed the Call button, and within minutes, they wheeled her into Labor and Delivery. The midwife was assisting another mother but would be in soon. According to the nurse, Jayson was in a hurry to get here.

That was good, because she desperately wanted to see her baby. And the lower back pain was intense. She glanced at the screen.

Uh-oh. Here we go.

"Hee hee whooo. Hee hee whooo," the nurse prodded.

Locking eyes with her, Courtney echoed, "Hee hee whoo. Hee hee whooo," repeating it until the contraction eased.

The nurse patted her back and adjusted the pillows behind her. "You did well. Let me get you some ice chips. I'm sorry to leave you, but we're short-staffed. Lots of women delivering tonight. Must be the full moon."

"It's okay. Thanks," Courtney said, trying to catch her breath and not panic, because those lines seemed to be increasing, which meant... "Ahh," she cried out, tears leaking down her face as she gripped the sheets. Maybe she needed to keep her eyes off the screen, because it was adding to her anxiety. No, it wasn't her anxiety. She sniffled. It was that she was alone. Her husband couldn't be here. Her sister was two hours away. And Brigg... Brigg was probably still mad at her.

A sob broke. Courtney hadn't thought of how being on her own during labor would feel. It was horrible, the very definition of misery and the pelvic pressure intense. Her heart twisted tighter than a Bantu knot. She would give anything to have even her in-laws by her side. Human connection.

Forgetting to breathe, her body began to shake. She was truly on her own. Leaning forward, curving her back, she put her head in her hands, her fears releasing into loud, wracking tears.

Suddenly, she felt a hand on her back, and she heard a voice she didn't know she was aching to hear.

"It's all right, Courtney. I'm here," Brigg said, lifting her upright and holding her hands.

"Brigg," she called out. "You found me." She was so

grateful for his presence, she could have cried, if she wasn't already. Another contraction hit.

"Breathe, Courtney," he said, walking her through the exercise until the wave died down. He wiped her face with a napkin. "You're doing great. You've got this."

All she could do was nod and cry and squeeze his hand, her knuckles white. The nurse returned with ice chips and a cool rag for her face.

"Can she get an epidural?" Brigg asked. His voice sounded filled with fear.

"I al-already asked. But they said I'm too far gone for that," Courtney huffed out. The contractions were coming faster and harder. Brigg rocked back on his heels and removed his hands to stretch his fingers. Panicked, she yelled out, "No. No. Don't leave me."

He lifted her chin and made eye contact. "I'm not going anywhere."

Something shifted between them at those words. Courtney inhaled and gave a nod. They joined hands and rode out another contraction together. And another. And even more as the hours passed and it was close to daybreak. Brigg grabbed the birthing ball from the corner of the room so she could rest her aching back.

In the early hours of the morning, the nurse finally breezed in, placed the ice chips on the tray, checked her progress and gave a thumbs-up. "Sorry I took so long. Had to help with another delivery. You're fully dilated. Let me go get the midwife." She waved a finger. "You're going to want to push. But don't. Wait until I get back," she warned before hurrying out of the room. Courtney dipped her head to her chin and gritted her teeth. She curled her fingers into fists. Man, she really wanted to push.

Using his thumb to wipe the sweat off her face, Brigg

said, "You are a champion." He pulled out his phone and took a picture.

"Are you nuts?" she huffed out.

"You said I could take your picture anytime, and this is it. Plus, I'm sure your sister would want me to capture every moment since she isn't here."

She cut him a glance. "Really? While I'm in labor. I look like death's raggedy breath."

"What on earth is that?" he chuckled.

"I don't know, but it sounds as terrible as I look and feel." She hollered as another contraction hit.

"You're bringing life into existence which is an amazing feat. You'll thank me after." Brigg continued to support her through the pain.

"My head's hot," she wailed. Her hair had come undone and copper ringlets fell down her face and back. Her scrunchie was probably tangled in the sheets. She was sure she looked like a tumbleweed. And, of course, Brigg decided to capture that moment as well.

Brigg fed her ice chips and then placed the cool rag on her forehead. Then, he scrounged for her scrunchie and wrapped her hair in a high bun. Grabbing his arm, she breathed out, "I'm glad you're with me. It couldn't be anyone else but you."

His eyes misted, and he leaned over to place a light kiss on her forehead just in time for another contraction.

A lady in a lab coat entered the room. "I'm Dr. Singh. I'm the pediatrician on duty and I'll be here to check on the baby once you've delivered."

"Okay, thank you," Courtney huffed, struggling to concentrate on the doctor's words while riding through a contraction.

The midwife scurried in and, after a quick look, commanded her to push. Ten minutes later, Jayson entered the world with a loud wail.

Upon hearing her baby's voice, Courtney slumped against the pillow and cried. "He's here. He's here."

Brigg squeezed her hand. "You did it. Good work, Mom." And he took another round of pictures, this time including the baby. He stepped back, his voice filled with amazement. "You are absolutely beautiful."

Courtney touched her chest, the tears streaking down her face. "I'm someone's mommy. Wow. I can't believe it." She and Brigg shared a laugh-cry before she held out her hands. "Can I hold my child?" She had watched enough movies to know this was the part where she got to savor the first moments with her son once he had been clean and swaddled.

Instead, there appeared to be a sudden flurry of activity before her.

"Is everything all right?" Brigg asked.

She wanted to snap that, of course, it wasn't or she would have her infant against her chest. But she drew in a breath, her body quivering, and told herself that Brigg meant well.

The nurses placed her baby in an incubator and the pediatrician inserted a tube down his nose. Courtney leaned forward and wailed, "Wh-what's going on? Why can't I hold my baby? What are you doing?"

"We're getting your baby nice and warm since he made an early appearance," one of the nurses said. "We want to make sure he's okay."

She blinked to keep from being blinded by her tears. They then attached the other end of the tube to a machine.

The nurse rushed to a corner of the room holding Jayson in her arms. Courtney stretched her hands and moved to get out of bed. "My son. Where are you taking him?" She watched them slap an It's a Boy card with her last name written with Sharpie onto the glass of the incubator. Jayson was seventeen inches but only 3.4 pounds. Slightly below the expected four to six pounds he should be. Next, they placed a security tag around his ankle before providing her with its corresponding wristband.

From her vantage point, she made out a small mop of hair that made her heart squeeze, but that was all she could see. He looked so…helpless.

Dr. Singh scurried to her side. "Mrs. Meadows, since your son was born prematurely, we're admitting him to the NICU to address some health concerns."

Her heart pounded. "What kind of concerns?" Brigg perched next to her, and she huddled under his arm, leaning into his strength.

"In your son's case, the top two are his low birth weight and his trouble breathing. We cleaned out his airways, and I've inserted an endotracheal tube and hooked it up to a ventilator, so he won't have to work as hard to breathe while his lungs continue to develop."

"How long will you keep him here?" Courtney sniffled, wiping her face and telling herself not to panic. Brigg got her some tissues from the side table and then paced while the doctor spoke.

"It all depends. We generally keep preemies until close to their due date. So, he will probably be here for at least six weeks. For now, we want to get him breathing on his own and we want his oxygen levels to go up."

"Will he be able to leave once he's breathing better?" Brigg asked.

The doctor cleared her throat and held up three fingers. "When your baby is steadily gaining weight, able to maintain stable temps outside the incubator and able to feed, whether by breast or formula, he will be discharged."

Courtney noticed the incubator had two openings for her to place her hands inside. "Can I touch him? He seems so tiny."

"Yes, you can lightly touch his hand or head." Courtney washed her hands and did just that. Her heart warmed. Her first contact with her son wasn't ideal, but he was here. "I promise to take care of you, little man."

The doctor came close. "We'll let him get some rest. Soon, you'll be able to engage in skin-to-skin contact to help you bond with your baby. It all depends on his overall health and development. But the nurse will walk you through everything when that time comes."

Nodding, Courtney thanked the doctor, and Brigg shook her hand. The nurses left with Jayson, and Courtney's heart squeezed. After a few words of encouragement, the doctor departed, promising to check on Jayson after her rounds. They moved Courtney to Recovery. As soon as they were alone, the tears flowed. Brigg rushed to her side, and she collapsed against him.

"There now," Brigg said, rubbing her back. "It's all right. He's getting the best care, and that's all that matters."

"This is my fault," she cried. "If I hadn't overdone it, maybe I wouldn't have gone into labor."

Brigg smoothed her hair out of her face and told her to look at him. "There will be no blame game. No would've, should've or could've. It's just what is now and what it will be moving forward." He cupped her face. "What is important now is that both you and Jayson are fine. When I came home and saw you passed out—" his voice cracked "—I was scared out of my mind."

Now she touched his face and smiled. "You rescued me, again. You're a good man, Brigg Harrington. Thank you."

She saw the warmth in his eyes, and an air of intimacy swirled around them, mingled with…something more. His eyes dropped to her lips, and he leaned toward her. She angled her head, her heart racing, already anticipating the sweet capture, the ravishing, the surrender. Their lips touched, fire ignited, then the door creaked.

She shoved Brigg away, moaned at the interruption and turned her head. Her mouth dropped when she saw who stood by the threshold. "Muriel! Robert! What are you doing here? How… How did you…?"

Brigg stood and moved to the other side of the room, placing his hands in his pockets.

Her mother-in-law folded her arms, looking between Courtney and Brigg, her eyes knowing, accusing. Courtney shrank against the pillows.

"Did you think you could hide from us? That we wouldn't find you?" Muriel asked, stepping into the room with Robert on her heels. "Ever heard of Carfax? Our PI gave us the address to the shop. Lenny was more than happy to share that a nurse he's dating said that you were in labor, and we rushed right over."

Ugh. Small towns and news were like a fire in a newspaper factory. Courtney inhaled sharply. They had tracked her car being repaired. *Wow.* It was then Courtney noticed Muriel had the baby bag under her arm. The other woman placed it on the edge of the bed. She bit the inside of her cheeks to keep from expressing her gratitude.

"Where's our grandson?" Robert demanded, looking around the room.

"He's not here…" Courtney shook her head, trying to gather her scattered thoughts, while hoping her face didn't betray the guilt fanning her heart. Nevertheless, she fudged through the introductions.

Brigg's eyes went wide. "You didn't tell me Robert Meadows was your father-in-law." No, she hadn't mentioned her father-in-law was a congressman and outspoken politician on women's rights, diversity and inclusion. A real stand-up man—except when it came to Courtney, apparently. She also resented the awe in Brigg's voice.

"I—I didn't see the need. It didn't come up," Courtney stammered, patting her hair and feeling as if her face were on fire.

Robert puffed his chest. "I can see there is a lot that Courtney hasn't told you."

"And I see she's been up to a lot." Muriel glared.

For a beat, words refused to leave her throat. Muriel must have seen her almost kiss with Brigg. Shame washed over her before she tossed it off like a used towel. Muriel and Robert had plotted to take her child. An underhanded move. She straightened. "You're not welcome here and you need to leave." She made a mental note to alert the staff that they weren't allowed entry to her room.

Muriel gasped, placing a hand to her chest. "I—I can't believe the gall. Why are you doing this?"

"You can't keep us from our grandchild," Robert said.

Brigg must have seen that as his cue to return to her side. He placed a hand on her arm.

"Oh, but you can prove me unfit and try to take him from me?" Courtney's eyes misted. "I heard you. I heard you."

Their shock would have been comical if their intentions weren't so devious and horrible. She felt Brigg stiffen next to her, and she reached up to squeeze his arm. A silent signal that didn't help his defense. She had found her voice and she was going to use it.

Muriel's face fell. She wrapped her arms around herself and stepped toward to the bed. "Oh, dear. I'm sorry. I didn't mean—"

Courtney lifted a hand. "Didn't mean what?" she snarled. "You didn't mean for me to overhear your scheme?" She pulled the covers around her. Her body quivering as her rage built. "You think that because you have money and resources, you can do whatever you want?" Her voice cracked. "I thought you cared about me because I loved you both, and I would have appreciated your support. But not after what you've done." She wiped her face with the back of her hand. "I asked politely the first time, but now, I am telling you to get out. Get out. I never want to see either of your faces again."

"But he's all I have…of my son," Muriel pleaded, holding out a hand. Robert flanked her side, hugging her close.

Seeing her ravaged face was almost Courtney's undoing. But she couldn't fall for their trick. "Nice try. I'm done being manipulated."

"My sincere apologies," Robert said. He sounded genuine, but again, she couldn't be sure this wasn't a ploy for her to trust them again and then snatch Jayson away from her.

"Mr. and Mrs. Meadows, let me escort you to the lobby," Brigg said, his voice holding steel but still somewhat deferential. They left without another word with Brigg in tow. But Courtney could hear Muriel's sobs echo down the hall, tearing at her insides, slashing at her heart.

Courtney clutched her chest and clamped her jaw to

keep from calling them back into the room, into Jayson's life and hers. She had done the right thing. She had a son to protect. She sniffled. If Brigg hadn't fixed her car, she wouldn't be in this situation and racked with guilt at turning her in-laws away. The thought wrapped around her mind while her emotions swirled. She reminded herself she had just given birth and her emotions were high and scattered. But it was no use. Anger ignited. She grabbed on to it, wielding it like a flaming sword.

Brigg. Brigg. Brigg. Invading her life, confusing her, making her feel things she wasn't supposed to be feeling.

Brigg. Brigg. Brigg. Fixing her car, rescuing her, leading her in-laws right to her door. Ruining her first hours of motherhood.

Her chest heaved. Yes, this was all because of him. Doing too much. Reason intervened, reminding her that Brigg had been by her side when she needed him most. But she pushed it aside. Her eyes pinned to the door.

As soon as he returned, she pointed at him, her tongue a blade. "This—this is all your fault."

Chapter Twenty-Two

"Whoa. Where is all this coming from?" Brigg asked, closing the door behind him. This hadn't been the reaction he anticipated upon reentering Courtney's room. He had prepared himself to console an overwrought woman, not fight off her jabs. At him? He took in Courtney's copper curls hanging on her shoulders, her blazing eyes and the fury emanating off her body and shook his head.

"It's your fault they found me," she said, while he struggled to recoup from being blindsided. How had they had gone from almost kissing to his getting yelled at? "This is supposed to be a happy time for me and because of your *helpfulness*—" she hurled the word like it was a profanity "—I had to deal with the most manipulative people masquerading as my caring in-laws."

He drew in a breath and walked to look out the window, telling himself not to take this attack personally. She had given birth and undergone a major emotional confrontation within a matter of minutes. Not to mention, she was dealing with this inexplicable attraction between them. He had seen the guilt in her eyes at their interrupted smooch, like she had been caught doing something wrong. The cop in him had soooo many questions…but experience as an officer, and with dealing with the opposite sex, told him now was not the time to ask.

Feeling the heat of her eyes on his back, Brigg turned to face her and prayed he would say the right words to diffuse the situation. "Courtney, you're entitled to your feelings, and I can't begin to imagine the emotions coursing through your body, but you're coming for the wrong person. All I mean to do is make your life better."

"Why?" she challenged, her tone calmer.

He took a tentative step. "Because since the day I've met you, I'm doing things I don't normally do. I'm feeling things I don't normally feel."

And he was falling for her.

On the inside, he cringed. *No. No.* That was taking things a bit too far. This wasn't what love felt like. This was attraction. A result of his lonesomeness. His unrequited sexual appetite. That's why, even now, with her misplaced ire, he wanted to feast on her exposed neck, those lips. Yes, this was desire kicking his butt, nothing more. He stuffed his hands in his pockets.

"It's because I care," he said, while she studied him, soaking up his words. "What I have done for you, I would do for anyone." *Liar.*

She seemed to relax at his words. "I'm sorry," she said. "I think my hormones are out of whack. I shouldn't have come at you like that."

"I agree, but forgiving temper tantrums works both ways."

She chuckled. "I guess." She slumped against the pillows, her hair forming a halo. To Brigg, she looked like a siren, and his feet moved toward her bed.

"It's true," he said. "Ask anyone in my family. I'm the most chill of my brothers, almost never losing my cool.

But you changed all that. It's because you're too cute for your own good," he teased, sinking down next to her. His legs brushed against hers, electricity sizzling between them.

She lowered her lashes, her cheeks rosy.

Brigg took her hand in his. "Don't get all shy on me."

She rubbed his cheek with the back of her hand. Her tender gesture made his heart smile. His lips widened. *Stop smiling.*

Courtney met his eyes. "So, do you kiss all the women you rescue?"

And just like that, he was back to falling, er, *desiring.*

"Only the ones with hair the color of a shiny penny skilled at sarcasm with a fiery tongue." He touched her hair. Sensations he wasn't ready to feel filled his heart. He decided to use humor as a twist tie to stem that flow. He moved close to her ear and whispered, "Although, you could use a hair stylist right about now."

"You need to rescue me with a hairbrush." She tilted her head back and laughed. Just as he expected. As he wanted. But then his eyes took in her graceful neck, and he had to take a taste.

"Don't go starting anything we both know you can't finish," she said, voice throaty in his ear. Then her stomach grumbled. Loudly. They both cracked up. "I'm sorry. I haven't eaten," she said, her tone not the least bit apologetic.

Oh, man, was he in trouble. Her sass and sense of humor turned him on. This woman could be his undoing if he wasn't careful. A nursing assistant entered to take her temperature and to bring her meal. The smell of food assailed his nostrils, and he swallowed.

"Yes, thank you," she said, snatching the tray close.

Without any aplomb, she dug into her meal and moaned and smacked and moaned some more. Fascinated, he watched her devour the eggs, muffin, fruit and juice in under five minutes.

"This food isn't as good as I'm making it sound or as it smells, but I am hungry." She pushed the tray out of her way and yawned. "And tired."

That's when he registered the dark circles around her eyes. Of course, she was tired. They had been up all night. "I'm going to go and let you rest," he said, pulling out his cell phone. Sure enough, there were texts and voice mail messages. The mayor had already called him twice. "Duty calls."

"You're going to work?" she asked in amazement. "But you were up right along with me, and you need to eat."

"I'm good," he said, liking how she sounded concerned for him. "A quick shower will revive me, and there's always some goodies at the station, so I'll be all right."

She gave a small nod. "You still need your rest." Her eyes shuttered close.

"I'll take a day or two when you come home."

"That reminds me. I never asked if I could stay with you while Jayson is here." Her words were just above a whisper.

"You don't have to ask," he chided.

Her answer was a snore. Brigg's heart melted. He placed a kiss on her cheek and closed the door behind him. Once outside, he moved with purpose.

An hour later, Brigg stalked into the police station carrying Courtney's small overnight bag that he had forgotten to grab when she had passed out. On autopilot, he beelined for his old spot before he remembered that he had a new office and rank.

"Good afternoon, Captain," Queenie said.

He stopped and placed his free hand on her desk. "Queenie, you knew me when I was a fresh-faced rookie and you've dabbed my tears a time or two. You're like the big sister I never had, so please continue to call me Brigg. Nothing has changed."

"I beg to differ, *Brigg*," she responded, her tone that of someone proud. "Heads up. The mayor is in your office. I left some of your favorite doughnuts to give you sustenance and fortitude."

"All right, thanks, Queenie," he said with a chuckle. Queenie and her five-dollar vocabulary.

He entered his office, holding his grimace. He hoped Adrian wouldn't be a regular visitor so he could do his job. "What brings you here?" he asked with congeniality, placing the bag on his desk and taking a seat.

"You've ignored my calls and we have a situation." Everything from Adrian's demeanor suggested he felt Brigg should apologize. But Brigg wasn't about to do that and set the tone for their relationship by cowering. There were times where he would be unavailable, and the mayor needed to understand that.

"Is it a dire emergency?" Brigg asked, squaring his shoulders.

"Um, no. But we have to act quickly."

He adjusted the new wider chair. A gift from the mayor though Brigg insisted this role was temporary. "What's going on?"

"I received word that Beckett intends to sue the department."

His mouth dropped. "What?"

Adrian stood and paced. "Yes. He has also included the academy in his suit. His argument is that neither the Love Creek police force nor academy adequately prepared him to cope with diverse youths and situations. He wants to get our arrest records, stating how many more minorities are targeted and given more stringent citations."

"Wow. I can't believe he would go there instead of accepting responsibility for his bad deeds."

"A classic case of shift of blame."

"A smoke screen for his guilt." Brigg picked up a pen and one of the three blank legal pads Queenie had placed on his desk. "Although his accusation has some credence. There isn't a functioning diversity, equity and inclusion committee or community outreach."

"Yes, but this is a small town," Adrian said, standing up to pace. "Our police force only recently expanded."

"An excuse and not an explanation," he ground out.

"True. But Beckett was captain and could have implemented some of these programs."

"Exactly. That's something I plan to do while I'm interim captain." Brigg then shared his community outreach plans, telling of his intentions to work with DJ on this effort. He couldn't contain his excitement at the opportunity to build meaningful relationships.

Adrian's eyes flashed. "Hire him."

Brigg shook his head. "I'm not following."

"Develop a strategic plan, put your thoughts on paper and present it to me. I have funds set aside, and we can offer him a great compensation package as the... community outreach coordinator." The mayor then rattled off a number and other ideas that made Brigg's eyebrows rise on his forehead.

"Whew. No wonder they call you Lightning Bug." Brigg's head swirled.

"They do?"

"Yeah. That's your other nickname. After you cleaned up the parks and built a new community center, people started calling you Lightning. Saying you bug people until they move like lightning to do your will."

He chuckled. "I'll take that over Greek Adonis any day." Pushing a lock out of his face, the mayor strode to the door. "I'll expect to hear from you soon, Captain. Have Queenie set up some dates on the calendar. This is going to take months of planning, but I think we can get things off the ground by next year." And with that, he was gone.

Brigg exhaled. "Months." He didn't intend to stay in this role that long. He liked being hands-on, keeping up with the beat of the community. Standing, he walked outside his office and approached Queenie.

"You looked exhausted," she said, handing him a stack of papers. "The mayor can be a tornado when he gets wound up, but as long you stand your ground, you'll be okay."

"Noted," Brigg said, eyeing the forms in his hands.

"Those need your signature before filing," she said. "I took the liberty of ordering your official dress uniform, and it's hanging in your office."

"Got it and thank you." He gestured for her to follow him into his office. Once inside, he rested the papers on his desk. "I have to develop a strategic plan, and I'm going to need your assistance. I know you have a bachelor's degree in program management, and it's time we put that to use. I also need you to work on a job description for a community outreach coordinator position the mayor wants to create. You'll work with his admin on both these initiatives, and we will review. This will be a joint effort across our teams."

By the time he was done, Queenie sat perched at the edge of the seat. "You don't know how many times I begged Beckett to—" She waved a hand and jumped up. "Never mind all that. I'm ecstatic to help, and I'll have something for you by next week, sir."

He swallowed a smile at her enthusiasm. "Wonderful. In the meantime, I need you to set up a meeting with Dominic Jones. I'd like to see him as soon as possible."

She marched around his desk to give him a hug. "Thank you, Brigg. You don't know what this means to me. I thought you were calling me into your office to trade me in for a younger model."

He held her shoulders. "One, you are only in your forties. Two, you're an asset to this department. And three, You are irreplaceable. Here's to twenty more years."

"It's nice to be appreciated," she said, breathy, slightly choked up.

"I'm simply acknowledging your worth." He couldn't wait for her to see the bonus he was setting up for her at the end of the year.

She gave a nod, made her excuses and rushed out of the room. Brigg watched her rapid departure. If he knew Queenie, she would be ensconced inside a bathroom stall until she composed herself. Then she'd be back to work in her quiet, efficient manner.

Brigg then focused on answering the emails and handling the tasks on his desk. By the time he was finished, it was close to dinnertime. He checked his phone to see if Courtney had texted or called. She hadn't. He pushed away his disappointment and reminded himself of how tired she was when he had left.

His cell buzzed. His mother had texted.

Did your GF have her baby yet?

He scoffed. His mom was tripping. Girlfriend?

Apparently, I'm in a relationship and don't know it.

His mom's text reminded him to also update his brothers' group chat with Courtney's status. When he was finished, another text from his mother popped up.

LOL. How is Courtney?

She had the baby, and when I left the hospital, she was resting.

You're at work???

He frowned. Why was that a surprise? Yes. I have a department to run.

You should be by her side. She's alone.

Shoot. His mother was correct. He watched the little dots appear, indicating she was still texting.

Get her a fruit basket. Believe me, she'll thank you for it.

His walkie went off. Brigg cocked his ear. From the sounds of it, it sounded like it was a rowdy drunk driver who was possibly armed, and one of his officers was en route to the scene. No way was he allowing her to handle this without backup. He sent his mother a quick text.

Got it. Have to go on a call. I love you.

I love you too. Stay safe.

Always.

Grabbing his walkie and keys, Brigg asked Queenie to drop the overnight bag off at the hospital for Courtney and rushed out the door.

Chapter Twenty-Three

Standing outside the glass door of the NICU ward, Courtney ogled her baby while he was fed her breast-milk through a tube. Her milk hadn't come in fully yet, but the nurse assured her that she had given enough. Courtney had come over right after finishing her own meal of country-fried steak. She battled dueling emotions of awe and powerlessness. Awe at her son's fighting power. Powerlessness at her inability to hug him, to hold him, to feed him.

She signaled to the nurse to ask if she could visit with Jayson.

"As soon as we're finished changing rounds, I'll let the next nurse on shift know to come get you."

With a nod, Courtney dabbed the corner of her eyes and returned to her room only to encounter another un-expected visitor. Only this was one was more than wel-come. And wanted.

"I can't believe you're here," Courtney said, closing the door behind her, her eyes glued on the occupant of the room. "How did you find me?" she asked, drinking in the sight of her sister.

Brigg had sent over an overnight bag, so she had been

able to shower and change into a pair of jeans and T-shirt, along with her sneakers. He had also packed her shampoo and a hairbrush, a much-needed necessity, adding a sticky note: *Hair to the rescue.* She had found it corny but cute.

He was such a thoughtful, considerate man.

Kaylin was dressed in a blue-and-white striped shirt, white short shorts and blue sandals, which was no surprise. Her sister was always color coordinated. What had changed was that Kaylin had a full face of makeup. The heavy, dark mascara and liner took some getting used to, adding mystery to her beauty. She sat with her legs crossed, the baby bag settled on her lap. There was a small paper bag on the floor next to her.

"Hello to you too, baby sis." Kaylin stood, placing the bag on the chair.

"Uh, sorry. Hello." She went over to enfold her into a tight embrace.

"That bus ride to Love Creek took way longer than it needed to," Kaylin said, running her hands through her bob, and settling back into the chair. "I was so hungry when I got off the bus that I decided to swing by your job to surprise you. That's when I heard you were in the hospital. Your coworker, Princess, gave me a ride."

"Ah, I see. The benefits of living in a small town."

"Love Creek is so small though. And quiet." Which was code for boring. Her sister loved the bustle of Miami and the nightlife, about an hour from where Kaylin lived. Like her, Kaylin hadn't stayed anywhere too long, and that's why they had both enjoyed cruising. But whereas Courtney had been ready for stability, Kaylin was still very much about the next adventure. Her sister loved the water and cruising to different ports and meeting all kinds of people.

"For the most part. I like it."

"Meh." The sisters shared a laugh.

"It goes without saying that I'm glad to see you, but if I had known you were coming, I would have told you to wait. Jayson might be in the NICU for a few weeks."

Her sister shrugged. "Not a prob. I got you covered." She picked up the brown bag and pulled out a long elastic band. Then she directed Courtney to pull up her shirt. While she put on the abdominal binder, she rambled on. "I booked an Airbnb nearby for a month, so you can bunk with me until then. It has three bedrooms and a swimming pool, so we can spread out." Courtney smiled. Her sister loved the water and would make use of that pool for sure. Though Kaylin was a strong swimmer, she tended to float or wade in the shallow end of the pool. "And since your car is fixed, I didn't bother to rent a vehicle. It will be just the two of us, like old times."

Courtney hesitated for a beat. She wasn't ready to leave Brigg's house. Then she reprimanded herself. Her sister had traveled hours to help her. "That sounds like a plan." The nurse entered the room to ask if Courtney was ready for a visit with Jayson. With a quick yes, Courtney hurried to her feet. "Can my sister accompany me?"

"She can watch through the window, but I would wait a day or two," the nurse said.

Kaylin stood. "That's fine. I can't wait to see my nephew. I ordered a personalized blanket, but it's not due to arrive until next week."

"Oh, how thoughtful of you."

The sisters walked arm-in-arm to the NICU nursery. There were four other babies visible through the door. The nurse scanned his badge, then held the door open for Courtney. Once she was inside, she had to put on a gown and mask. He then led her to the sanitizing station and talked her through how to scrub her hands. Next, he scanned her security tag and asked for her name and date of birth. Courtney rattled it off, tapping her feet. She appreciated all the efforts to maintain a secure environment, but she needed to see her son. After scanning the baby's tag, the nurse brought over a chair so she could sit and visit with the baby.

Finally, she was sitting in front of her newborn's incubator, heart pounding and expanding with love. She looked over at Kaylin and waved. Her sister had tears rolling down her face and gave her a thumbs-up before taking pictures.

You did good, she mouthed.

Overcome, Courtney lifted her thumb in return. Turning her focus on Jayson, Courtney whispered, "I can't wait until I can hold you for real. Keep fighting, my son." Watching his tiny chest rise and fall, all the things she thought significant faded. Her grief at Jet's untimely passing. Her anger at her in-laws. They lessened in magnitude as she watched her son on a ventilator. Praying for him to thrive. She sang and spoke to him for a few more minutes before ending her visit. By then, Kaylin had returned to Courtney's hospital room. The sisters oohed and aahed over the pictures, including the ones Brigg had texted of her during her delivery.

"When are you getting discharged?" Kaylin asked.

"Tomorrow. I'll have to swing by Brigg's to get my stuff once I'm released."

"Speaking of Brigg, when am I going to get to meet that fine man of yours in person?"

"He's not my man," Courtney said. "He's a…a friend. I'm sure he'll pop up at some point. He's now the interim captain for the police department, so he had to go into the station."

"Another man in uniform," she teased.

"That's precisely why he's not long-term material." She splayed her hands. "Not that I'm looking for anything permanent. I'll have my hands full with Jayson. It's all about him now."

"You still have needs. I don't think being a mother wipes out your sex drive."

"Nope. In fact, it was quite the opposite when I was pregnant." Especially when it came to a certain lawman.

"Then you'd better get on that saddle and take a ride before coming back to Fort Lauderdale."

Courtney gasped. "You are a hot mess." She had googled how long she needed to wait after having a baby—for informational purposes—and had been surprised to learn there was no set wait time, though most doctors recommended four to six weeks.

She told Kaylin as much, to which her sister replied, "Recommended is not required."

Shaking her head, she said, "I can't with you."

There was a rap on the door, and upon given entry, a staff member walked in holding a huge bouquet. Marching over to the window, he placed it on the sill and departed.

"These are gorgeous," Kaylin said. "Who do you suppose they're from?"

Courtney pointed to the card sticking out from the arrangement. "Read it."

Kaylin's eyes scanned the tiny paper. She shook her head. "You're not going to like it."

"Who sent it?" she asked, though she now suspected it might be her in-laws.

"Muriel and Robert sent them."

And she was right. "They are too beautiful to toss. Do me a favor and take them out to the nurses' station?"

With a nod, Kaylin did her bidding. But when she returned, she said, "Family is important. I won't argue with your decision, but I will say, I hope you reconsider. When we were taken from Mom, we cried for days and days, and our biggest wish was to see her again because she was our blood, our bond. Next to Mom, Jet was family. He had his flaws, but he loved you. Now he's gone. Another loss." Kaylin shook her head. "I just want Jayson to have as much love available to him because as the saying goes, it takes a village. The more support he has, the better."

"We have enough love for him, and right now my only priority is getting my son in the best of health and flourishing," Courtney said, gently. But her sister's' words took root. And something about the way she said them made Courtney wonder if there was something else Kaylin wasn't telling her.

"Fair enough. Text me when you're discharged so I can come get you." Coming over to kiss her on the forehead, Kaylin pleaded jet lag and scheduled an Uber to get to the Airbnb.

Courtney grabbed her sister's arm. "Are you all, right?" she asked. "You don't seem yourself. I can't put my finger on it, but something's wrong."

For a second, Kaylin's sorrow shone through her eyes before she lowered her lashes.

"Talk to me," Courtney pleaded.

Kaylin patted Courtney's hand. "We'll talk, but not today. Now I know what they planned to do to you was messed up but I'm still pushing for reconciliation, if possible. Promise me you'll think about what I said regarding your in-laws."

Unease settled in the pit of Courtney's stomach, but she let Kaylin go without pushing any further, simply giving a nod. She knew Kaylin would share when she was ready. Then, as she promised, she mulled on the next steps with her in-laws.

What they had planned to do had been underhanded and deceitful and had annihilated her trust. But maybe now that Jayson was here, they had had a change of heart? The only way to know would be to have a conversation with them. The genuine distress on Muriel's face had gutted her. She wasn't sure she was ready to reach out yet though. When Brigg returned, she would talk to him about it. She yawned. This had been one long day.

She turned on the television to the news channel and snapped to attention when she saw Brigg. The mayor was giving a speech, something about the department being sued, but her eyes were trained on Brigg, who stood behind him. He looked smart in his captain's uniform. Her own personal superhero. Her libido went into overdrive.

What a delicious specimen. Her sister was right. Courtney should help herself to a full meal instead of settling for a sample before she left for Fort Lauderdale. She chuckled. She must be physically hungry to be thinking about lovemaking using food metaphors. Maybe she would ask the nurse for a snack when they came in to check her vitals.

A couple hours later, Brigg sauntered in, carrying roses, a teddy bear and a fruit basket. She salivated looking at the oranges, the peaches and the plums. She gave him a kiss on the cheek and thanked him before washing some of the fruit. Brigg sat on the edge of the bed. She sunk her teeth into a juicy plum and moaned.

"This is so good," she said. "How did you know this was what I needed?"

"I can't take credit. My mother advised me," he said, zoned in on her lips. His eyes darkened. "I'm glad I took it, because watching you eat is a treat."

Some of the plum juice ran down her chin. Brigg reached over to lick it away, and her brain went to mush. She closed her eyes.

"Are we a thing?" she breathed out. "We can't be because you know I'm leaving soon."

"We don't have to be," he said, now nibbling on her ear. "However, we could do something about this insane attraction between us."

She opened her eyes and gave him a little push to get his attention. "A temporary agreement of sorts. Is that what you mean?"

"Yes. I can get with temporary."

"I like the sound of that," she said, kissing his full lips. Her hand reached to cradle this thigh before inching upward. "Can you wait four weeks?"

He nodded. "Of course. There's a lot we can do without actually doing the deed."

Oohhh. This man was naughty. She liked it. A lot. "I like the sound of that but…later."

"All right, bet." Brigg held out his little finger. "Let's pinky swear on it."

She joined her pinky with his. "Let the countdown begin."

Brigg's voice deepened. "You have no idea what you signed up for. What time do you need me to pick you up tomorrow?"

She placed a hand over her mouth. "I was so caught up that I forgot to tell you I'm moving out."

He stilled. "Moving out?"

The air cooled.

"Ugh, yes." She touched his shoulder. "My sister's here, and she rented a place for a month. She's coming for me when I get discharged."

He took her hand. "Can't you tell her you don't want to leave?"

"But she came all this way. How is that going to look?"

"Like you got a man. A temporary man." He argued his case with a tender kiss. A kiss with promises she believed he could keep. And then some.

"Things have progressed with us so fast—I can't keep up."

Brigg shrugged. "Sometimes you just…know. This is bigger than us, and we just have to strap in and enjoy the ride while we can. Besides, we're not talking about forever. Your sister will have you to herself once you're back in Fort Lauderdale. Just let me savor you for the next few weeks."

"What a tempting proposal." Courtney studied him. "It feels good to be wanted, especially after going through labor. That wasn't a pretty scene."

"It makes you more desirable to me. I couldn't have endured all you went through to bring life into the world." Brigg scooted close. "We shared a momentous occasion together, and I think that's what speeding things up between us."

Those words tempered her anticipation. He could be right… All this could be because his adrenaline and her hormones were off the charts. They had withstood a hurricane and a delivery together. Two over-the-top situations. No wonder their passion was out of whack. They needed a heavy dose of normal.

Courtney rested her head against the pillows. "I agree with you. But now it's making me doubt if this intense attraction is legit. Let's cool things down for a bit. I'll stay with Kaylin, and over the next four weeks, we'll go out and get to know each other. Since we're crunched for time, let's make it a daily date so we can spend as much time together as we can." She wagged a finger. "First base only. If, after that, we still feel the same, I'll move in with you for the remainder of the time I'll be in town. In your bed." Plus, she could schedule a check-up with an OB-GYN to make sure everything was in working order.

"I could get with that." Brigg rubbed his hands together. "Twenty-eight dates in twenty-eight days, followed by two weeks of lovemaking." He held up his pinky finger. "Another pinky swear?"

With a laugh, she agreed. "We can take turns planning our activities. Let's not get too outrageous. Keep them low scale."

"All right, bet. It's on."

Chapter Twenty-Four

Dating only? Brigg scoffed. This woman had no idea what she was in for. This fire between them could only be quenched by one thing: a hot, nasty, can't-look-each-other-in-the-eyes-the-next-day union of their bodies and minds. And that was the truth. But for now he would go along with her plan.

Tomorrow was day one. She had said to keep it small. That was so not going to happen. The Harrington men didn't half step anything. And he had six brothers to help him brainstorm. This was going to be fun. He had agreed to keep his hands off her body, but Courtney hadn't said he couldn't use his words. And, oh, was he going to use them.

"Do you think they will let me see the baby?" he asked.

"Yes." Courtney didn't meet his eyes. "I told them you were my birthing partner. I think it was only fair since you were there for his unforgettable entrance in the world." She was cute when she rambled. Her chest and cheeks were pink. Ooh, he couldn't wait to see if that was a full-body blush.

That's it. He wouldn't survive twenty-eight days of

limited physical contact if he allowed his mind to take him into dangerous territory. Brigg got up off the bed and went to sit on the chair.

"Thanks for doing that. I feel an attachment for the little guy," he said, stretching his legs. "When can we go see him?"

Brigg had been so glad his officer had deescalated the drunk driver before he arrived at the location, so after a brief check-in, he had rushed over to the mayor's office for the press conference. Adrian wasn't one to drag things out, but Brigg had struggled to remain patient throughout the mayor's update. All he could think about was getting to Courtney and getting his first good look at Jayson.

"I was just there a few minutes ago, but we can visit anytime."

"Awesome. I'd like to make that our first date. I'll let you get some sleep, but I'll come by tomorrow morning, and we can visit him together."

Her eyes misted. "I like that idea. How thoughtful."

Brigg departed the hospital with a smile. There were several messages from his family, but he vowed to answer them after he had gotten some sleep. His eyes burned, and he faded out as soon as he showered and got into the bed.

Early the next morning, Brigg jolted awake at a loud bang. Someone was in his house. Seconds later, he saw Ethan duck his head and enter the room. "What are you doing here?" Brigg released several breaths to calm his heart rate. He slipped into a pair of pajama pants since he was only in his underwear.

"I came to do a wellness check. Nobody's seen or heard from you." Ethan said, running a hand through his long, curly locks, a tribute of his Native American mother.

He was dressed in a pair of swimming trunks, a long yellow tank and flip-flops. If Brigg knew his brother, Ethan had stopped by on his way to the rec center or the beach again, judging by his tan, making his skin the color of deep brown sand.

"It's been one day," Brigg said. "And I'm pretty sure I answered the group chat." They headed out into the living area. The sun was already up and showing off its impressive strength. Brigg went to adjust the thermostat by a couple degrees.

Ethan held up his phone. His left earring sparkled. "You didn't."

"Showing up here is a bit much." Ethan was prone to overreact to the smallest things. Maybe it was because he was used to putting on a show for the cameras in his swimming days.

"Well, we wouldn't be worried about your big head if you didn't have such a dangerous job."

"This is a small town. Nothing much happens..." Brigg checked his phone. *Shoot.* Ethan was right. He tossed a throw pillow at him. "Okay, now that you've seen me and can confirm I'm breathing, get out."

"Catch up with you later," Ethan said, heading out the door.

Brigg got dressed and headed over to the hospital. As he was walking through the parking lot to the entrance, he spotted a woman with the same copper-colored hair and slender build as Courtney. She was dressed in a white crop top and a long colorful flowing skirt. He knew that could only be one person.

"Kaylin," he called out, taking off his sunglasses. The sun's rays scorched the side of his face and exposed skin. He quickened his stride to catch up to her.

She stopped and turned around before waving. "Brigg. It's great to meet you in person." They shook hands. Though the sisters shared many physical similarities, he didn't feel any of the electrical pull as he had with Courtney. He only had to be in Courtney's presence for him to feel sparks.

Kaylin used her hands as a sun visor over her eyes. "Let's go inside. It's hot out here."

"For sure." They walked through the automatic doors and entered the lobby. Robert and Muriel Meadows were seated in the small reception area. As soon as they saw them, the couple got to their feet.

Brigg paused, deciding to follow Kaylin's lead. He hadn't broached that topic with Courtney yesterday, but he hoped she would feel comfortable to share the back-story. Kaylin squared her shoulders and went to greet them.

He folded his arms and observed the exchange, giving the older man a head nod. They were dressed like they were going to the country club, looking regal and composed. But tight lips, furrowed brows and red eyes told the true story. They were hurting real bad.

"We were hoping to run into you," Muriel said, her chin quivering. "We made a terrible mistake." She placed an arm on her husband's shoulder. "Going for custody was my idea and I pushed Robert into it. Now Courtney wants nothing to do with us, and I can't blame her, but I can't stay away." She covered her face with her hands.

Custody? Brigg blinked. No wonder Courtney had put them out of her room. That would explain why she had run off in an unreliable vehicle at eight months pregnant. He clenched his fists. If he hadn't been there, Courtney would have been alone in the midst of a thunderstorm. He slid them a glance. Because of their selfishness.

Kaylin gave her an awkward hug. The women rocked in their embrace.

"We were hoping you could talk to her," Robert said, clearing his throat. He pierced Brigg with a determined look. "I believe she will listen to you."

Brigg broke eye contact and lifted his hands. He wasn't about to speak on Courtney's behalf in this situation. He also didn't feel comfortable with Robert deferring to him. He wasn't a part of Courtney's circle like that. They weren't family. They weren't in a relationship. They were a step above friends. A step. That was it. And that would end once she left Love Creek.

"I think she will come around," Kaylin said after the women separated.

"How is Jayson?" Muriel asked. Robert handed his wife his handkerchief, and she wiped her face. Brigg admired how tender the other man was with his wife.

"He's a trouper," Kaylin supplied.

"We spent all night reading up on premature babies," Robert added. "I'm so scared for him." Brigg knew they were fishing for information, and Kaylin was willing to satisfy their unspoken request.

"He's a little over three pounds and a good seventeen inches." She dug in her purse for her phone. "I took pictures." The couple hovered close while Kaylin tapped on her screen to access the photos.

Brigg watched their faces light up.

"He has the look of Jet," Muriel declared, enthralled.

"Yes, and he's got Courtney's hair," Robert murmured, enlarging the picture with his index and thumb.

"Oh, can you send these to us?" Muriel asked, placing a hand over her heart.

"I'm sorry but I would have to talk to my sister about that."

"Okay, we understand. How about we give our contact information if she changes her mind?"

Kaylin was happy to grant Robert's request, and they exchanged numbers. While she had her contacts list up, Kaylin asked for Brigg's number as well, then sent him a text so he would have hers. Brigg didn't see the need for that gesture, but he didn't want to be impolite.

Exhaling, she looked at her watch and addressed the Meadowses. "We have to go. Until I speak with her, please respect my sister's wishes."

With a nod, Muriel touched Kaylin's arm. "Can I ask why you don't hate us? We thought we were going to have to beg and plead for your understanding."

"I have my reasons," Kaylin said. "But the biggest is that I am thinking of Jayson. He's going to need his grandparents." She patted Muriel's arm and then looked up at Robert. "Just give it time."

Brigg and Kaylin made their way to the elevators. As soon as the door closed, she exhaled. "I sure hope I did the right thing. Courtney will be furious with me for giving them a glimpse of the baby." Her tone indicated that she wasn't too worried about that though. Something Brigg understood from having brothers. They could go from feuding to joking in minutes.

"She doesn't stay mad for long," Brigg said.

Kaylin laughed. "Yep. She generally has a forgiving nature but the Meadowses wronged her big-time."

"I can see their love for their grandchild. It's obvious they are going to be doting grandparents. But I can't say the same for how they feel about Courtney," he ground out, barely able to contain his fury. The picture of Courtney pregnant and soaked in the rain was one that would stay with him for some time. They stepped out of the elevator.

"I get why you're upset, but if they hadn't done what they had, you would have never met my sister." Her whispered words hit his core.

"Good point." Brigg couldn't remember what his days had been like before Courtney. He didn't even want to think about what it would be like when she left.

"There's always something positive to find, even in the direst of circumstances."

He studied her. "Do you always look for the silver lining?" he asked, referencing the well-known cliché.

"Yes, but I appreciate the clouds as well. They teach me life lessons." She must have seen the quizzical look on his face, because she said, "You'll get it when the time's right."

Kaylin stepped inside Courtney's room while he followed behind her, pondering Kaylin's mysterious words. Kaylin yammered away about running into Robert and Muriel before she gave Courtney a brief hug. Courtney appeared to be half listening, but she didn't seem upset that Kaylin had shared photos of Jayson with her in-laws. His eyes connected with Courtney's, and all thoughts of clouds and silver linings left his mind.

She glowed. And it wasn't from the sun beaming into the room.

Her eyes lit up when she saw him before her lips widened in the most welcoming smile. His chest puffed. Her smile was a gift to his heart. He smiled in return.

She held out a hand. "Ready for our date?"

"Date?" Kaylin asked, looking between them.

He listened while Courtney gave a brief rundown of their plans, minus her intention of spending fourteen days in his bed.

"I think that's so romantic," Kaylin breathed out, giving him a once-over. "Do you have any brothers?"

"I have six, but two are off the market, and possibly another," he chuckled, viewing Courtney's sister as a harmless tease. He could imagine her being the life of the party, with Courtney as her unwilling sidekick. She was a mass of energy in constant motion, while Courtney was more his speed, more even-keeled, but there was no denying both sisters had wit and sarcasm in abundance.

Kaylin bounced in her chair. "Hmm… Maybe my time here might lead to some interesting adventures. How about we do a double date before I leave? You can bring one of your brothers."

"That can be arranged," Brigg said. His brothers had been dragging him for being unavailable when they wanted to hang out, so this was a great solution.

"I can't believe you're trying to get Brigg to play matchmaker," Courtney said, getting to her feet and stretching out a hand toward him.

Kaylin waggled her eyebrows. "A girl can have some fun."

"Well, I got word I'm getting discharged today. Probably in the next hour or so."

"Awesome," Kaylin said. "How about we get together later today? I'll grill some salmon steaks and make an arugula salad."

Whoa. Kaylin moved at rapid speed. Brigg could hardly keep up with the conversation.

Courtney lifted a hand. "Slow down, sissy. I've met all the Harrington men, and they are gems. I don't want you ruining them or breaking one of their hearts before you dash off to sea."

It sounded like Kaylin liked the water. Hmm... She and Ethan might hit it off, and then he could have Courtney to himself. "Maybe I'll invite Ethan to come along with me."

"Ugh, don't encourage her," Courtney said, placing a hand on her forehead.

Kaylin rolled her eyes. "Quit being dramatic." She reached in her pocket to pull out a stick of gum. Then she settled in the chair and pulled out a magazine. "It will be a mini celebration of you embracing motherhood, since you didn't get a shower."

"That's because Muriel was adamant that I didn't need anything." She lifted her shoulders. "You see how that turned out."

"This doesn't count as one of our dates," Brigg made sure to point out, though his mind was centered on the fact that Courtney hadn't had a baby shower. Realization hit. There was no crib, no car seat, nothing.

Now he was glad he had Kaylin's number. He knew exactly what he had to do.

Chapter Twenty-Five

This man was trying to make her heart trip. But based on what she had learned about him so far, it was just Brigg being Brigg. It was literally his job to help others which was why he had thrown her the baby shower she had never had. So she had no right reading any more into his grand gesture. But she was.

She most definitely was.

Seated on her decorated armchair under a small tent, Courtney's eyes roamed her sister's backyard, which had been transformed into a party zone. For her. Blue and white balloons pinned in the grass formed the words Welcome, Baby. Paper garlands of the same colors pinned to tiki torches crisscrossed the length of the yard.

After everyone had screamed, "Surprise!" she had changed into a pair of shorts and a bedazzled shirt that read, Jayson's Mom, a gift from Kaylin.

Some of the Harrington clan had turned out, a testament to their devotion to Brigg. Brigg's father, Patrick, manned the grill along with his brother Drake. His mother, Tanya, fussed over the punch and cake table. His brother Ethan was the appointed DJ for the night and Kaylin was right by his side, swinging her hips to the seventies jam. They looked a bit too chummy, but she trusted Kaylin knew what she was doing.

Princess, Nancy and other staff from the diner, as well as Brigg's admin secretary, Queenie, had also shown up. Courtney immediately liked the other woman's quiet, effective demeanor. Even Lenny had made an appearance. The mechanic hadn't stopped eating since he had arrived thirty minutes ago.

Walking up to where she sat, watching the festivities, Brigg dragged one of the plastic lawn chairs and came to sit next to her. He had changed into a pair of light blue jeans and a white shirt.

"Having a good time?" he asked.

"I can't believe you did all of this in a matter of hours," she said.

"As you can see, I had help," he said.

Courtney pointed to the stack of wrapped gifts by her side. "This was above and beyond, but I appreciate the gesture. I can't thank you enough." Once Brigg had gotten his first glimpse of Jayson, he hadn't stayed long, promising to catch up with her for dinner later.

He waved a hand. "Queenie was more than happy to spend the day shopping with my mother and Kaylin." He tucked her under the chin. "I hope you'll allow yourself to have a good time for a few hours. Jayson is in good hands."

"How did you know I was thinking about him?"

"It's a given. You're a good mother. It's my job to put your mind at ease."

She touched his face. "Thanks, Brigg."

"I couldn't have done it without Kaylin. Your sister had the task of getting you here."

"Yes, she practically pulled me out of the NICU, saying I needed some me time." Come to think of it, the nurses must have known about her party because they had urged her to leave the ward and get a breather once Kaylin had returned for her.

"Not a problem." He smoothed his shorts. "Love Creek takes care of its own."

She placed a hand to her chest. "But I'm passing through…"

"Doesn't matter. For whatever time you live here, you're one of us."

Her heart melted. The small town felt like home. She looked at Brigg. There were a lot of benefits to belonging somewhere. Then she gave herself a mental shake. She couldn't get attached. Anything between them had to be short term. Neither she nor Brigg sought anything permanent.

Soooo, she might as well live it up now.

Snatching Brigg's hand, she pulled him to her feet and led him to the makeshift dance floor. Swinging her hands in the air, all she could do was a light two-step to the funky tune, but Brigg was getting down enough for the both of them. At one point, Kaylin joined them and so did Drake and Brigg's twin, Caleb, once he had shown up.

Courtney and Brigg moved off the dance floor so she could go pump. When she was finished, she joined Brigg, who was watching from the sideline. Everyone else shook their butts until sweat poured down their backs. Once Patrick and Tanya had departed, Ethan put on a playlist, and he and Kaylin started grinding against each other like he'd known her all her life. They paused for her to open presents, and by the time she was finished, she had everything a baby would need and more, which warmed her heart.

Courtney stood and stretched, intending to get something to drink, but Brigg got to his feet.

"You thirsty?" he asked.

"I could use some punch."

"Be right back." He patted her back. That's when she saw the Meadowses standing at the perimeter of the lawn. Hovering. Watching. Judging.

She froze, trapped in the median between guilt and joy. Guilt for having a good time when Jet was gone. Joy for new life, a new zing, if you will. She took a deep breath and chose joy. She squared her shoulders and trudged forward. This was a conversation that needed to happen, so she might as well do it now when she had backup around if needed.

Behind her, she heard a splash and a shriek. Her sister must have cannonballed into the pool. Courtney looked behind her for confirmation, and Kaylin gave her a big wave before making her way to the shallow end.

"You look like you're having a good time," Muriel said, eyeing her shorts and T-shirt.

Courtney folded her arms in front of her. "Yes. Yes, I am. Something wrong with that?" she challenged, tapping her feet to the beat of the music. "What are you doing here?"

"Your sister invited us."

Ah. She should have known. For some reason, Kaylin was determined to play peacemaker.

"We hope you don't mind us coming," Robert said. "Jet wouldn't have wanted you moping around. He would be right here with you celebrating, so we're here on his behalf."

"Though it seems you've already found his replacement," Muriel scoffed. Of course, she uttered those words as soon as Brigg approached with their punch. Robert gave his wife a quelling look. Brigg's face was stoic. After a nervous laugh, Muriel apologized. "I'm sorry. Seeing you with someone else is jarring. A blatant reminder that Jet isn't here, and I miss him."

She heard Ethan announce the last song and asked for help with clean up.

"This isn't what it looks like. Brigg and I are two friends having fun. Celebrating life. There is no replacing Jet. He's Jayson's father and I'll never forget him. And before you call me a bad mother, I have every intention of spending the night with my son at the hospital." From the corner of her eye, Courtney thought she saw Brigg stiffen before he excused himself to help dismantle the tent.

Robert gestured to a chair. "Can we talk?"

She gave a jerky nod, and the three of them went to sit by the gifts.

Her father-in-law didn't belabor the point. "Muriel and I figured you must have overheard us that day in the library that you left. In hindsight, we realize you were telling us goodbye in your own way—taking pictures and all that." Courtney shrank into her chair. He reached for her hand. "I wanted to extend my sincere apology for our actions, including disregarding your right to give your son his name. We promise that Muriel and I will never interfere with your decisions or try to override your authority as a parent. All we ask is that you include us in Jayson's life."

"I'm happy to do that," Courtney said, "but no more games."

There was a beat before Muriel admitted, "I didn't

think you would give us a second chance so easily. Especially after my stupid emails."

"It's easy to release the past when my future is bright," Courtney said, her eyes searching for Brigg. "What you both did hurt me in ways I will never be able to express, but I'm not going to carry a grudge forever. Jayson needs all my energy. He's my number one priority."

"Thank you," Muriel whispered. "You're a better woman than me."

"I know."

Muriel's brows rose at her swift agreement. But, hey, Courtney spoke the truth.

Robert reached into his pocket and pulled out two envelopes and handed them to her. The first contained a trust in Jayson's name for his care and all future expenses. She gasped. "Wow. This is generous." Courtney wasn't going to play coy and not accept their offer. She was a single parent and she wanted the best for her child. Period. She could take care of herself, but like Kaylin said, it took a village.

Now that the music was off and the tiki torches extinguished, Courtney could hear the night sounds of crickets and frogs, and she could see the mosquitoes circling. It was a good thing Kaylin had made her put on insect repellant.

"Open the next one," Muriel prodded, voice giddy with excitement. She swatted at a palmetto bug that landed on her hair with the calmness of a woman who had grown up in the South.

Courtney opened the envelope to find a key inside. She held it up. "What's this?"

Robert asked her to follow him. Tentatively, she trailed behind the couple to the front of the house. She saw the oversized bow first before her mouth popped open. It was a black luxury sedan and it was a beauty.

"I can't accept this," she said. "I have a car. Don't need one."

"Please don't say no," Robert said. "If it helps, I only want what's best for my you and my grandson."

Courtney snorted. "Thanks, but I don't need this."

"It drives like air," Muriel breathed out, dangling the key. "Take it for a test drive."

"You're the daughter we never had." Robert pleaded. "We didn't know how much we loved you until you left us in the middle of the night. That was the second time in my life I was scared out of my mind." His eyes saddened. "You know the first."

She placed a hand on his arm. "I would have never gotten through most of this pregnancy and losing Jet if it weren't for you." She eyed Muriel. "Both of you." Once she had uttered those words, Courtney realized the depth of their truth. The Meadowses had been a rock and her support. Remembering that gruesome time made her forgive them even more. Her voice cracked. "I love you guys. Don't hurt me like that again."

They gave a solemn nod before the three of them hugged it out. Courtney's heart lightened.

"I'm still not taking that car though."

"How about you come back to Druid Hills with us instead?" Muriel asked. "We plan to return in a few days."

Courtney shook her head. "I need to be independent. I think I want to open my own event planning business. Or even a restaurant." She scrunched her nose. "I'm not sure yet, but whatever it is, I've got to be able to stand on my own two feet."

"I understand, and we're more than happy to help

however you need in the meantime," Robert said, his voice tinged with respect and admiration. "But you can drive that car to your new venture, whatever it is."

She patted his arm. "That's a good idea. I'll think about it." After another round of hugs, Courtney arranged for them to meet her at the hospital the next afternoon so they could finally meet their grandson. Muriel pulled away in the vehicle, and Courtney had to admit, it looked sleek and smooth turning around the corner.

Right before he left, Robert pulled her aside. "I know you declared you're just friends. But I know a smitten man when I see one. I recognized the same look on Jet's face when we were on the cruise. You remember what happened seven weeks later?"

"This is different," she assured him, though her heart had its doubts. Because the entire time she stood talking with Robert and Muriel, Courtney's mind had been in the backyard wondering what Brigg was up to.

He eyed her with skepticism and opened his car door. "If you say so…"

"I do. It's too soon for anything serious."

"For the record, I would be glad if you found love again."

"For the record, my love life is no longer your concern," she said, giving him a peck on the check. "Now, see you tomorrow."

After watching them leave, Courtney returned to the backyard to look for Brigg. Everything was almost cleared away. Kaylin and Ethan were stuffing a large garbage bag.

Brigg had his back turned as he emptied the ice from the cooler on the lawn. Courtney hugged him from behind. He tensed. "How did things go with your in-laws?"

"Very well. We've buried the proverbial hatchet, so to speak."

"That's good." Brigg started folding the rectangular table. He had yet to meet her eyes. He marched over to Ethan's truck to put the cooler in the back. According to Brigg, the tents, tables and chairs had been on loan from his parents' house. The Harringtons hosted a lot of parties.

"Something wrong?" she asked.

"Nope. Why would you say that?"

She grabbed his shoulder. "You're not saying much and you're acting like a mosquito bit your butt."

"You said it all when you said we were just having fun," Brigg said, whipping around to face her.

She frowned. "Aren't we?"

"Yes, but—" he scratched his head and groaned "—it's more than that for me." He stormed off to get another chair.

Courtney was right behind him. "What do you mean by *more*?"

"I don't know, okay?" he grunted out, placing his hands on his hips.

Robert's words about Brigg being smitten came back to her. Her heart thumped *yes-yes-yes*, but her brain issued a big fat no. She cocked her head. "Brigg, are you developing feelings for me? Because that's not our deal." Her heart thudded in her chest.

"Do you sleep with your friends?" he snapped.

"No…"

"Well, that's what you told Robert and Muriel, and I didn't like it."

She raked a finger through her curls flattened by the humidity. "What did you want me to tell them?" she shot back. "That I'm trying to get in your pants and ride you like I'm running from the police when I just gave birth to their grandchild less than seventy hours ago?"

"No." He blew out a long plume of air. "I don't want what we have put in a box."

She gritted her teeth. "We put ourselves in a box. Together. We even pinky swore on it. Twenty-eight days of dating, and then fourteen days of lovemaking until I go to my sister's. Am I right?"

His left eye twitched. But after a moment, he nodded.

"Good. We're on the same page. Now tell me if you've changed your mind."

"No, I haven't changed my mind. Okay?" He flailed his hands. "Just let me work my frustration out by packing up these chairs. I'll take your gifts to my place, and we can sort it out another day. I'll be all right tomorrow for our second date. See you then." He stomped off.

Courtney shook her head, inwardly fuming. He had better not be falling in love with her. The last man in uniform she loved had died because of his job, and Brigg was very much attached to his. She couldn't see him giving it up, and she didn't want him to, because then he would resent her. And that was the last thing she wanted him to feel for her.

Ugh. Maybe she should just call the whole thing off. Nope. She couldn't.

She craved him. Throbbed for him. She had to appease her physical needs even if it broke her heart in the long run. She would rather have some of Brigg than none at all. And in the long nights ahead, she would have something to remember.

Chapter Twenty-Six

After twenty-three days, Courtney would finally get to hold her son in her arms and she hadn't slept a wink the night before. Most of her night had been spent questioning her preparedness as a mother. That's why as she sat at the breakfast table dressed in her pjs, across from her sister, she poured out her misgivings. Rain had been falling since before daybreak, and she hoped the sun would come soon.

"I need to do something with my life besides float from port to port, state to state. I want to give Jayson the stability I never had growing up."

"What do you think you want to do?" Kaylin spooned the scrambled eggs into two platters and then grabbed their wheat toast before cutting it into slices. Then she poured two glasses of orange juice. Her sister had stuck a hibiscus in one side of her ear, and though it was super early, she already had her glam face on with dark eyes and dark lips, which was a direct contrast to her pink shirt dress and flip-flops.

Courtney had broached that topic twice, but each time, her sister had blown her off with a wave of the hand, saying she just felt like changing things up. Courtney believed differently. Her sister looked amazing, but months ago at Jet's funeral, her makeup was fresh, playful, typical Kaylin. This was edgy and flawless, but it was as if there was something suppressed in the inside that she had to release. Like she was literally wearing her emotions on her face.

But she couldn't make Kaylin talk until she was ready. They were alike that way. Kaylin brought their plates and Courtney got the juice. Then they settled to eat.

Her sister raised her eyebrows. "Did you hear me? Have you decided?"

"Yes, I have enrolled in an event planning course to earn my professional certification at FAU." What she liked about Florida Atlantic University was that she could attend online while caring for an infant. So if Brigg asked her to stay... Not that he would. He was all about the fun, just like she repeated as often as she could to remind herself of the rules. She needed to stay chill with their arrangement.

Kaylin smiled. "Sis, that's great you've made a decision."

"Yeah, well. I realized I had to choose something. It was the only way to overcome uncertainty." She shrugged. "It's better to try and fail than remain in limbo."

Kaylin clapped her hands. "I agree. Do you need money to pay for the course? Living on a ship allows me to save a lot on expenses."

"No, in my short time at the diner, the Harrington men left *extremely* generous tips, so I am good with paying for the program." Her chest puffed. It felt good not relying on anyone. "Once I finished the application, I felt a calm within myself, a certainty. It's odd, but hitting that

Complete button was a major step for me. My heart was pumping in my chest, but I did it."

"You did. You did." Her sister took her hand and gave it a light squeeze before continuing to eat. "I know I'm not your parent, but I am soooo proud of you."

"Thank you. There are seven modules, and I can't wait to get started. There's a live virtual option, so I can arrange my schedule to fit around it."

"Are you sure you want to do this with a newborn?"

"Yes, it's the best time. Imagine me trying to attend classes with a toddler."

"Good point. Either way, I'm happy for you, and I'll be your biggest cheerleader." Kaylin raised her arms. "Go on with your bad self."

"Me too. I'm happy because going into business for myself will help me set my own hours, and I will be able to spend quality time with Jayson. By the time he is old enough, I will have a career." She squared her shoulders. "I want my son to be proud of me." She finished up her breakfast.

"Oh, honey, I know I don't have children, but I imagine as long as you love them, fill their tummies and keep their butts clean, they will think you are the best mommy in the world."

"Ha ha. You have a point though." Courtney sipped her juice.

"Don't I?" She wiped her mouth with a napkin placed in the center of the table. "I know we would have wished that from Mom." For a second, Kaylin's lips turned down, and she appeared as if she were going to say something else. But she took another drink of her OJ instead.

"Ain't that the truth." Courtney said, using a term that

they had learned going to church with one of their foster mothers.

"Sure 'nuff is."

They high-fived each other and Courtney changed topics. "So, what's going on with you and Ethan?"

Kaylin lowered her lashes, thickened with extensions. "We're just having fun. Nothing wrong with a summer fling."

"Are you sure that's all? Because it looks like you're sweet on him."

"Yep. That's all I have time for. You know I live on the water."

"Yes, I'll never forget the day you played mermaid in the pool, staying submerged for a good ten minutes."

Her sister laughed. "Yes, and you blamed me for us having to leave that home."

"Going back to Ethan, you have a lot in common. You know he was an Olympian."

"Of course. You know I google and stalk the social pages before I get into any entanglements." *Entanglements* had become her sister's word to use for her short-term affairs. Kaylin had been engaged to her swimming instructor, who was twice her age, when she was fresh out of high school. Since then, she avoided any kind of serious commitment. She often joked that Courtney was all she had heart space for, which saddened Courtney, because her sister had so much love to give.

"Don't shortchange yourself. You're an overcomer in many ways."

Her sister twisted the napkin in her hands. "I've started swimming again. Just laps. With Ethan." Besides traveling, swimming was her passion. In fact, she too had been an Olympian hopeful. Until her instructor had been arrested for bribery, ending not just their relationship but her chances to compete. The breaststroke had been her specialty.

"That doesn't sound like an entanglement…"

"Yeah, well, sometimes, the heart wants what it wants. But ultimately, I'm in control. And when I say I'm never putting myself out there again, I mean it." Her sister's voice took on an edge.

Courtney leaned forward and met her sister's eyes. "Kaylin, what's wrong?" The pitter-patter of the rain on the glass was the only sound for a few seconds.

Then Kaylin spoke. "I found Mom."

If she wasn't sitting, Courtney's legs would have folded like a broken accordion. "What do you mean, you found Mom? When?" Her voice rose. She couldn't have heard right. There was no way her sister had kept this from her.

"Four months ago." Tears welled in her eyes.

"F-four months…" She could hardly get the words out. Courtney placed a hand across her abdomen. "And you're just now telling me?" Her chest tightened. "Why would you hide something of this magnitude from me? Where is she?"

Kaylin held up a hand. "Give me a chance. I'll answer all your questions." She finished off her juice and plopped the glass on the table. "I got tired of wondering what happened to our mother. Being at sea for weeks at a time gives you many opportunities for reflection. After Jet's funeral, I started to think of family and how a key member was out there somewhere who would never know she had a grandchild. I felt an overwhelming urge to find her. I think deep down a part of me thought she would rescue us. After making inquiries on my own with no success, I decided to hire a private investigator." She swallowed. "Four months ago, they found her and I'm sorry they did."

"Was she strung out?" Courtney asked.

Her sister shook her head. "She looked good too, considering…"

"Considering what?"

"She was in rehab and wanted nothing to do with me. With us. She lives in Ohio."

"Ohio? That seems so random. How did she end up there?"

"Who knows? Probably followed a man out there." Yeah, that sounded like something their mother would do.

"Did she recognize you?" Courtney asked, hungry for information about the woman who birthed them.

Kaylin dipped her chin to her chest. "Yes." The tears came then, and her body shook. Courtney wanted to be furious at her sister for keeping this from her, but Kaylin was so distraught that she rushed around the table to comfort her. "I'm sorry I didn't tell you," she hiccuped. "But be glad I didn't. Mom screamed at me, called me outside my name in front of everyone in the facility, then told me in not so friendly terms to get out. At first, I thought it was because she was embarrassed…" Kaylin wiped her face. "But she just didn't want to see me. According to her, she signed us over to the court for a reason." Kaylin scoffed. "Me being me, I asked her about our father, and that's when…that's when…when she…said…" She sobbed. "I can't. I can't utter her horrible words."

Courtney pulled her sister to stand and led her over to the living room. Kaylin plopped on the brown leather couch and closed her eyes. The tears blotched her makeup and left dark streaks, but Kaylin was oblivious, mumbling to herself. Courtney decided to make them both a cup of tea. Her hands shook, but she needed to occupy herself before she prodded Kaylin to finish the tale.

Once she had steeped the peppermint tea and they had taken their last sip, Courtney quietly asked, "What did she say, sis?"

"She said our father was dead and she wished we had both died with him. Said we weren't worth the mud on the bottom of her feet." Kaylin delivered the words in a tone devoid of any emotion.

Courtney gasped. "What kind of a mother would fix her mouth to say something like that?" Now that she was a parent, she couldn't imagine wishing any harm on her child. Then she answered her own question. "I know why. Because she wasn't a mother to us. She couldn't be. Drugs snatched her away." She put an arm around her sister and they huddled together. Surprisingly though, she didn't hurt as much as her sister did. Maybe it was because she had a child to cherish.

Kaylin's nose was red from crying. "That wasn't just the drugs. She felt that way. And her blood runs through us." She looked at Courtney. "Neither of us wanted to have children, remember? We were afraid that if something happened to us, they would end up in foster care like we did."

Courtney's heart sliced with regret for the two young girls who had felt the need to make that vow. "Yes, but as you see, sometimes life decides for you."

"Yes, it does," Kaylin said wryly.

"But when I look into Jayson's face, I know he was meant to be here, and all I feel is overwhelming gratitude that I get to claim him as my own." Her lips quivered. "Between you and Jayson, my life is complete."

"What about Brigg?" Kaylin asked. "Is there room for him?"

She ran her fingers through her hair. "I don't know." She wasn't sure if she wanted to truly know the answer to that question.

"I see the way he looks at you when he doesn't think you're looking. He is hooked on you, and he's good people. Worth the risk."

"Look who's talking."

"You're braver than me," Kaylin confessed. "You shine when you're in his presence, and he is protective of you. You two have a good vibe. A good energy between you that you don't see often. It surpasses the physical."

She felt seen. Exposed. "Our connection is off the charts, but I can't put my heart out there with another man in uniform. The risks are too high. If something happened to him…"

"You can't think like that. It's better to take a risk and lose than not to risk at all."

"Um, I don't think that's quite how the saying goes, but I get your drift."

"Your refusal to analyze the depth of your feelings doesn't negate the fact that they exist. You put your heart out there before, why can't you do it again?"

"Moving on with a baby without Jet was tough. Doing the same without Brigg would be unbearable. Unimaginable." She touched her chest. "I don't know if I would recover. Falling for Jet was like falling down a hill. Falling for Brigg would be like falling over a steep cliff with no end."

"Nonsense." Her sister's tone was firm. She patted Courtney's leg. "You would get through. It would be tough, but you would do it because you have a son who needs you. He would be your reason to get up in the morning. To keep fighting."

"I guess, but why put myself in that position in the first place?"

"Because love is worth it. For as little or as long as you have it. Despite Mom crushing my heart, I remember her before the drugs. She was the best, and I want that for you. You deserve it."

"So do you. Mom's wrong, you know?" Courtney said, rubbing her back. "You're worth more than your weight in diamonds."

She gave a little laugh and rested her head on Courtney's shoulder. "Now who's botching the cliché?"

Courtney chuckled. "We are a sorry pair, the two of us."

"Aren't we though? But at least we have each other."

"Yes. You and my son are all I need."

Kaylin gave her a pointed look. "Tell that to your heart."

"Since when does my heart listen to me?" Courtney asked, shaking her head. For that, neither had an answer.

Chapter Twenty-Seven

Brigg had never run, jogged and showered in his life as much as he had been doing for the past three weeks.

He had also never had so much fun with a woman.

Courtney went for the quality-time activities that didn't cost much, like walking along the pier, watching movies, chasing each other on the beach and so on, while he dropped his money on extravagant experiences like a helicopter flight, a balloon ride, horseback riding and five-star dining.

Without the pressure of sex, he and Courtney had discovered each other's likes and dislikes while deepening their friendship. She was the first person he spoke to in the morning and the last at night, unless he had a shift. It seemed like every day he was learning something new about her, and he concluded that he liked everything about her.

And he was going to have a hard time letting her go.

However, he had run out of ideas, and today, day twenty-three, was up to him. Courtney had them bake their favorite cookies the day before—his was chocolate chip and hers oatmeal—which he found really creative.

So here he was sitting at his kitchen table, eating his

breakfast and debating what to do next. The biggest issue was that they couldn't travel far. They had daily visits with Jayson, who, as of yesterday, had reached an ideal weight. He just needed to be able to regulate his body temperature and keep tolerating the breastmilk. Today, Courtney was going to begin skin-to-skin contact. She would hold her son for the first time. Brigg had to be there to witness that even though he had several meetings today.

One with DJ about the community outreach coordinator position. Another with Queenie surrounding the strategic plan. And then a work lunch with the mayor about transitioning from his interim captain role. Brigg was more than happy to be on the interview committee.

Before he left the house, he texted the brothers' group chat to see if anyone had any suggestions.

He pulled into the captain's designated spot. This is one luxury he would miss when his time was up. As soon as he got out of the car, he heard a familiar voice call out to him from behind. He looked at his watch. DJ was due to arrive in fifteen minutes and he didn't want these two crossing paths.

"Not today, Beckett. In fact, not ever." He heard the rush of footsteps before Beckett was walking in step with him. Goodness, this man was determined. Brigg stopped and faced him. "What do you want?"

"I know I'm the last person you want to see, but I can't let you go that easy. I care about you too much." Beckett looked like he had lost even more weight since Brigg last saw him, and he had more lines around his eyes, but at least he didn't reek of alcohol. He was dressed in a checkered shirt, jeans and had on a baseball cap.

Brigg looked into the other man's blue eyes and remembered DJ's admonition to forgive him. Maybe if he did that, Beckett would leave him alone.

"All right, I forgive you, but I think it's foul that you're suing the department. Now, if that's all, I really have to go." He made a move to leave, but Beckett was persistent.

"I'd like to talk more over a cookout. We'd love to have you over. Like old times. We're the town pariahs and could use some friendly company."

Beckett needed to leave well enough alone. "It's a little soon for all that. Forgiveness doesn't mean things go back to the way they were. It's a means to move forward without the baggage of the past." Brigg patted him on the shoulder. "But I'll call soon."

"Fair enough. I'll be in touch," the other man called out. "And for what it's worth, you're doing a bang-up job as interim captain. I hope you make it permanent. After that video, this town can use a Black face as head of the police force."

And just like that... Brigg frowned. "What do you mean by that?" He didn't give Beckett a chance to respond. "Are you saying that the mayor appointed me because of my race and not my talents? My experience? My skills?"

"No, uh, that's not what I meant," he stammered. "Remember, I'm the one who recommended you to take my place. But you have to admit, it's genius for race relations between the police and the town."

"Is that why you recommended me?"

Beckett took off his baseball cap and wiped the sweat off his brow. "No. But I know you."

Brigg cocked his head. "That makes one of us, because the more I talk to you, the more I realize I don't know you at all. You didn't do me any favors, Beckett. I earned this temporary promotion, and the mayor wanting to promote me permanently has nothing to do with race. Now if you'll excuse me, I have work to do." Brigg stormed off without a word of goodbye.

He walked through the automatic doors to the precinct just as his cell rang. It was his father calling. He drew in a deep breath and counted to three before answering the phone.

"Everything all right?" he asked his father after greeting him. He hoped his agitation wasn't evident in his tone.

"Have you seen the newspapers?" his dad asked.

"No, what's going on?" He noticed a few eyes on him and heard a few snickers. He nodded at Queenie, who handed him a copy.

"You're front-page news. You and Adrian. They are calling you Love Creek's Dream Team. And get this, you're in a cape. He's Lightning, and they've dubbed you Brigg the Brave."

His brothers were going to tease him about this for years. And Axel is going to see it as payback for all the ribbing Brigg gave him when he was made the Sexiest Man Alive in a national magazine.

"They call that news?" Brigg opened the newspaper and began to turn the pages. "That explains why everyone is looking at me like I have horns on my head. There were a few times I thought I saw cameras flashing, but I thought I imagined it." Sure enough, there was a picture of him coming out of DJ's house.

"We're proud of you, son."

"Thanks, Dad." Distracted, Brigg started to read the caption and inhaled. "No. No. No." If DJ saw this article, he might get the wrong impression.

"Wh-what's wrong?" his father asked.

"Dad, I've got to go." Brigg ended the call and rushed out to Queenie's desk, holding up the paper. "Please tell me this is an advanced printing." He squinted. If he wasn't mistaken, it looked like Queenie was wearing lipstick and had changed her hair color. Brigg wasn't about to ask though, in case he was wrong.

"No, I don't think our little town does advanced issues." Queenie tilted her head. "Your nine o'clock is here."

He lifted a hand in greeting, but DJ barely gave him a smile. As soon they entered his office, Brigg asked, "So, I guess you saw this morning's headline?"

DJ made his way to the conference table and confronted Brigg head-on. "Yep. I don't appreciate being a pawn. Being used for your gain. The new superhero captain befriends the town's most renowned paraplegic. How altruistic."

Brigg placed a hand on the table. "I'm not using you. I can't control what the media does. I had no idea I was being followed and the subject of an exposé. And I'm not offering you this job out of pity. I'm asking you to take it because you've started making a difference on a small scale, and I have the funds, resources and the full support of our mayor to help us reach more of our Black sons. Everyone."

DJ studied him for several seconds. "I don't want to be seen as a charity case."

"You are far from it. In fact, I would like you to share your story before you start. You are a living, breathing example of someone rising above his circumstance, and I think that needs to be applauded. The mayor would like to honor you publicly."

"I don't do it for the accolades."

"Think of the youth in your position who will see themselves in you." He pointed. "You are the real superhero."

He exhaled. "I'm in."

"Done." He pumped his fists. "I'll get Queenie to review the compensation package."

"Cool. I just have one thing I need to know before I sign those papers." DJ's serious tone gave Brigg pause.

He sat across from the other man. "What do you need to know?"

"How do you fit your cape under that ridiculously tight uniform?" DJ busted out laughing.

Brigg eased back in his chair. "I see you got jokes. Just wait until you get your own nickname."

"Bring it. In fact, my headline should be 'The Real OG.'" DJ cracked up. "By the way, don't forget I owe you a beatdown."

"It's on. Drake and Ethan are ready for a rematch."

Brigg then called Queenie inside. She came in, swinging her hips, and greeted DJ shyly. DJ fumbled over his words. He hid a smile. DJ might end up with more than a job.

Brigg cleared his throat and decided to play matchmaker. "Queenie, since DJ has accepted the position, I'll leave you to review the plans with him first. Then we can set a date on the calendar to meet."

"Yes," DJ said. "Let's talk over a long lunch."

"Well, I guess that should be okay?" Queenie looked Brigg's way for confirmation.

He waved them off. He finished up some paperwork and met with a couple detectives regarding some cold cases before his cell phone beeped with a message from the mayor, pushing back their lunch meeting. He smiled. Now that he had some time between appointments, he'd better check on one of the most important women in his life.

Chapter Twenty-Eight

"I thought I was going to have to come searching for you," Tanya said, cutting through the cantaloupe she had picked from her garden. "It's been a couple weeks since I've seen you." She also had honeydew, pineapple and strawberries washed in a colander hanging over the sink.

"I've been so busy. This interim captain gig is no joke. I'm in charge of everything. Plus, I try to go out and help the team when I can. I have a meeting with the mayor in a half hour, but I said I have to come see my mom." Brigg snatched a piece of the fruit and plopped into his mouth. He groaned. "This is sooo good."

"You can't do both jobs," his mother said. "You have to choose." She reached for the melon and used the santoku knife to deftly slice it in two, then began cutting it into chunks.

Brigg's mouth watered. "I can't believe you grew all this in your backyard."

"Well, I didn't do it alone. Your father helped me a lot before he started volunteering at the school district. I tell you, that man does not know the meaning of the word *retired.*"

"You and Dad are my couple goal," Brigg said, grabbing one of the plump strawberries.

"Yes, he is wonderful. When Axel's father left, I thought I was going to have to do this alone, and I was all right with it. But then I met your father and his two wonderful boys, and my heart went into overdrive." She tucked him under the chin. Brigg smiled, having heard this story many times. He never tired of hearing how his parents bonded during karate lessons. Tanya had knocked Patrick out. Literally. "I've never regretted a day since, especially when you and Caleb came along. I wish the same for all my sons."

"Love isn't for all of us. It's no biggie for me."

She tossed the strawberries in the salad, then began working on the pineapple. Brigg went over to the pineapple upside-down cake on display and cut himself a slice in the meantime.

"The devil is a lie. You say that because you've never been in love. But it will happen. When you meet the right woman and everything falls in line, you'll see what all the fuss is about."

Courtney's face flashed before him. "Is it possible to meet the right person at the wrong time?"

"I don't think there's such a thing as the wrong time," Tanya said, dicing the pineapple into chunks. The smell permeated the air. "If you've found the right person, you adjust your life to fit them, and the telltale sign is you don't mind doing it. That's what makes it right."

"Dang, that's some sound advice."

"Of course." She kissed him and served him fruit salad in a container.

His mother's words stayed with him on his way to lunch with the mayor. It had been sprinkling most of the day, and Brigg's wipers scraped against the glass.

He couldn't help but notice how many adjustments he had made to his routine, his rules, since meeting Courtney. If his mother's theory was right, then he might have caught the lovebug.

Nope. He wasn't entertaining that possibility any further. He had already made up his mind about not falling in love. Since the sun wasn't out, he felt safe leaving his fruit in the truck. He jogged into the restaurant, forgoing the use of an umbrella. Once again, there was a camera flash and he suppressed a groan. He wished these reporters would find something else to do with their time.

The mayor had already arrived. There were two garden salads and what looked like iced teas on the table. Brigg sauntered over and took a seat.

"I got a chance to review the strategic plan, and I've got to say, I think it's stellar." Adrian poured some of the vinaigrette on his salad and picked up his salad fork.

Brigg did the same. "Queenie worked on it with DJ. He's supposed to start in a couple weeks."

"Excellent work securing him. I am excited about the idea of a Love Creek PD's Got Talent as our first outreach. I think it's creative, and it will help the community see our officers in a different light."

"The reaction has been exciting so far. The PD has been posting small clips on social media, and there's been a lot of hype. Plus, we're getting caterers. Food is another major draw."

"What do you plan to do?" Adrian asked.

"I'm the emcee."

"No. No. You have to do something."

Brigg splayed his hands. "If I'm going to open myself for ridicule, then you need to join me."

"I don't think so." The mayor focused on his salad. A

server came over and took their lunch orders. Brigg chose a roast beef sandwich, and Adrian ordered the salmon.

"Let me know what you will do," Brigg said, ignoring the shutdown. "It's an election year."

That made Adrian's head pop up. "I don't do a song and dance. I let my work do the talking."

"We will do something together."

"Fine." The mayor then changed topics. "Before I forget, I received notice that Beckett withdrew his lawsuit."

Brigg leaned forward. "He did? Did he say why?"

"Not a word. Just a simple statement." Adrian shrugged. "I'm too relieved to push for answers. Maybe Beckett realized he was in the wrong."

Hmm... The Beckett he knew didn't give up that easily. He remembered the dejection on the other man's face, and unease lined his stomach wall. He had brushed off his former mentor, treating him like a speck of dust in his life. Not that Beckett didn't deserve it, but still...

The mayor brought him out of his musings. Brigg was surprised to see the other man had cleaned his plate. "So, have you decided to stop dragging your feet and make your decision?"

"I need a little more time." He began eating his sandwich.

"Fair enough. You have two weeks." Adrian looked at his watch and stood. "I'll be in touch."

Brigg straddled the road of indecision. He had an opportunity to make top-down change and he was hesitating. That wasn't like him. He prided himself on his ability to make rapid decisions, a necessary part of his job. Especially when he was on the street or in the schools. Brigg had lost count of how many situations he had to defuse in a spur of the moment. Everyone praised his skills and spoke about his career with admiration.

Everyone but Courtney.

Whenever he was in uniform, he could see the appreciation in her gaze when she checked him out. But there was no disguising her rigid stance, the fear in her eyes when he left. Almost as if she didn't expect him to come back and she was trying to be brave. Her fake bravery rattled his confidence. Made him question the only thing in life he ever wanted to do.

Huh!

That's why he couldn't give the mayor an answer. A part of him wondered if he would be taking the desk job to make her happy. The funny thing is, Courtney would be leaving soon, so he didn't know why her unspoken opinion impacted him. But it did.

He cared what she thought.

And she hated his job. To her, it represented certain death. But to him, it represented honor and service. He loved being a cop. But he didn't know how to ease her mind, offer her a guarantee where there was none.

So he'd enjoy all she had to offer, and then in a few weeks, because he cared, he would let her go.

With his mind settled on a course of action, Brigg made his way to the hospital. Courtney was in the waiting room on the NICU floor. As soon as he crossed the threshold, Courtney gave him a bright smile. Brigg knew he had been waiting for that all day. Her smile injected a feeling of contentment, matched only by the beautiful view of the skyline in the large bay windows.

Brigg gave her a tight hug and kissed her on the cheek. She smelled like almond and shea butter. And her cheek was so soft under his lips. Five days. Five excruciatingly long days, and he would be able to kiss her, touch her, make love to her. His body grew taut just thinking about it.

"Are you ready for today?" he asked.

"Am I ever." She trembled. "I don't know why I'm so nervous."

"Today is the day you get to hold your son in your arms. You get to kiss him and just love on him. I'm honored I get to share this moment with you."

"It couldn't be anyone else but you."

That warmed his heart. "This might sound odd, but I'm glad you broke down on the side of the road and that I was the one on duty."

"Yeah, well, I can't say I'm glad you gave me a ticket."

He chuckled. "I did get it dismissed."

"That you did."

Brigg's chest expanded. He loved their easy banter. Courtney was good with the comebacks. He held out a hand. "Let's go see Jayson. Let's go see our—I mean—your son."

Chapter Twenty-Nine

Five hundred and fifty-two. Five hundred and fifty-two hours of waiting had all come down to this moment right here. The first of two big moments Courtney had planned for today. That's why she had dressed with care. Her hair was in a neat bun and her white sundress with bright yellow flowers and yellow sandals matched the weather and her outlook. Courtney squeezed Brigg's hand.

"I can't imagine what you must be feeling right now," he said.

"My heart feels like a drum in my chest," she said, her breath shaky. "In a few minutes, my baby will be against my chest. I'll be able to feel his heartbeat."

He gave her hand another squeeze. "I made sure my phone is charged and ready to go."

"Yes. Kaylin, Robert and Muriel told me to make sure I record this moment. They've already texted me reminders twice." Ever since the baby shower, her relationship with her former in-laws had improved. Courtney had created a family album online and posted pictures regularly to keep them in touch with their grandson. They had also ensured that Courtney was added as her son's beneficiary so she had access to funds to care for Jayson.

"Thank you for choosing me to be here with you," Brigg said, solemn. "I'm honored."

She nodded. She would never admit it, but there were secret times where she traveled down the path of what-ifs: What if this were her and Brigg's child?

It could be...

She clamped down on that thought and glanced his way from the corner of her eye. He was dressed in his uniform. A visual for why she couldn't be with him.

Courtney used her security band so they could enter the unit. From there, they donned the gowns. She wore her gown with the opening in front and skipped the mask, but Brigg put on a mask and grabbed a pair of gloves. They washed their hands, and he donned the gloves before heading to Jayson's area. The nurse on duty gave them a wave.

"He's waiting for you, Mom and Dad," she drawled out.

Hearing Brigg referred to as Jayson's dad always gave her a jolt, but Courtney and Brigg just nodded and smiled.

"He looks like he gained a pound since yesterday," Brigg said, sounding proud. *Just like a dad...*

"Maybe not a pound, but he sure did." Like most of the nurses, she sounded chipper and upbeat. "All right, let's get you settled."

"I'm shaking," Courtney admitted, settling in the armchair. Brigg held up his phone to capture the nurse picking the baby up out of the incubator. Her eyes welled. "Oh, goodness, this is really happening. It's happening." She lifted her hands, her lower lip quivering.

"You're doing great," Brigg murmured.

The nurse placed the tiny bundle into her palms and Courtney cried. "Hello, little one. It's Mommy." Her shoulders shook with tears and joy as she slowly brought her son close to her chin and collarbone. "It's Mommy." She closed her eyes, the tears streaking her face, while she savored all the sensations going through her body.

She felt Brigg come close and opened her eyes. "Guys, there's nothing like it. I wish I could describe what I'm feeling right now."

The infant squirmed and made a little sound, which was a delight to both Courtney and Brigg.

"Look at him move," Brigg said, sounding as enthralled as she was.

"Do you want to hold him?" she offered, ready to share this experience with him.

"No, I'll wait until he's bigger before I take a chance." Brigg ended the recording. "I think we have enough to share with everyone." His voice sounded choked up, and his lashes appeared spiky, but Courtney decided not to tease him about it.

Courtney snuggled Jayson close and exhaled. "Mommy doesn't mind keeping you all to herself." With the nurse's assistance, she breastfed him for the first time and fumbled through a diaper change before the nurse stated Jayson had to go back to the incubator.

"He's getting good at maintaining his body temperature," she said. "But we want it to be consistent. He did well with his feedings today, so I think he might be going home sooner than you think."

"That's wonderful!" Brigg exclaimed.

"Fantastic," Courtney echoed. But when they left the ward, the elevator ride was somber. "I know what you're thinking," she said.

"I am happy for Jayson but sad our time is coming to

an end." They stepped into the lobby. "Did you drive?" Brigg asked.

"No, I had Kaylin drop me off so we wouldn't have to return the car before we go out on our date."

Brigg froze. "Our date. Courtney, I got so caught up today, I didn't finalize anything."

"That's okay," she said. "I was going to suggest a change of plans anyway. I have something else I would much rather do today."

"Okay, but I'll arrange the next two dates. They'll be epic. I promise. Thanks for being so understanding." When they stepped out into the lobby, Brigg asked, "So, what do you have in mind?"

She said in a lilting tone, "I had an appointment with my OB-GYN today and she gave me the all clear."

"What does that mean?"

"It means I'm ready to bump up our twenty-eight-day plan to twenty-three days." She could tell by the look on his face, Brigg didn't get what she was trying to say. She stood on her tiptoes and whispered in his ear.

His eyes went wide. "Oh." Then he sprang into action, almost dragging her out of the building. "Your place or mine?"

She giggled. "Let's go to your house, because my sister and your brother have been having way too much fun, if you get my drift."

If she wasn't hanging on to the sway bar in the car and praying the entire drive, she would have found it hilarious how fast Brigg drove to his house. He jumped out of the car and raced over to open the passenger door to help her out. Brigg used the home app to open the front door and then swung her into his arms. The minute he crossed the threshold, he stalked into the bedroom and tossed her on the bed. She landed with a light bounce.

Before she could catch her breath, he had her undressed in less than thirty seconds. She shouldn't have bothered with the matching underwear, because Brigg was all about getting down to her bare skin, and he threw them across the room. He kissed her on her feet and trailed an electric path up her legs. Stopping at her core, he feasted on her until her toes curled. She screamed as her body erupted into ecstasy.

"It's time to return the favor," she said, pulling off his pants and yanking his shirt open. A couple of buttons flew onto the tile. "I'll sew that later."

"Don't worry about it," he said, tearing out of his clothes before returning to kiss her senseless. His hands stoked her fire once more, making her call out his name, begging for release. He sheathed himself and plunged into her, then stilled. She gasped. "You feel so good," he said, gritting his teeth.

Her body widened to acclimate him before the tremors started. Grabbing his butt, she began to move, bidding him to ride with her. He was more than happy to oblige as she urged him into an earth-shattering climax.

Sweating, chest heaving, Brigg collapsed beside her. "That was amazing," he breathed out.

"Ready for round two?" She flipped over and then began to love on him, giving him all he had given her and then some, determined to drive him over the edge. And she succeeded. Brigg screamed her name as he came for a second time. She inhaled his unique scent and closed her eyes, flopping by his side.

"Hungry?" he asked once their breathing tempered. He turned to her and cupped her face with his hand.

"I don't think I can take any more tonight," she said, wiping her brow. Her body was slick and wet, and she was feeling that good kind of sore. The kind that said she had received some good lovemaking. The kind that would make her smile that secret smile tomorrow because she had been in between the sheets of an expert lover.

"No, I meant, food food." He grinned. "I know I gave you more than enough pleasure for tonight. I doubt you could handle more."

She cracked up. "Someone's sounding real cocky. Speak for yourself."

"Let me self-correct. What I should say is, I know I can't handle any more of your goody box, or I might dry out from overexertion." The man had force and stamina, so she knew he was messing with her.

She sucked on his lips. "That's what I thought. Because I'm like the Energizer Bunny. I can keep going and going, if you wind me up right."

He laughed. "Take it easy on me, woman. I need sustenance, and then I'll see what else I can do." He got out of bed, and she held out her hand. After feeding on fruit and some of his mother's cooking, Brigg led her into his bathroom, filling up the spa tub before surprising her with an exquisite round three.

He loved on her until she shed actual tears. Tears.

Brigg carried her and rested her on his bed. The moonlight provided the right backdrop for him, giving her an eyeful of his strength. And his sword.

"Thank you for making me feel desirable and wanted. I know you saw my stretch marks," she whispered.

He bent over and splayed his large hands on her stomach. "Those are battle scars," he said, using his tongue to lick on them and then going lower. "I can't get enough of you," he murmured, inciting her own passions.

She didn't think she could be ready again so soon, but he stirred an animalistic hunger she didn't know she was capable of, and there was only one person who could feed her need. In time, Brigg lay next to her in repose, but Courtney remained awake. Contemplating.

The intensity of their connection. Their insatiable desire. How they fit. How they moved in tandem, instinctively knowing what the other required.

For her, that could only mean one thing. The very thing she warned him against had befallen her, which terrified her. She released a staccato breath and looked at Brigg. Running a hand down his face and over his lips, she wiped away the sudden tears and whispered, "I'm in love with you, Brigg Harrington. I'm in love with you something fierce."

No doubt about it. She was in deep dog doo. She would laugh if she weren't already crying.

Chapter Thirty

Every part of his body ached. Courtney was a machine and he had no regrets. Brigg had the scratches on his back and butt to prove it. The physical reminder of her prowess. Her marking her territory. Then his baby had rubbed him down with some oil from her bag to soothe his love wounds.

Yes, she was his baby now. His boo thang.

If only she would quit joking and move in with him permanently. But she had given him a sweet "No, you get eighteen more days," when he had dropped her off at her sister's this morning, and she had swished that track-star behind all the way to the front door.

His hands gripped the wheel. Brigg didn't know how he was going to explain his shiny face and hands. All he could do was hope no one noticed. He felt like he had lost ten pounds of liquid from the night before and this morning.

Yet, he would do it again. He was ready for the replay. Last night was a personal best, but he felt he could beat that record. Because of Courtney. He had never had an addiction, but he could see this woman becoming a habit. One he didn't want to break.

A message popped up on his dashboard. He had the car play it since he was driving.

How about we meet for pizza at noon? Code for *lunch time loving*.

That sounds good, he dictated.

Your place?

See you then.

You're out of condoms.

Brigg rushed through his morning tasks, and by 12:15 p.m., he and Courtney were tangled between the sheets, having wolfed down their pizza slices. Her bags were in the corner of his room, and seeing them made his heart lift. He had already cleared drawer space for her.

This was their pattern over the next two weeks. Every free moment Brigg and Courtney found outside of visiting Jayson at the hospital, they were making love. He didn't think there was an area of his house they hadn't made memories, screaming from pleasure.

Before her sister's Airbnb contract ended, they decided to go with Kaylin and Ethan to the movies. Since Courtney wasn't able to leave with Jayson still in the hospital, she gave Kaylin the Kia to drive back to Fort Lauderdale as Kaylin had a cruise job. Courtney had decided to accept the luxury sedan from her inlaws. Her new wheels would arrive in a matter of days.

They purposely chose a film that had been out for a while so it wouldn't be crowded and they could make out.

Brigg and Courtney sat a few rows behind their siblings, sharing a large popcorn. There were only two other couples in the large theater. Like randy teenagers, Brigg and Courtney started out with heavy petting, but soon, she was trying to muffle her screams. "I would normally be arresting kids for doing this very same thing."

She planted those luscious lips on his. "Well, when you're the captain, you can break the rules."

He slurped on his Cola in an attempt to cool his insides. As soon as the movie ended, they waved off Ethan and Kaylin.

"I'll talk to you tomorrow, sis," Kaylin said, giving her sister a knowing glance. "Be sure to do what I would do."

"You bet." The sisters shared a giggle.

Oh, he and Ethan were both in trouble. He looked over at Courtney. Good trouble.

They rushed to his truck. "I can't wait to be inside you," Brigg said, starting up the vehicle and backing out of the parking space. He gripped the wheel to keep from speeding down the row.

"Then why aren't you?" she teased.

He gave her a side glance. "What are you suggesting?"

"You must know a good place we could stop?"

"I don't think that's a good idea," he said, though he sure was tempted. "One, I'm sworn to uphold the law. And, two, being interim captain means having your picture taken at the oddest of times. Let's just say, I don't want to end up with my pants down on the front page. You can wait ten minutes."

From the corner of his eye, he saw her shimmy out of her undies from under that ridiculously short skirt. He groaned. "All right, bet." Brigg made a quick turn and pulled into a well-known make-out spot. As soon as he put the car in Park, she jumped on his lap. "You're going to be the end of me," he said as she zipped down his pants and settled on him.

"I needed you," she said, releasing a moan, her curls bouncing up and down. "I've always wanted to do this. Make love under the moonlight."

He closed his eyes while she rocked her hips and took him to the brink of coming. Just as he was almost at that point, there was a heavy rap on his window, followed by a huge flashlight. He froze. This could not be happening. With a yelp, she jumped off him. The windows were foggy, giving Courtney some cover while she pulled down her skirt. He adjusted his clothing, just knowing his face held nothing but mortification.

He sighed and rolled down the window to meet the eyes of a shocked rookie, Mendez, whose mouth hung agape. "Cap—captain?" The man covered his mouth. "Wh—what are you doing?"

Brigg grunted and flailed his hands. "Go on home. Nothing to see here." His mortification increased when the man dipped his head to shine the light into the cab.

"Are you okay? Are you here against your will? It was so dark, I didn't recognize your car."

"No." He exhaled, willing himself to remain patient. "I'm good. See you at the station tomorrow."

"We were just admiring the moonlight, Officer." Courtney had her arms folded around her, the picture of innocence.

Understanding dawned. Mendez pulled his lips into his mouth in an effort to hold his laugh. "Apologies, sir. Be safe, Cap." He dipped his head and walked off, swinging his flashlight in his hand and doing an off-key whistle.

Brigg exhaled. "This is going to be all over the station

tomorrow. I guarantee you, I won't live this down." Despite everything, Courtney wanted to continue. "Nope. We are going home," he said.

"There goes my dream of getting laid in your police vehicle eventually." She pouted.

Brigg pictured her perky butt in the air and smiled. "That can be arranged. With careful planning."

"Let's add handcuffs."

"Do you know how many cases I've had where the keys got lost?"

"How many?"

"Too many."

She swung her legs. "Then don't lose the keys."

Maybe now would be a good time to share his minor claustrophobia. They entered the house and got undressed, leaving their clothes in a pile near the front door.

"I'll race you to the bedroom," she said, darting down the hallway.

"All right, bet." He took off after her, snatching her up and pinning her beneath him on the bed.

Goodness, this woman was fun. Her spontaneity had his insides all twisted. He didn't know how he was going to let her go. Her glorious chest heaved under him. He shifted so all his weight wasn't on her and dipped his head to kiss her.

Courtney's phone rang early the next morning. She lifted up a hand and got up. "I've got to get that in case it's the hospital calling." She went into the hallway, and he heard her answer the call. Seconds later, she marched into the room, her movements harried, her smile withered. His ardor cooled and he dashed to her side. "I'm on my way!" she yelled sounding panicked. Dragging the drawer open, she took out a jumpsuit and fresh underwear and started to get dressed.

"What's wrong?" Brigg asked, putting on his underwear, then shoving a leg into his pants, doing a small hop to get the other leg in.

"I don't know. They said I needed to get to the hospital," she said. "I can't believe my baby was in trouble while I was…" She trailed off and wiped the corner of her eyes. "I'm a terrible parent and I'm failing my son."

"Stop it. You were by his side all day today. He was doing fine when I saw him earlier. This is not your fault." He got his shirt from the pile by the front door and slipped it over his head.

"I hate feeling like he's suffering," she said.

"He's in the best hands. Let's just wait to see what's going on before you fall apart." Those words were as much for him as they were for her. His heart thumped like a criminal in pursuit.

Putting the portable siren on top of his truck, Brigg shot out of his driveway and pulled into the lot, parking by the visitor drop-off, ignoring the No Parking sign. With a hand on her back, they ran inside the building, then toward the elevators. Once inside the car, he tucked her under his arm.

"Jayson will be okay," Brigg said.

"If he was, they wouldn't have called me at this time. It's almost 6:00 a.m." She sucked in a breath. "I forgot to text my sister."

"Let's find out what's going on with Jayson before we make any calls."

She sniffled. "I don't want to lose him."

"You won't," he said.

"Did your Spidey senses tell you that?" she said. Then

immediately apologized. "Sorry, you know what happens when I get worried."

The door swung open. "It's all good." Holding hands, they rushed into the unit. While he saw the beaming face of the nurse on duty, all Courtney had eyes for was her son. She pulled out of his grasp and ran over to the incubator. "What happened? What's going on?"

"We have some really good news," the nurse said, resting a hand on her hip. "The doctor came by after hours and said Jayson is ready to go home. We debated waiting until it was a bit later, but we figured you would want us to call."

Thank you, God!

Brigg rolled back on his heels and waited for Courtney to process the words. He watched her eyes go round, and she gave a big whoop. "Are you serious? You're not pulling my leg?" she rambled. "Of course you wouldn't do that." She jumped up and down. "My son. My son is coming home. He's coming home."

"Yes, we have the discharge papers. We'll get him ready to go for you."

Courtney dissolved into tears. Brigg held his arms open and snatched her close. Her shoulders shook. "I can't believe my baby is coming out of the hospital. I've been praying and hoping." He rocked her close and let her cry her ugly cry. Tears soaked his shirt, hers and his. She leaned out of his arms. "We didn't bring his car seat."

"I've got it in the trunk," Brigg said.

"You really are my hero," she said. Just then, Jayson wailed. Courtney pushed out of Brigg's arms and placed the receiving blanket over her clothes before lifting Jayson into her arms. "It's me and you, son. We're finally united for real. For good."

Her words gashed his heart. How he wished this was *their* son, *their* reunion. But he was a bystander in her life. His time with them would was about to end. Unless…he came clean. Told her how he felt. A declaration she didn't want to entertain.

She was all for what he could offer physically, but emotionally, she was as distant as the horizon on the beach when it came to him. All she had, she poured into Jayson, as any new mother would. But it was like Brigg no longer existed. She spoke about going to Fort Lauderdale with such joy, like she wasn't leaving anything of importance behind in Love Creek. Like she wasn't leaving him.

Once they were home, Brigg set up the bassinet and placed it on Courtney's side of the bed. His radio went off with a distress signal of a potential volatile hostage case and Brigg gasped when he heard the address. He knew that house.

"We got it, boss," the officer said. "We can update you."

"No, I'll be there."

Brigg rushed to join the other officers on call. He preferred working over wallowing with misery, and he knew the person in question, which added to his urgency. This time when he departed, there was no tension or fear on Courtney's part. He doubted she noticed he was gone.

Chapter Thirty-One

From the moment the doctor said Jayson could leave the hospital, Brigg's attitude had changed. Though solicitous, Brigg had appeared sullen and withdrawn and Courtney didn't know what to make of his sudden mood shift. Since Jayson was asleep, she curled up into the bed and continued her contemplation.

Maybe he had been upset at her assumption that she was coming back to his place. Maybe Jayson's discharge signaled the end of their temporary arrangement, and he was too polite to say she was overstaying her welcome.

Courtney had swallowed her disappointment when Brigg hadn't seemed as enthused about Jayson's thriving as she was. He wasn't the father. That's what she told herself and forced herself to stay chipper. During the drive to Brigg's place, she played with the baby, making sure to mention her impending departure for Fort Lauderdale so Brigg would know she wasn't trying to take advantage of his kindness. Jayson had a follow-up appointment in a couple days, and after that, she would relocate to her sister's apartment.

She debated going to a hotel until she left but decided

she would endure Brigg's standoffish behavior, because she needed to be close to him until her departure. Apparently, falling in love resulted in a lack of pride.

Her heart had ached when the call came in and Brigg got dressed. She knew he wasn't scheduled to work, but he had rushed out. Like he would prefer to be anywhere where she and her baby weren't. Normally, she would have confronted Brigg, but she didn't know if her heart could handle rejection from his lips. Lips that knew every part of her body.

Why should she stop being who she was? she pondered, then sat up. She needed to call him and find out what was going on. Decision made. Courtney called Brigg on his cell phone.

"Are you okay?" he asked when he picked up, sounding a bit frazzled. She heard heavy winds in the background, which meant Brigg was driving with the windows down.

"No. Why are you acting like I'm a bother all of a sudden?"

"Wh-what? Did you call me to argue with me? You're not a bother. Where is all this coming from?"

"From the moment you heard Jayson was coming home, you had an attitude."

"I did not have—" He exhaled loudly in her ear. "Listen, I'm almost at the location, can we talk about this when I get in?"

"Okay, I guess you have more important things to do than talk to me." Goodness, she was sounding like a spoiled brat.

The outside noise went quiet. A signal he had rolled up the windows. "Courtney, you're important to me. Don't you know that?" He was shouting now. "You must know how I feel about you. About Jayson. If I had an attitude, it's because I wish you were mine. I wish Jayson were mine. And as for bothering me, bother me, baby. Bother me a lot. Bother me forever. Because I'm in love with you, all right. I am in love with you so much I can hardly think. I can hardly breathe."

She inhaled. He'd called her his baby. Tears misted her eyes. "I—I'd better go. We can talk later, like you said."

"Really? I tell you how I feel and now you want to end the conversation?" Brigg yelled.

"No—no, it's that I think the first time I hear you say those words, it shouldn't be in anger." She didn't want to tell him she felt the same when he was like this.

"Well, it is what is at this point," Brigg said, sounding flustered. He asked her to hold on, and it sounded like the windows were back down, because she could hear him telling the person he would be there in a minute.

"Baby, I've got to go, but it would have been nice to hear 'I love you, Brigg.'"

Forget about waiting. "I do, my love. I do love you."

"Woo-hoo! You just made my day. Let's have a proper do-over when I get home. I shouldn't be long. Okay? See you soon, honey. I love you. I love you. I don't think I'm going to get tired of saying that."

"Okay. I love you too," she rushed out before he got off the phone. Her heart sang. She kicked her feet in the air and whooped. He loved her. That incredible man was in love with her. She replayed their conversation over and over in her mind.

He had to wait for the do-over to hear Courtney utter those three words in person. And, he had to wait to look her in the eyes and tell her how much he loved her. Because he had a job to do.

But in a matter of hours, Brigg would get his chance. Getting out the vehicle, Brigg approached Mendez and the lead cop on duty, Winkler, who was in his forties with a paunch, standing a couple inches above five feet, but he could outrun men in their twenties. The officers stood outside the home of his former boss and captain, Beckett Sparks. Winkler had the bullhorn in his hand as they had set up about twenty feet away from the entrance. Built in the 1990s, the one-story ranch home sprawled across an acre and a half. Judging by the vehicles in the circular driveway, only Beckett and his wife were inside.

Winkler updated him. "Mrs. Sparks called. Said Beckett had become withdrawn and wasn't acting like himself since everything went down. He sent their daughter on a vacation to Mexico with two of her friends. And he tried to get rid of his wife as well by asking her to go to the store. She forgot her purse and returned to find him with a gun in his hand. That's when she called 911, and he threatened to kill her and himself."

"How long before the mediator gets here?" Brigg asked. This moment felt surreal. He couldn't imagine Beckett would try to take his life. He heard his cell ding and reached in his pocket to press the button to put it on silent.

"She's fifteen minutes out."

They heard a loud crash and a woman bellow out for help. Brigg grabbed the bullhorn. "Hey, Beckett, it's Brigg here." His heart hammered in his chest.

After a few seconds, he saw the door crack. "Why are you here?" Beckett called out from the shadows. He was wise enough not to give them an open shot, though harming him would be a last resort.

He adopted a neutral tone. "Just wanted to talk to you. Can we do that?"

"Too little too late," Beckett shot back before slamming the door.

Tara screamed, "Help me."

Seconds later, Brigg heard a gunshot go off. His adrenaline spiked. There was no time to wait for the mediator. He called out to Mrs. Sparks, but there was no response. Brigg dropped the bullhorn and started running toward the front door. Banging on it, he begged Beckett to open the door.

Winkler and Mendez brought the bar to break the door down.

"By the time you get in, we'll be dead," Beckett shouted out.

"Let her go," Brigg yelled, stepping aside. He went to peer into the windows even though he was leaving himself open to get shot. Then he remembered that the sliding doors were almost always left open. He signaled to Mendez before going around the backyard.

What he saw made him freeze. The once well-tended lawn had become overgrown, and there were beer cans scattered across the perimeter of the house. He picked his way up to the sliding door. Fortunately, the blinds were closed. He gently pulled the door and exhaled. It was unlocked. He wiped his brow and opened it just enough to slip through.

Beckett and his wife were rolling back and forth on the rug. She had her hand on the gun, and he was attempting to wrench it out of her grip. Brigg inched close. He stepped on a broken vase, and the sound alerted Beckett of his presence. The other man swung around, snatching the weapon and shoving his wife to the floor. Then he aimed it at Brigg and fired.

Chapter Thirty-Two

Courtney hummed under her breath while she hunted for her razor and face mask. Looking in the mirror, she gasped at the state of her hair. There was no way she was exchanging her in-person *I love you*s with troll hair. She needed to give her hair a good wash.

Scurrying into the bathroom, Courtney showered and scrubbed every part of her body. Then she moisturized with body butter before working on her hair. Her heart raced, fearing Jayson would awaken while she was still primping.

She dug into her drawer, searching for the nightgown she had purchased at the secondhand store. This was the perfect occasion to wear it. She shimmied into it, loving the feel of the sheer, stretchy material on her skin. She felt desirable. She gyrated her hips and lifted the hair on her nape before striking a pose.

Ooh. She would take a picture and send it to Brigg so he knew what was waiting for him when he arrived home. A teaser. She snapped the pic and hit Send, then snickered. She wished she could see his face when he saw her.

She heard a tiny wail the same time her new app dinged. Jayson was up. She had installed the app to track his feedings, sleep times and diaper changes. One of the other mothers in the preemie ward had recommended it. Courtney dashed over to the bassinet and picked him up. Goodness. He felt so tiny in her arms. Her stomach clenched.

Realization hit. This was her first time alone with her son. She had to feed him and change him on her own. There was no one around to help or make sure she was doing this right. Her heart pounded. What if she messed up? Unbidden tears welled.

Jayson continued to wail. Courtney wavered, unsure if she should do the diaper change first, nurse him or warm some of the breastmilk she had stored. She patted his back and bit on her lower lip while his little body shook from his cries. His only means of communicating his needs. Her palms felt sweaty, and she had a sudden urge to pee. Courtney placed him back into the bassinet.

She released a long plume of air and raked her hand through her curls. His face had reddened from his crying and now he had the hiccups. She rocked back and forth. "Okay, you can do this, Courtney. You did it in the hospital, you can do it now."

No. No, she couldn't do it. Panicked, she gave Muriel a video call. Both Muriel and Robert popped on and assured her she would be fine. Muriel advised her on what to do, her experience soothing and calming.

"Babies are resilient," Robert added. "You've got this."

After making her promise to call if she needed anything else, Courtney ended the call.

Courtney trekked into the kitchen to get a bottle of water and a snack. Then she darted back into the bedroom and placed a receiving blanket on the bed before changing Jayson's diaper. Her hands shook, and she had to toss a couple diapers before she got it right, but she did it, singing to him along the way. When he latched on and began sucking away like a little champion, Courtney's chest loosened.

Wow. She sighed, feeling like she had finished a marathon. In a few hours, she would have to do this all again. Courtney took a huge gulp of water and snapped a pic, basking in her small accomplishment. She sent it to both Brigg and her sister.

Once Jayson had fallen back asleep, Courtney fought the urge to keep him in her arms, kissed him on the forehead and laid him in the bassinet. Looking down at him, she had to take a couple more photographs. He was the most beautiful baby she had ever seen. "I hope you're ready to have your picture taken at least a hundred times per day, little man."

Her sister responded with heart emojis. Brigg hadn't at all. He must still be working on the scene.

Thinking of Brigg, Courtney decided to put on the news. She turned on the TV, keeping the sound at a low volume and putting on the closed captions. She eyed Jayson to make sure the sound hadn't disturbed his sleep. He had his mouth open. Poor guy had tuckered himself out trying to feed. Courtney returned her attention to the screen.

Brigg's ex, Pilar, stood before a large house and sounded like she was fighting back tears. Courtney read the caption: LCPD CAPTAIN SHOT AT FORMER BOSS'S HOME. There was a flurry of activity behind Pilar—police officers milling about, cameras flashing, an ambulance.

Courtney's chest caved and she lost her breath. "Brigg." Courtney hastened to turn up the volume with her shaking hands. She stood, pacing back and forth. "Don't over-react. It might not be him," though deep down, she knew it couldn't be anyone else.

Pilar's eyes appeared red and her cheeks blotchy. "Now that the suspect has been apprehended, EMS workers are inside working on Bri—Captain Harrington. We have no information on the extent of his injuries…"

It was him. Her head lolled backward. Brigg was hurt. He had been shot. Her greatest fears realized. She curled her fists, tightened her lips and released a long, muffled scream. "Please. Please let him be okay," she choked out. Her eyes remained pinned to the screen to see if there was any more update on his condition. To hear that he was still alive.

Oh, goodness. This was like Jet all over again. Her body chilled. The tears flowed. The fear fanned each time they replayed Pilar's words. She paced and prayed and paced and prayed. "Brigg. Brigg. Please, sweetheart. Please."

She called her sister. "Kaylin, please tell me you're back on land," she rushed out, on the edge of hysteria. "Brigg's been shot and I don't know what's going on. I have the baby, and I don't know if I should take him out when he hasn't gotten his shots yet. I don't know what to do."

"Take deep breaths," she said. "I'm on my way up there, actually. Once I heard Jayson was out, I hit the road. I'm about an hour away."

"Oh, thank goodness." Her legs wobbled and she dropped to the floor. "Brigg could die just like Jet. I can't lose him."

"You don't know where he's been shot," Kaylin said. "It could be a graze. You know how the media likes to hype things up."

"I don't know what to think," she bawled. "All I know is he was shot while on a case, and I don't know if he's okay."

Kaylin forced her to take calming breaths. "Remember, you have Jayson. Babies feed off your energy. Try to calm down. I am coming as fast as I can."

Ten minutes later, she heard a bang on the door. It was Ethan. "Kaylin begged me to come over so you can get to the hospital. I'll stay with Jayson until she gets here."

Her mouth dropped. "Are you sure? I know you're worried about your brother."

He hesitated but dipped his head. "Yes, you go ahead. If I know Brigg, he will be looking for you if he's not…" He gulped and grabbed her arm. "Go. He's going to need you."

"Okay." She showed him where to find the bottles and diapers, before yelling, "I'll call on my way and tell you what to do," then bounded to the door, but Ethan called her name just as she gripped the door handle.

"I know the situation is dire, but you might want to change your clothes." He averted his eyes and she hurried into the room to put on a pair of jeans and a top. She was too frantic to be embarrassed. Seeing the spare key to Brigg's vehicle, she grabbed it. Since Brigg had taken the official police truck, she would use his car.

"Bye," she said. "Jayson should sleep for hours." She jumped into his truck and put on the portable siren. The tires squealed as she backed out of the driveway. Tears clouded her vision and she rubbed her eyes. Her heart hurt. Her head pounded. Memories of a similar drive to Jet's bedside engulfed her, but she held it together. She had to get to Brigg.

"No news is good news." She repeated that mantra

until she arrived, tearing into the lot. She parked right in front.

Police vehicles packed the curb. The mayor, who was giving a statement to the press, appeared somber. She couldn't tell from his expression if Brigg were dead or alive. Courtney skulked between the growing crowd and scuttled through the Emergency Department entrance. She spotted Tanya and Patrick speeding down the hallway and ran to catch up with them.

"How is he? Is he… Is he…?" she asked, her heart pounding, her chest heaving.

"Courtney? What are you doing here? You should be home with the baby," Patrick said.

"I had to be here," she said, her chin wobbling. "I had to come. Ethan's with the baby."

Tanya patted her shoulder. "We were told they're operating. So we know he's alive." Courtney marveled at how calm the other woman sounded. But then she saw how Tanya gripped her husband's hand and the worry creasing her brows. This was a call every parent feared.

Courtney's shoulders slumped. "He's alive. He's alive," she sobbed.

"Come," Tanya said. They opened the door and entered the waiting room. Within seconds, Courtney found herself surrounded by the rest of the Harrington men.

Chapter Thirty-Three

His shoulder felt it housed a volcano and his lids felt like a sumo wrestler squatted on them. He pried his eyes open. Even with his vision slightly blurred, he would know those copper curls anywhere. He blinked into focus. Courtney sat in an armchair near the window of his room. Her eyes were closed and her mouth open wide enough to catch flies.

"Courtney," he croaked out, resting his head on the pillows. His bed was tilted upward. Reaching across his chest, he realized his entire chest was bandaged.

She jumped awake. "Brigg," she cried out, coming to his side. "You're awake."

He smiled. "You're stating the obvious."

"Whatever," she said, relief evident in her voice. "Oh, honey, I was so worried about you." She plastered his forehead and cheeks with kisses. Then she rested her head against his chest and spread her arms around him. "I'm so glad you're okay. In addition to getting shot, you broke a couple ribs when you tackled Beckett to the ground." Her head popped up. "I've got to call your parents. They made me promise to let them know as soon as you awakened. Your entire family stayed until you got out of surgery. They left at about midnight. I had to beg them to let me be the one to stay."

"Wait a few minutes." He tapped her back. "I just want to look at you." His mind registered the brightness of the sun and the time. It was just after 9:00 a.m. "Where's Jayson?" He tried to look around to see if he spotted the baby carrier.

"He's with my sister."

"Oh, good. I was worried he was here." Brigg's head pounded. He leaned back against his pillows.

She kissed his hand. His chest. "I was praying most of the night. I haven't been this scared since..." She trailed off and went to get him some water.

"I'm sorry," he said, taking a sip. "When the call came in that there was a hostage situation at Beckett's house, I knew I had to get out there. He was waving a gun around, threatening to kill his wife and himself. I thought I could get through to him."

Courtney tensed before standing up. "You knew he had a gun and you went inside the house?" Her voice held disbelief.

He gave a painful nod. "I was trying to help and this is merely a flesh wound. I'll heal."

"Merely?" She took a step back. "So, you knowingly put yourself in danger? A bullet pierced your body. You could have been killed." Her chest heaved and her voice sounded devoid of feeling. He felt unease wriggle like a snake in his chest.

"But I wasn't." His matter-of-fact comeback seemed to tick her off. "His wife was begging for help," Brigg explained. "It was an intense situation. I had to act fast."

She folded her arms. "Don't you have a special task force for this circumstance?" she asked, slightly accusatory.

"The situation escalated..." He stopped. Her face said, *I don't want to hear it.* "It sounds as if you think I shouldn't have tried to help. To do my job." He tried to sit up, but he couldn't move his arm.

"Ding, ding, ding." She flailed her hands. "You have a special team to deescalate hostage situations. But you're all about being a hero like there's no one else to do it. Never mind that I had just poured my heart out to you moments before on the phone. Never mind that I have a young baby to take care of. You knowingly put yourself life at risk."

He clasped his hands. "Tell me, Courtney. What would you have me do?"

"Delegate."

"Dele—" *This cannot be happening right now.* "The man was my former boss. My mentor. I had to go," he huffed, annoyance rising within. "I was a cop when you told me you loved me."

"You don't get it, do you? You chose to go. There's a difference." She lifted her chin.

They engaged in a visual standoff. Brigg refused to feel guilty for doing his job. "Not to me, and if it came down to it, I would do it again."

"Wow." She released short staccato breaths. "I left my baby who had just come home after weeks in a hospital to be here for you because I love you. But I can't do this. What was I thinking? I cannot do this. I cannot go through this again." She picked up her purse and looped it around her shoulder. Then she walked over to the door.

Panic spread like fire to paper. "What are you saying?" he asked, his heart hammering in his chest.

She faced him. "I knew better than to open my heart

to another man more devoted to his job than to me. I knew better. But I fell anyway."

"It's not like that," he pleaded. "I couldn't have my men in danger."

"But you can have me scared and worried. I see how it is." She gave him a tender smile. "Listen, it was fun while it lasted, but reality is back with a bang, and it's time for me to face it."

"No. No. Don't leave me, baby." He swung his legs, but the pain in his head and arm was too intense. He flopped back on the pillow. "I've never loved anybody in my life like this before. Don't go."

"Unlike you, I have a son to think about. You have your priorities and I have mine and they are not aligned. I can't see us having a future this way." Her voice cracked right along with his heart. "Goodbye, Brigg." She slipped out of the room, shutting the door and him out of her life.

He clutched his chest, already feeling the loss of her presence. Brigg knew the answer would be to tell her he would accept the captain's position and work from the sidelines. *Delegate*, to use her word. But he couldn't guarantee never getting hurt.

Neither could she.

They were at an impasse.

Maybe she was right, that there was no way for them to have a future. He gripped the sheet. But there were millions of couples where one spouse was in a service-related field that could put them in jeopardy, and they made it work.

But how many of them could say they already lost a spouse in the line of duty? He understood her fear. He slumped, dejected. If he hadn't been so weak, he wouldn't have fallen in love, and he wouldn't be battling tears on a hospital bed.

A few minutes after the nurse came in to administer his meds and update his vitals, Brigg received a text. His phone was on the tray next to his bed and someone had put to charge. It was from Kaylin. Hope rose in his chest.

Find the silver lining.

??? What does that mean? he asked. There was no silver lining when the love of your life walked out on you.

At that moment, Lynx strutted into the room. "Shanna sends her love and Mom's making soup. She said to tell you she's getting your old room ready."

Brigg groaned, but it was just for show. He needed his mama, and it wasn't because of his physical wound. His heart was hurting like it had been shredded by a food processor.

"Axel and Hawk are flying in and should get here sometime this afternoon. Don't tell him I said so, but Hawk was pretty shaken when I called."

Brigg nodded. He felt so blessed to have such a close-knit family. "I'm hoping they release me tomorrow. I'd rather recuperate at home than sit here all day."

Lynx sat in the chair, crossed his long legs and studied him. "You look like crap." He was dressed in a polo with his school's logo and a pair of khaki's. His hair had grown longer so he had it swept back in a ponytail.

"Feel like it too," he said. "And I'm not just talking about getting shot."

Blue piercing eyes met his. "What's going on, bro? You good?"

It was his gentle, knowing tone that broke him. Brigg sobbed. "I lost her. I lost Courtney." With Lynx's prodding, Brigg told him all that had transpired between himself and Courtney up until her final exit from the hospital and subsequently his life.

"Where is she now?" Lynx asked.

"Probably packing as we speak." He pictured her trying to stuff her bags and Jayson's things in her trunk and the back seat. Even though the new car was much larger, she wouldn't have room for everything. "Do you think any of the guys could give her a hand?"

"I'll reach out to Caleb and ask him to hire movers," Lynx said. "Let me take care of it. You concentrate on getting well so you can get your woman back."

"Get my woman back?" He frowned. "She said she's done with me for good reason. I don't see her changing her mind. You didn't see her. She was terrified. Besides, I'm not begging anybody to stay if they don't want to. I have my pride."

Lynx stood. "Pride is a lonely bed partner. And it's not begging. It's fighting for the woman you love. Unless you don't think she's worth it?"

"Would you beg?" Brigg shot back.

"For Shanna, I'd be the first one on my knees. I like the view from down there anyway," he teased, coming to stand by the bedside. "Is she worth it? That's the question."

"Oh, she's more than worth it. She doesn't think I am though. She strutted out of here with her head held high."

"That's not the woman I saw yesterday." He folded his arms. "Dude, she left her baby at home for hours to sit and wait for you to get out of surgery. She refused to leave even when we told her we would call. She insisted on staying the night when we all told her to go home. Those are the actions of a woman in love. What do your actions show?"

Brigg felt sucker punched. "I'm an idiot, aren't I?"

"Yep. That's the smartest thing you've said since I got in here."

"So… I should have apologized?"

"Right again." Lynx picked at the IV drip and examined it. "What's in this thing, because it's increasing your IQ by the minute?"

Brigg laughed and touched his chest. "Stop it. You're making my chest hurt."

"From what you told me, it wasn't about your profession, though she had her misgivings. In her mind, you put yourself at risk on purpose without thinking about her or her child."

Boom. Her words, *You have your priorities and I have mine and they are not aligned,* came back to him. "But of course they are my priority," he sputtered. "I opened my home and then my heart to them."

"But did you tell her that?"

He sat up. "Not in so many words, but…it's obvious."

Lynx splayed his hand. "If it were, she would still be here."

Brigg sucked in a breath. "I can't stand you, sometimes." He tried to sit up, but Lynx placed a hand on his arm.

"Oh, no. You're not going anywhere. You've got to get well first. I'm not facing Mom's wrath by making you do something stupid like try to run after Courtney in your condition."

"But she'll be gone by then."

"Good. You need to feel what it's like to be without her so you'll never make that mistake again."

"I'm already miserable," he moaned.

"Quit being dramatic," Lynx said, rolling his eyes. "You have a small rectangular tool that can be very effective. Use it."

Chapter Thirty-Four

"Even from his hospital bed, Brigg is thinking about you," Kaylin said, carrying a box to the small pod on Brigg's front lawn. Courtney had just placed the unopened stroller box inside the unit, the last of her possessions from Brigg's house. Jayson was asleep, which was customary for babies his age, so they were able to get a lot done before he woke up from his nap. Especially since Caleb and Ethan had been on hand to help. Both men had shown up in T-shirts and jeans to help them pack.

The sisters began walking toward the front of the house.

"Yeah, he's thinking of how fast he can get rid of me," she muttered, even though she appreciated his thoughtfulness. The moving company would come for the pod and keep it in storage until Courtney was ready for it. She had decided to look for her own apartment in Fort Lauderdale instead of cramping up Kaylin's space.

"Now you need to quit it, because that's not true. That man loves you and you know it."

"Yes, he loves me, but his career comes first."

"We'll be on our way," Caleb called out, closing the

unit and attaching the lock. "The movers should be here tomorrow to get it."

Ethan rubbed his hands. "If you don't need anything else, we're going to get going." He snuck a glance Kaylin's way and winked. Kaylin bobbed her head but didn't head over to where he stood. Courtney noticed her sister kept her distance the entire time. Their summer fling appeared to be truly over.

Courtney asked, "Are you sure you don't want any lemonade? It's freshly squeezed."

"No, we've got to get to the hospital," Caleb said pointedly. A silent reprimand that she should be there as well.

She gave a cheery wave. "All right, thanks for all your help." She closed the front door. The house was back to the way it had looked before she moved in. "Thank goodness for AC, because outside is like a furnace." Fanning herself with a hand, she addressed Kaylin. "Let's finish our juice and we can head to the doctor's office." Courtney had already called the pediatrician's office and was fortunate there had been a cancellation. Jayson would get his shot and they would hit the road. They sat around the table and she poured them each a glass.

Her cell pinged. She saw another notification from Brigg—three in the past hour—and sighed. He kept sending her love songs on YouTube.

"Which one is that now?" her sister asked.

She pressed play only to hear "bittersweet memories…" The iconic rendition of Whitney Houston's of Dolly Parton's "I Will Always Love You." Courtney rolled her eyes and pressed Pause. Inside though, her heart thumped its approval. It seemed like Brigg wasn't blasé about her walking away from him. Good. Not that she was going to change her mind.

Kaylin snickered. "He's coming for you hard. As he should."

"He can come all he wants, but it's not going to change anything." Except for the rhythm of her heart, which was racing with anticipation. She finished her juice and washed their glasses, humming to the song. Of course, she didn't realize that's what she was doing until her sister pointed it out.

"Stop playing hard to get. You know you two belong together."

Courtney lifted her hands. "It won't work. He's set on putting himself in harm's way, and that's too much dedication for me."

"How can you be jealous of a job?" Kaylin asked, suddenly serious.

"What? I'm not jealous. That's preposterous."

"It sounds like it to me." Her sister guzzled the rest of her lemonade and licked her lips.

"You think I'm wrong for leaving?"

"Not wrong. Just stupid."

"Stu—" Wiping her hands on the kitchen towel, Courtney returned to take a seat across from her sister. "Explain yourself."

"Fine, *stupid* was a harsh adjective to use. From my perspective, I see a man who loves and who wants to take care of you the only way he knows how. He's not doing anything illegal. In fact, he's trying his best to uphold the law. But above all, he accepted you and cared for you even though you were carrying another man's child. How many people have the capacity to love like that? Loving Jayson requires selflessness, and I was there to witness him showing up at that hospital every day for you. For Jayson. What more can you ask of him to do?"

She sat back in the chair. "Humph. Well, if you felt that way, why did you help me pack?"

"Because I'm ride or die with you. I'm going to support you while I'm telling you I don't agree." Kaylin's brown eyes held mirth. "And, sis, for the record, I don't agree."

"I could lose him." Courtney confessed the fear in her heart. Her eyes misted. "Yesterday proved that."

"And you just as easily could not. Brigg could work another twenty years and never get injured another day in his life. Or he could face his end another way tomorrow." Kaylin lifted her hands. "That's life. No one knows. What it comes down to is whether or not he's worth the gamble."

"I'm scared," she sniffled, her stomach churning. "Being with Jet taught me tragedy could strike at any moment. I'm trying to be prepared this time."

"There's no dress rehearsal to prepare for tragedy. What you're scared of is joy. Brigg gives you joy and you can't take it. Acknowledge your fear but embrace your vulnerability. Lean into your joy," Kaylin said, leaning forward to squeeze Courtney's hand. "I know it's terrifying, but you can't live your life waiting for the shoe to drop. You need to live your life so you have no regrets."

Dang. Her sister was dropping some serious nuggets, like she'd been through some things. Courtney pondered Kaylin's words. "Sis, you're an old soul… Maybe I can find a place in town instead of moving to figure this all out."

Kaylin tapped her fingers on the table. "That's a good first step."

Spurring into action, Courtney called the diner to see if the apartment above the restaurant was ready and available. Princess squealed, yelling that it was, and told her to come by that afternoon.

She got off the phone and smiled, her heart feeling light. That's when Brigg sent another YouTube clip. This time it was "Stay" by Rihanna featuring Mikky Ekko. Tears in her eyes, she showed her sister the video. "I think this is a sign. What do you think?"

"I have to agree. Like life, plans can change in an instant. Now, if deep down, you dread being with him because of his job, then you need to see what it's like with just you and Jayson."

"I don't get it," Courtney said. "Weren't you encouraging me to stay?"

"I am. You should. But I don't want there to be any doubt in your mind of what you can live with. Now that you have an idea of what things could be like with Brigg, you need to see what it would be like without him."

"I told you how I think I would feel already."

"Thinking and knowing are two different things. Besides, you walked out on him earlier, and I don't want you to do that again, ever. Unless you are 250 percent sure. Cut contact with him for a short time and see how you feel."

Despite her doubts, Courtney agreed to the experiment. "I don't know if I will survive," she said, "But I'll do it." She held out her arms. "I'm going to miss you."

"Of course, you will," Kaylin said. "I'll come visit often."

Courtney used the number on the pod to call the movers. They were more than happy to get her unpacked at her new address that very day if she needed.

The sisters hugged.

"Once again, I'm heading back to Fort Lauderdale

without you." Kaylin looked at her watch. "I'd better get going."

"Don't go," Courtney pleaded. "Love Creek might grow on you, including one of its famous bachelors."

"That ship has sailed. On to the next destination."

"You have a serious case of wanderlust. Do you think you'll ever slow down?" Courtney asked.

"Not if I can help it." Kaylin sighed, then furrowed her brow. "I didn't notice it before you said it, but there are a lot of famous men from this one little town. Must be something in the water. That's why I'm getting out of here this evening. I don't want to drink from this water too long. Or who knows what will happen?"

Since she had drank the town's water, Courtney didn't contest her sister's logic but remained silent. In her gut, she felt something had gone down with Kaylin and Ethan, but she wouldn't push. As usual, Kaylin would talk when she was ready. She strolled inside Brigg's room and looked around for what wouldn't be the last time, she hoped. Then she picked up Jayson off the bed and slung the baby bag onto her shoulders.

"Let's go check out my new place."

Her sister was already at the door. "A new place for a new beginning."

"Yes." Courtney smiled. "Except this time, I didn't break down on the side of the road and I'm not seeking refuge. This time it's my choice."

"Yes, sis. You got this." Kaylin high-fived her. "And since you're choosing, choose joy."

Chapter Thirty-Five

After three long weeks recouping at his mother's house, Brigg stepped out of the doctor's office at lunchtime and pumped his fists in the air. He'd finally been given the all clear, and that meant two things: (1) he could go back to work on light duty, and (2) he could travel.

The first call he made was to the mayor to accept his job. The second was to Courtney. She didn't answer. Just as she hadn't the numerous other times he had called. But Brigg wouldn't let that deter him. His game plan was to drive to Fort Lauderdale and convince her to come back with him.

He sent a text to the group chat to let his family know he was good to go.

Brigg's cell phone rang just as he got into his truck, intending to head to the freeway. It was Caleb.

"Hey, bro, we're at the diner. Why don't you come have lunch with us?" Caleb asked. His phone must be on speaker because Brigg could hear his brothers in the background.

"We've already ordered your favorite item on the menu," Lynx said.

He hesitated. "I really want to get on the road. Can I

give you a rain check?" He was now by the same inter-
section where he had pulled Courtney over.

"Boy, you'd better get your butt here," Hawk yelled.

"Hawk? What are you doing here?"

Brigg exhaled. He felt bad that Hawk had driven all
this way only for him to skip out on them. "All right,
bet. I'll roll through, but I can't stay more than an hour.
I've got plans."

"Yeah, yeah, we know you've got to get to Courtney,
but fam first," Drake said.

"She is my fam." Or, he wanted her to be if she would
have him. He patted his jeans pocket holding the engage-
ment ring his mother had helped him pick out.

"See you soon," Caleb said and ended the call.

Brigg executed a U-turn and headed into town. He
pulled into the diner and frowned. His parents were here,
as well as Axel. He shook his head. Trust his family to
turn every event in a major celebration. Axel and Hawk
were racking up some major flier miles though. They
might as well move back to Love Creek.

Getting out of the truck, Brigg stretched, appreciating
the beautiful sunny day. He thought about Jayson. Little
man must have grown a bit since he'd last seen him. He
sent Courtney a text, asking for a picture of him, though
he didn't expect a response.

Thank goodness for Kaylin. She had kept Brigg updated and encouraged, or he wouldn't have survived the
past twenty-one days of no contact.

He entered the diner and stopped. The place was decorated in white and gold balloons and streamers, which
blocked the entrance. It almost looked…bridal. He stepped
past the streamers and looked around. A quick glance confirmed there was no one else in the diner besides the serv-

ers, which meant his family had rented out the space. So extra. His heart warmed. The tables had been joined to form one long table, and it had been dressed with white linen and white and gold flowers.

It was absolutely gorgeous.

Brigg walked through the streamers to hear his family yell, "Surprise!" They were huddled together.

He cracked up. "How is this a surprise when you told me you all were here?"

"You'll see," Ethan said, his eyes shining.

They slowly parted down the middle, revealing a private table with two fancy chairs. When he saw who was sitting in one of them, his mouth dropped.

Brigg rushed forward and grabbed Courtney's hand to make sure she was real. "Courtney, you're here." She touched his face, causing his heartbeat to go into overdrive. That was a touch of love he felt, but he hated to hope.

"There you go, stating the obvious," she said with tenderness. "But, yes, I'm here. I never left."

He gasped. "You've been in town this whole time?" When she nodded, Brigg twisted around. "You guys knew and didn't tell me."

"Courtney asked us not to say a word. She wanted to prepare all this," Drake offered.

"You planned all this?" What he really wanted to ask was, why? She was dressed in a long flowery dress with sheer material and some ruching. He touched her hair, "You look breathtaking." A blush rose against her skin. He looked around the room. "Did everyone know?"

They all nodded with huge grins before settling into the seats at the table. Kaylin entered the diner and joined them. All Brigg could do was shake his head. His eyes fell on Jayson in his stroller by Courtney's chair. The baby was alert, and those brown eyes were pinned on Brigg. Leaning over to kiss his cheek, Brigg cooed, "Hello, little man." He couldn't keep his eyes off Courtney for long though. "Where have you been staying?"

"In the apartment upstairs," she said, sounding breathless and happy. Her copper curls shone under the bright lights.

"Are you serious?" He felt the quiet behind him, but Brigg needed to talk to her one on one. He had so many questions…and he couldn't wait to get them answered. "We need to talk." Brigg tugged her toward the back room, but she pointed up the stairs.

The steps creaked with their ascent, but he did enjoy the view. There were windows and a cheery space that Courtney had made her own. He took in the wall decorations and the wooden letters spelling out Jayson's name. She had a twin-size bed, and Jayson's bassinet was right next to it. He liked her little decorative touches, the photos on the wall, which made the space cozy. But many of her possessions were still in boxes.

When he mentioned that, she said, "That's because I don't plan on being here long."

"What made you stay here in Love Creek?" he asked. "Because the last time we spoke, you made it clear you were out of here and you were done with me."

"Not *what*, but *who*." She touched her curls. That's when he noticed her ring finger was bare.

"I don't get it."

She led him over to the bed, and they sat together. "I'm here because of you. I wanted to leave because I was scared to lose you, scared to love you like I do. But my sister called me out on it, told me to cease contact with you until I figure things out."

"What did you figure out?" he asked, plucking the fitted sheet.

"I do not want to live without you!" she exclaimed, clutching his hand.

"I want that too, but at what cost?" His heart hammered. "Being with you means that I have to make changes, which includes thinking about the risks before acting on them." She opened her mouth, but he gestured for her to wait. "I admit I don't have that all figured out, but I do know I want to spend all my days and nights with you and Jayson. So, I'm prepared to—"

She placed a finger over his lips. "You've got to do what you love. I realize that now. After losing Jet, I was scared to open myself again, but you made my heart heal and hope. Because of you, I was able to recover from the past, and I'm eager for a new start with you."

His heart sang at her words. She continued, "If you want to be in the thick of things to help people, then go with what's in your heart. I know the thought of losing you is terrifying, but as of this moment, it is just a thought. I didn't lose you. You're here, and I need to soak up all your love for however long it lasts. I will never be 100 percent comfortable but I won't live each day waiting for impending doom."

He kissed her fingers before kissing her on the lips. "I accepted the captain's position."

She slumped her shoulders. "You did?"

"It took some time, but I love it. I'm recruiting a special task force to give the department crisis and mediation training. I also have Queenie working on surveying the officers and researching their strengths so that we can assign them accordingly." He touched her chin. "I promise to do all I can to not just keep myself safe but also my officers and the community at large."

"I love you," she said. "I can't ask for anything more than that."

He stood and pulled her flush against him, then kissed her briefly. "Now that we have this settled, let's get back downstairs. I'm pretty sure everyone is waiting on us to eat, and trust me, my family aren't nice when they get hungry."

They went down the steps holding hands. His family cheered when they turned the corner. By then, the mayor and some of his officers had turned up, along with Robert and Muriel. Then Courtney stopped and pulled on his hand. When he turned to check on her, he saw Courtney slip to the floor, ignoring the fact that her dress could get dirty.

Everyone circled, but Courtney only had eyes for him. "Brigg, I am so in love with you, I wanted to ask if—"

"No, no. Stop." Brigg fell to his knees, so now they faced each other. "You're not taking this moment from me." He pulled the ring out of his pocket and held it up for her to see. Her eyes went wide. The room went silent. "Courtney, I love you and I need you in my life. These days without you showed me I could survive. But I couldn't live."

"That's good," he heard behind him and stopped to give Drake a quelling look.

"That ring is on point," Ethan said.

Brigg did his best to ignore his brothers and pressed on. "Being with you gives me joy, and I'm sorry if I ever made you doubt that for even a second. If you will do me the honor of becoming my wife, I'll do my best to make it up to you every day for as long as I am on this earth."

"Dang. Did anyone record this?" Caleb asked.

"Shush," Tanya said. "You're ruining his proposal."

Courtney cupped his face. "Yes, Yes, I'll marry you." They kissed while his family whooped. He slipped the ringer on her finger, and then they stood. The Harrington clan surrounded them.

"Best proposal ever," Shanna said, giving him a hug.

Lynx gave her a light jab. "Hey, I thought I was pretty romantic."

"I'm sure Maddie will say I got all y'all beat when I asked her to marry me," Axel said, pulling out his phone. "Let me call her and ask."

Shanna laughed and embraced Courtney. "Welcome to the family. It will be good to get more estrogen in this clan. As you can see, they can be competitive at times."

Courtney giggled, "I'm loving it. All of it. And I can't wait for couples' nights, because I'm sure Brigg and I will be bringing it."

Joy filled his heart. He was already loving the vibe between Courtney and his family. His parents approached to extend their warm wishes.

Patrick embraced Courtney. "Thanks for giving me my first grandchild."

Courtney's eyes misted. "Oh, thank you for saying that."

"We would like to keep him for a couple days," Tanya said, "To give you two a quiet celebration and to get to know our grandson. If you feel comfortable entrusting him in our care."

"Thanks, Mom and Dad." Brigg said, moved by their gesture.

Courtney nodded. "You've raised seven children and they turned out swell, so of course, you can keep him if you'd like." Brigg's parents went over to sit with the baby, and Ethan started up the music. "Thank you, Brigg, for loving me and for giving me something I have always wanted—a big family." She spread her hands, "And if you agree, I'd like us to us to get married today in front of everyone who loves us. The mayor agreed to grant us a special marriage license if you're in."

"I see no reason to wait another day. I hope you're ready for it," he said, drawing her close.

"I'm ready, my love," she said, "I'm ready for it all."

* * * * *

COMING NEXT MONTH FROM

H HARLEQUIN
SPECIAL EDITION

#3039 TAKING THE LONG WAY HOME
Bravo Family Ties • by Christine Rimmer
After one perfect night with younger rancher Jason Bravo, widowed librarian Piper Wallace is pregnant with his child. Co-parenting is a given. But Jason will do anything—even accompany her on a road trip to meet her newly discovered biological father—to prove he's playing for keeps!

#3040 SNOWED IN WITH A STRANGER
Match Made in Haven • by Brenda Harlen
Party planner Finley Gilmore loves an adventure, but being snowbound with Professor Lachlan Kellett takes *tempted by a handsome stranger* to a whole new level! Their chemistry could melt a glacier. But when Lachlan's past resurfaces, will Finlay be the one iced out?

#3041 A FATHER'S REDEMPTION
The Tuttle Sisters of Coho Cove • by Sabrina York
Working with developer Ben Sherrod should have turned Celeste Tuttle's dream project into a nightmare. Except the single father is witty and brilliant and so much more attractive than she remembered from high school. Could her childhood nemesis be Prince Charming in disguise?

#3042 MATZAH BALL BLUES
Holidays, Heart and Chutzpah • by Jennifer Wilck
Entertainment attorney Jared Leiman will do anything to be the guardian his orphaned niece needs. Even reunite with Caroline Weiss, his high school ex, to organize his hometown's Passover ball with the Jewish Community Center. Sparks fly...but he'll need a little matzah magic to win her over.

HSECNM0224

Get 3 FREE REWARDS!

We'll send you 2 FREE Books plus a FREE Mystery Gift.

FREE
Value Over
$20

Both the **Harlequin® Special Edition** and **Harlequin® Heartwarming™** series feature compelling novels filled with stories of love and strength where the bonds of friendship, family and community unite.

YES! Please send me 2 FREE novels from the Harlequin Special Edition or Harlequin Heartwarming series and my FREE Gift (gift is worth about $10 retail). After receiving them, if I don't wish to receive any more books, I can return the shipping statement marked "cancel." If I don't cancel, I will receive 6 brand-new Harlequin Special Edition books every month and be billed just $5.49 each in the U.S. or $6.24 each in Canada, a savings of at least 12% off the cover price, or 4 brand-new Harlequin Heartwarming Larger-Print books every month and be billed just $6.24 each in the U.S. or $6.74 each in Canada, a savings of at least 19% off the cover price. It's quite a bargain! Shipping and handling is just 50¢ per book in the U.S. and $1.25 per book in Canada.* I understand that accepting the 2 free books and gift places me under no obligation to buy anything. I can always return a shipment and cancel at any time by calling the number below. The free books and gift are mine to keep no matter what I decide.

Choose one:
☐ **Harlequin Special Edition**
(235/335 BPA GRMK)

☐ **Harlequin Heartwarming Larger-Print**
(161/361 BPA GRMK)

☐ **Or Try Both!**
(235/335 & 161/361 BPA GRPZ)

Name (please print)

Address _____ Apt. #

City _____ State/Province _____ Zip/Postal Code

Email: Please check this box ☐ if you would like to receive newsletters and promotional emails from Harlequin Enterprises ULC and its affiliates. You can unsubscribe anytime.

Mail to the Harlequin Reader Service:
IN U.S.A.: P.O. Box 1341, Buffalo, NY 14240-8531
IN CANADA: P.O. Box 603, Fort Erie, Ontario L2A 5X3

Want to try 2 free books from another series! Call 1-800-873-8635 or visit www.ReaderService.com.

*Terms and prices subject to change without notice. Prices do not include sales taxes, which will be charged (if applicable) based on your state or country of residence. Canadian residents will be charged applicable taxes. Offer not valid in Quebec. This offer is limited to one order per household. Books received may not be as shown. Not valid for current subscribers to the Harlequin Special Edition or Harlequin Heartwarming series. All orders subject to approval. Credit or debit balances in a customer's account(s) may be offset by any other outstanding balance owed by or to the customer. Please allow 4 to 6 weeks for delivery. Offer available while quantities last.

Your Privacy—Your information is being collected by Harlequin Enterprises ULC, operating as Harlequin Reader Service. For a complete summary of the information we collect, how we use this information and to whom it is disclosed, please visit our privacy notice located at corporate.harlequin.com/privacy-notice. From time to time we may also exchange your personal information with reputable third parties. If you wish to opt out of this sharing of your personal information, please visit readerservice.com/consumerschoice or call 1-800-873-8635. **Notice to California Residents**—Under California law, you have specific rights to control and access your data. For more information on these rights and how to exercise them, visit corporate.harlequin.com/california-privacy.

HSEHW23